"This is a great story. It grabs you and takes you on an emotional journey. The European settings are richly presented and deftly woven through the narrative. O'Driscoll delivers the details that give dimension to the personae of the story, just enough to pique our interest in these conflicted characters and to want to learn more about them."

Bill Thompson, Editor

"I've read a lot of novels. *Who Burried Achilles?* is the best book I've read in several years. It is imaginative and compelling, a well-crafted and complex story. The author reveals a deep understanding of humanity."

Joy Dodds, RN

Who
Buried
Achilles?

To Wayne Horner,

Jeff O'Driscoll

Who Buried Achilles? is a fictional story about fictional characters. Any resemblance to actual people or events is purely coincidental.

Library of Congress Control Number: 2017909061

JeffsPublishingCompany.com

Cover design by Lisa Hildebrand

ISBN: 978-0-9986102-3-8

TO MY LOVING PARENTS

ACKNOWLEDGMENTS

I am grateful to my son, Joseph O'Driscoll, for taking more than one patient slog through my work-in-progress and providing more than one set of useful notes.

I am also appreciative of Bill Thompson, a talented and experienced editor who read an early version of my manuscript and wrote a note to his assistant: "I think Mr. O'Driscoll is worth encouraging. Give him my number." Thank you, Bill.

Thanks to others that read my work at various stages and gave useful feedback and encouragement. And to Lisa Hildebrand for my cover image.

Who
Buried
Achilles?

Jeff O'Driscoll

1

A NIGHT IN PARIS

NO ROOM," the maître d' said in French, his tone decidedly dismissive.

Meth glanced over his shoulder at the line forming behind him. He looked at an empty table near the woman in a snug coral sweater and pointed with his chin; then he waited. The maître d' glimpsed at the table and turned back. Meth tightened his expression and pushed a fifty-euro bill toward his foe, making sure the other patrons couldn't see what was happening. The stern-faced host gripped his pedestal, one hand on either side of his reservation book, like a self-absorbed evangelist at a lectern with a bible. Without softening his expression, as if reluctant to admit defeat, he accepted the bribe. Meth would end up exactly where he intended.

Meth usually ended up where he wanted to be. He would act indignant about the exchange, but he actually liked the challenge. And he liked to win. He'd once dropped more cash on the concierge than on the hotel room he was initially told did not exist. But he'd won; at least, that was how he viewed it.

At his table, Meth noticed the glances of the auburn-haired diner in the coral sweater. He'd felt her eyes follow him to his seat. Her jade pendant dangled between the abundant cowl neck of her sweater and her feminine curves and reflected light from a nearby candle. She gazed at him almost continually. Even as she ordered, she looked at him instead of her server. Hearing her order, Meth recognized a Parisian accent. He seldom smiled but forced a half-grin in her direction while resisting the temptation to invite her to his table. He couldn't risk being seen with her. He ordered dinner, swirled his Pellegrino, and fiddled with his phone to avoid further eye contact.

When the calamari carbonara arrived at Meth's table, the hot rounds of squid glistened under a layer of slightly cooked egg white; the yolk, nestled in the center of the dish, still waited to be ruptured. He inhaled the aroma and reached for his fork. As far as he knew, it was the only restaurant serving calamari in a style generally reserved for pasta.

Meth's phone blinked and danced across the table. He kept it on silent out of respect for other diners, but he couldn't turn it off. Some calls had to be answered, even in the middle of dinner. He snatched the vibrating phone with one hand and waved off the sommelier with the other; he'd neither ordered wine nor wanted it. He never imbibed, even in Paris. He pushed back from his small table in the softly lit Restaurant Jean-François Piège, assured the server he would return, and started for the exit.

As Meth passed the woman's table, her necklace again captured his attention. He eyed the delicate chain, tracing it upward until his eyes locked with hers. He noticed her matching jade ring as she rested her elbow on the table and dropped her chin into her palm. He also noticed the prescription bottle next to her champagne flute.

Meth pushed toward the exit, agitated by the phone call and the disapproving look from the maître d'. He emerged onto Rue Saint-Dominique. Noisy patrons from the restaurant and the nearby pub huddled near the entrance, smoking, drinking, and laughing. A subtle tic momentarily wrinkled the right side of Meth's face when a slender blonde dropped her glass and spat a curse at the shards as if the mishap had somehow been their fault. Meth hated the way his face twitched when people swore, but he couldn't prevent it. Trying to suppress it seemed only to make it worse. For decades, he'd put up with it. Fortunately, others seldom noticed.

Meth swatted dense cigarette smoke from his face, sending it swirling upward through the vertically oriented letters of a red neon hotel sign, THOUMIEUX. Moving from the crowd, he stepped onto the cobblestone street, his phone still vibrating as the lights of the Eiffel Tower flickered over his shoulder. He had noted the caller ID at the table and knew he couldn't ignore the call. If he tried, it would only ring again. He finally answered, conversing at first in French, then switching to increasingly animated English.

"Save your obscenities, Karl," he snapped, pacing in the red hue of the neon sign. "Why are you being so pedantic? I told you, I *will* take care of it."

Pedantic was one of those words Meth trotted out when it seemed appropriate, not to impress anyone, just to be precise in his speech. Ironically, Meth was more pedantic about his speech than Karl was about business. That, along with his succinctness and his lack of contractions, drew occasional criticism from the few people who knew Meth well enough to tell him he sounded arrogant. He didn't care. Meth was nothing if not direct. He rarely initiated a conversation and he struggled when forced to maintain one. Speaking on a phone only accentuated his brevity and mechanical tone.

"I *am* in Paris!" he groused after a long pause. Meth paced while speaking, then stood still as Karl spoke, as if walking and listening were mutually exclusive. "I told you . . ." Meth said, stomping along the cobblestones. Then he froze; a small black dog shivering in the gutter held him silent and motionless.

"What's wrong?" Karl finally asked.

Meth looked away from the malnourished pup, reengaging the long-distance conversation and gesturing his frustration as if Karl could somehow see him through the phone. "Nothing," he said. "Like I told you, I *will* take care of it."

Karl continued his rant, but Meth was done. "Tonight!" he said interrupting. "I will be there Thursday." He stabbed the phone with his index finger, aborting the call with Karl still talking. He lamented not being on a landline so he could slam the handset down on the receiver. He shoved the phone into his pocket and started back to the restaurant.

"Got a fag, mate?" a disheveled English panhandler asked with an outstretched hand. Uninvited, he shadowed Meth's steps as they moved toward the sidewalk.

"I do not smoke," Meth replied, pushing his way back to the restaurant entrance. "I hate everything about cigarettes," he added, as if smoking was some grand moral breach. He disappeared through the crowd, leaving the panhandler empty-handed.

Meth's appetite had dissipated somewhere between the phone call and the cigarette smoke. He navigated his way back to his table only to survey his cold food and shake his head in disappointment. He nodded to his server and dropped a hundred-euro bill next to his half-eaten meal. The server raised a brow and returned a smile.

Meth grabbed the remaining baguettes from the small cutting-board on his table. He dropped them on top of his carbonara and tipped a variety of cheeses and meats from his charcuterie platter onto the pile. He lifted his sparkling water and stared, as if waiting for one last bubble to surface, then drank the last two swallows and returned the glass to the table. Hoisting the bowl of scraps, he turned toward the exit. He noticed an empty chair in place of the coral sweater. Her champagne flute and prescription bottle were both empty. Further irritated by the effects of the phone call, he scanned the room for her auburn hair, but she was gone. In one smooth pass toward the exit, he dropped a bill on the counter near the cash register, grabbed a box of Dunhills—*Might as well buy the best*, he thought—and quickened his step to the door.

Outside, red shadows danced across Meth's face as he again passed under the neon sign. After a quick survey of the area, he spotted the sweater passing a nearby streetlight. She staggered slightly. He took a step in her direction as he tossed the cigarettes into the panhandler's partially-gloved fingers. Without waiting for acknowledgment—Meth was never comfortable accepting thank-yous—he turned to follow her.

He kept the coral sweater in view as he again eyed the timid, still-shivering dog. He inched closer, gradually stooping. He lowered the bowl of scraps and slid it across the rough concrete, leaving tiny bits of fine china on the sidewalk along the way, until the hungry stray dropped his jowls into the bowl. Meth ran his fingers through the tangled hair on the back of the dog's neck before standing to move on. He glanced back at the glow from the satisfied panhandler's new treasure. Tightening the neck of his thick gray sweater, he headed down the rue.

Agitated, Meth walked fast, quickly closing the gap between him and the woman from the restaurant. He knew she'd be back. He could have waited for her at the hotel, but he followed anyway. A fastidious insomniac, he knew there was no point in heading to his room. Sleep came reluctantly to Meth when he was calm; it never visited when he was upset or had a task to complete.

He took a long jaunt, first around the Eiffel Tower and then under the cold stone eyes of the eagle on the southeast pillar of the Arc de Triomphe, all the while maintaining a fix on the bouncing auburn hair. He wondered why she would take such a tourist-worn route, but he was nonetheless impressed with her pace and endurance. With no further hint of a stagger, she navigated cobblestones in three-inch heels and covered the first few kilometers in less than an hour. She stopped occasionally as if seeing something she'd never before noticed, or to inhale the aromas wafting from bistros and cafes out into the night air. When the streets and the spaces between the buildings lined up, Meth could occasionally see the distant lights of Montparnasse. He was glad the towers and modern architecture had not metastasized to the rest of Paris.

He followed her back to Hotel Thoumieux, located above the restaurant where they had exchanged glances. The neon sign still buzzed, but the panhandler and stray pup were gone. Still careful that he not be seen with her, Meth took the stairs. He finally approached only as she neared the door of her fourth-floor room. He made sure she saw him approaching. He offered a smile and a slight nod. He casually pulled a room key from his pocket, the old-style fob conspicuously dangling—HOTEL THOUMIEUX ROOM 406—announcing him as a neighbor without saying a word. Her shoulders relaxed. She returned his smile. No longer a stranger, he slowed his pace and veered toward her.

"Share a bottle?" he asked in French with his distinctively raspy voice, at the same time producing a Côtes-du-Rhône he'd hastily purchased as she blithely strolled the Champs-Élysées. She offered a demure look, as she had in the restaurant, like she'd been waiting all night for him to speak. She invited him in with no apparent curiosity about how he had happened to find her again at that particular moment. She pushed the door closed behind them.

Meth leaned to reach the corkscrew on the credenza. He uncorked the bottle and filled one glass. He turned toward her, took a step, and brought the glass to her hand. She took a sip. With her other hand, she touched his arm and coaxed him closer. He caressed her cheek with his left palm, his fingers simultaneously tracing the ridges of her ear, pausing briefly near the jade dangling below her lobe. He inched his right hand along the arm of her sweater, taking a tantalizingly slow pace from her wrist to her shoulder. His left hand slid down the back of her head. He felt the tiny mounds of flesh arising on the nape of her neck. He heard a stutter in her breath—bordering on a moan—as she smiled and rolled her eyes. With her lids closed, she took a long drink, swallowed, and relinquished her empty glass back to him as she reclined onto the bed. He set the glass on the nightstand near her purse.

"Détends-toi," he whispered.

• "I *am* relaxed," she replied in English. "I took a sedative with champagne at dinner, then a long walk. And, now, the wine . . ."

She was relaxed. That was certain. Too relaxed to complete her sentence. Not too relaxed to enjoy the moment. She writhed under Meth's continued touch. He reached his free hand past her purse to the prescription bottle on the nightstand. She had many such bottles. Confirming his research, he saw her name, Brigitte Fournier, on her stockpile of narcotics.

"May I have one of your oxycodone?" he asked in his characteristically proper style.

"Help yourself," she mumbled.

Continuing his caress with one hand, he deftly opened her bottle with the other. He'd practiced to be sure he could. He had practiced everything.

Her eyes still closed, she remained unaware and apparently unconcerned about his actions. He tapped one pill, then a second, then a third onto the nightstand, but ingested none of them. Instead, he grated them together in his closed fist until they crumbled into her glass. Then he added more wine.

"Here," he encouraged, bringing the dangerous concoction to her lips, "have some more."

FIVE HOURS later, Meth checked the pulse in her right wrist. He had checked it several times through the early morning hours, and this time it was still. He rolled the neck of her sweater out of the way and checked her carotid. Still. The result was the same when he rested his cupped hand in front of her nose to check her breathing. Still.

He abruptly dragged her from the bed to the floor, his feigned tenderness now absent, replaced by the cold countenance that was his norm. *It is just a job,* he reminded himself, trying to assuage the guilt he pretended not to feel, the guilt he told himself was undeserved. *It had to be done.* The first few were the hardest. He was still a teenager then. He'd lost count somewhere in the twenties—somewhere in *his* twenties—when his memories and nightmares blurred into uncertainty. For more than a decade he'd felt nothing—certainly not guilt—and he liked it that way. But something about Brigitte Fournier reminded him of the mother he had loved in a childhood that now seemed more than a lifetime away.

He drew a handkerchief from his pocket and carefully wiped the amber-colored prescription bottle before placing it into the left hand of the motionless figure still wearing her coral sweater. In the process, he tapped three more pills out onto the carpet. He wiped the glass and half-empty bottle—he'd poured a generous portion down the drain—before carefully wrapping her right hand sequentially around each. He repositioned them, with their fresh prints, back on the credenza. He wiped the corkscrew and the furniture. He did his usual meticulous sweep of the room. Forcing thoughts of his mother from his mind, he stepped back over Brigitte's flowing auburn hair and casually straightened his cufflinks.

"It is just a job," he muttered aloud, looking back. He stood silent, looking longer. To say he was conflicted would be the epitome of understatement. He repositioned her body into what he imagined would have been a more comfortable position and stroked her hair away from her face.

After another long pause, still using his handkerchief, he quietly opened the door and surveyed the hallway. He had watched her check in to the hotel earlier in the day and, after checking in himself, had disabled the hallway security camera near the elevator. He had rehearsed every detail. He stepped into the hallway, hung the Do Not Disturb sign, and slowly pulled the knob. Brigitte's perfectly manicured hand disappeared as the shadowy wedge of light narrowed behind the closing door.

2

HEADING HOME

METH ENTERED his hotel room at the end of the hall, just two doors from the lifeless woman with the jade jewelry and auburn hair. He pushed the door closed behind him and leaned against it just long enough to take a deep breath. Trembling muscles in his right thigh sent a ripple down his pant leg. He pulled off his sweater and his creased black jeans, like peeling away an unwanted persona, and flung them over a chair. He flopped onto the bed. He massaged his quivering leg and took another deep breath.

Better me than of one of Karl's goons, he thought. *Better a peaceful sleep than fear and violence.* For a time the money was enough—enough, that is, to sustain the rationalizations he'd carefully woven through the early years. Now he didn't need the money. He knew what he was doing was legitimate, even justifiable. Many would thank him if they knew. But it had still taken him years to quell his ruminations about the ethics of his craft. Now, thanks to Brigitte, the questions and doubts had clawed their way back.

Soft light spilled from the street through the partially open drapes and cast shadows across the walls until he turned on the bedside lamp. His eyes darted from one corner of the room to the next, as if searching, then slowly scanned the door and settled on the bedside clock at 5:02 a.m. He looked toward the window, the rumblings in his leg slowing under his continued massage. The moment his tremor subsided, Meth's countenance calmed. Agitation ebbed from his face and the tension around his eyes softened; he became a different man when the trembling stopped. He rolled off the bed as if nothing had happened and headed for a quick shower.

After his shower, Meth wrapped a towel around his waist and listed slightly to locate his reflection in the steamy mirror. He pulled a brush

7

through his thick dark hair and rubbed his hand back and forth across his whiskers, leaving his three-day beard intact. He paused, focusing on the small vertical offset in the middle of his right eyebrow. He winced as he touched it, as if it were still tender. The scar, nearly thirty years old, sparked memories still painfully fresh. Touching it brought the reflection of another scar into view. He eyed the Q-shaped mark on the back of his left hand in the mirror. He turned his hand over and looked at it directly. He glanced back at the mirror, at his eyebrow.

A few minutes later Meth cinched his belt, left the top button of his tab-collared shirt open, and donned a leather-trimmed sport coat. He avoided ties whenever possible; they reminded him of funerals and the people no longer in his life. He stepped toward the large windows of his hotel room. He drew the drapes, swung the windows wide, and leaned into the unseasonably warm January air. Looking beyond the decorative wrought-iron rail, he surveyed the glowing streetlights below and the few lit windows that marked the early-risers in nearby buildings. The cobblestone street four stories down, still wet from a midnight rain, glistened in the predawn light. He leaned into the fresh air, took a cleansing breath—in through his nose, out through his mouth.

I love Paris, he thought. It was a strange word for Meth. He didn't love anything. He hadn't used the word in twenty years except to ridicule the whole concept of love. That the word rolled through his mind surprised him.

As a general rule, Meth was not keen on France, though he always enjoyed its capital city. He began his life in Bayeux, in Normandy, but recollections of Bayeux were mixed at best. His few cherished memories of childhood sprang from his trips to Paris with his maternal grandfather, Truman Hamstead. Truman loved life and took Meth along whenever he could. As an adult in Paris, Meth liked the food, the women, the art—particularly le Musée d'Orsay on the left bank of the Seine—and the history. He frequented upscale restaurants, like 1728, now housed in what was once the Hotel Mazin La Fayette and named for the year in which the hotel was originally constructed. He felt equally comfortable grabbing a petite baguette au fromage at a corner pâtisserie and eating it while walking Île de la Cité. He looked up the street, then down, toward the Eiffel Tour. He took another deep breath, as if to sniff out one of those bakeries.

"I *love* Paris," he whispered, determined to prove he wasn't afraid of the word, pretending he knew what it meant.

Meth turned back to his room without closing the windows. He walked past his bed and gripped the doorknob. He paused and took a deep breath, hearing the air rush in then out through his nose. He pulled the door open and propped it with his foot. Grabbing his leather satchel, he draped his cashmere overcoat across his arm and wrapped a gray silk scarf twice around his neck. Leaning into a new day, he passed into the poorly lit hallway and strode toward the elevator.

Meth strutted through the lobby as if he owned the hotel. When he started to move—when he had a destination in focus and a timeline in mind—he walked smartly toward his goal without looking back. He never looked back. He dropped his room key onto the counter and continued toward the waiting taxi. A uniformed clerk scooped the key from the desk and offered a perfunctory, "Merci, monsieur. Au revoir." Meth didn't respond. He just kept moving.

"Gare de Lyon," he requested, passing the driver who held the open rear door of a black Mercedes. Meth slid onto the creaking leather. The driver nodded, closed the door, and hustled around the taxi to his seat. The tires squeaked on the damp cobblestones as the car jerked away.

After a silent ride, the taxi stopped below the clock tower at Gare de Lyon, the sun still refusing to start the day. Travelers hustled toward the gare, dragging bags of various shapes and sizes. Meth exited his taxi, ducked a passing umbrella, paid the driver, and added a sizeable tip. As he turned to leave, he shoved his hand into his pocket and noticed something. Turning back, he pulled half a dozen coins from his pocket and dribbled them into the diver's still-open hand.

"I have no use for these heavy coins in Zurich," he explained, as if he didn't want to be accused of being generous. "They should make these things lighter, like Swiss francs."

Apparently less concerned about the weight than the value, the taxi driver clenched his hand. "Merci, monsieur."

Meth pushed through the gare, paying no attention to the surroundings or people except for a wistful glance toward Le Train Bleu, his favorite Parisian restaurant and a landmark in Gare de Lyon for over a century. He felt strangely at home in the station. He liked the rumble of distant undecipherable voices and the rub of leather soles on smooth concrete, and he relished the aroma of coffee and croissants and fresh newsprint. His pace—a jog for most people—and his impeccable timing found him approaching his car exactly one minute before its scheduled departure.

Near the coach, a small red ball bounced across the platform in front of him. Meth reached out and caught it mid-stride, like a goalkeeper in the World Cup. He paused, turned, and, with an uncharacteristically empathetic expression, gently handed it back to a smiling five-year-old boy.

For a just a moment, maybe less than a moment, Meth's countenance changed. He was a boy again. Then it was gone.

The child's mother attempted to thank Meth, but he'd already turned his focus back to the train, unaware and unconcerned about anyone except the boy. He saw a spark from an arriving train and paused just long enough to inhale the unmistakably electrical smell of newly-formed ozone. If others found the smell objectionable, it had a different effect on Meth. He could never identify anything specific, but it always triggered some primal sense of familiarity. With an almost-satisfied expression, he stepped onboard.

When boarding a double-level train, Meth always chose the upper level. He liked to see as far into the distance as possible, and he liked facing the front of the train. He preferred a seat near the middle of the coach, away from the noise of the pneumatic doors at either end. As with most things in Meth's life, his train routine was predictable. He settled near the window and opened his laptop on the table. He dropped his Tusting satchel and overcoat into the aisle seat, turning it into his personal buffer zone. When he sat down, he straightened his legs and plopped his shoes onto the facing seat. The aisle seat, diagonally across the table, usually remained unoccupied. Today proved no exception.

He reclined his seatback and closed his eyes, partly to sleep and partly to dissuade others from initiating conversation. As beautiful as the French countryside was, sometimes he closed his eyes just to avoid painful memories.

On the other side of Meth's closed eyes, a particularly attractive woman with a large bag ogled discreetly as she boarded. Still standing in the aisle, she dropped her bag and grabbed a seatpost to catch her balance as the train lurched into motion. It was hard to not notice Meth; dark, six-foot-one, well proportioned, he looked like an escapee from the cover of *GQ*. The small vertical offset in the middle of his right eyebrow was not so irregular as to be unattractive. It was just enough to add a distinctive signature to his look. And when he raised his brows, the right lagged ever so slightly below the left, like a younger brother trying to keep up. His infrequent words telegraphed an aloofness that only added to his mystique.

The eyebrow was a gift from his father, a permanent reminder of his seventh birthday. Meth refused to call him a father. For many years he had refused even to speak his name. He referred to him simply as Le Soûlard—The Drunkard—one of the few French words Meth liked. As far as Meth was concerned, the man was a malevolent, booze-addled waste of human flesh who somehow managed to close his fist that day, amid a cloud of vulgar French expletives and angered by some still unidentified trigger, and send Meth flailing across the room in front of his childhood friends. Le Soûlard left Meth bleeding in the corner. As quickly as he'd staggered uninvited into that party, he left again, abandoning Meth to the rest of his life, marked inside and out.

Meth's placid style, his abhorrence of alcohol, cigarettes, and foul language, all grew largely from a vow he'd made that day to never be like the despicable animal who left his hateful mark and then left altogether. Meth's reluctance to speak French, though fluent, grew largely from the fact that the man who was once married to his mother spoke only French.

That birthday party proved a turning point for Meth, supplanting most of what preceded it and changing everything that followed. In a sense, the only three things Meth got from Le Soûlard were a determination to take a different path, a set of scars—one on his hand, one on his face, and others more insidiously buried in his psyche—and a name.

A cabin attendant approached Meth's table and paused. The purple TGV on her lapel pin, an acronym for Train à Grande Vitesse (high-speed train), accented her standard gray suit and purple blouse. The uniform looked nicer on her lithe figure than it did on most employees. To add a personal flair, she had woven a matching purple ribbon through the long dark braid that bounced across her back as she walked. She stopped her cart at Meth's table and pretended to not notice his eyes were closed.

"Petit déjeuner, monsieur?" she asked.

Meth raised his good brow just enough to make eye contact and forced himself to be polite. "Breakfast?" he asked, his sleepless voice deeper than usual.

Taking his cue, she responded in English. "It's included with your ticket, monsieur."

Meth would not usually have this exchange; he would not have purchased a ticket with a meal. Somebody in the office, probably Alex, had purchased the ticket for him. Normally he slept through these morning trips. And, since he had not yet been to bed, sleep was a higher priority than food. He nevertheless nodded affirmatively before again closing his eyes. She placed a tray with a croissant, coffee, orange juice, a cup of granola, and a package of yogurt on the small table in front of him and lingered a moment, smiling, as if contemplating what she might say to draw another glance.

Meth drew in the scent of fresh coffee and held it. It took him places: to an inviting home in Geneva where he had first tasted coffee with his maternal grandfather, to Le Train Bleu with that same loving grandparent, to happier times. He wanted to be there again. He recognized the Italian accent in the attendant's French and English. Without opening his eyes, he indulged her continued presence. "Bello accento," he commented. "Da Italia?"

"Sissignore," she said, her eyes brightening.

Meth looked up, reestablishing eye contact. He admired her slender figure. *None of those ridiculous bags of American silicone*, he thought.

"Sicilia? Sardegna?" he asked, further pinpointing her accent.

"Sì, signore. Sicilia. I'm leaving tomorrow for a week in Val di Noto." She smiled and lifted her brows. "Tonight I'm at Merian am Rhein in Basel."

Meth eyed her up and down and then up again without speaking.

"Michaela Idoni," she said, flicking her nametag as she spoke.

"Grazie," he said, pointing to the meal. "Ciao."

She moved on reluctantly, looking back twice.

Meth turned his attention to the passing hamlets and fields, the power poles now flashing past like pickets on a fence. The rising sun cast blue and pink hues across a few small clouds. Wisps of fog obscured buildings and gave one steeple the appearance of floating freely in the morning air. Puffs and swirls escaped cottage chimneys. In the deepest reaches of his imagination Meth pictured the homes as safe and comfortable, the families as loving. In reality, he feared such absurd notions existed only in his mind, spawned by romantic movies in his distant past. If forced to talk about such fantasies, he would admit neither expectation nor hope that such a family actually existed.

He gazed intently at the smoke swirling from one cottage chimney until his eyelids sagged and closed.

3

HAPPY BIRTHDAY

SIX-YEAR-OLD METH, his arms loaded with firewood, gazed upward at the smoke escaping his chimney. He labored a few more steps through deep snow to his front porch and then to the door. His only cherished possession—a three-month-old puppy, the runt of the litter and a gift from old man Charbonneau up the lane—bounced along behind him. Meth had heard his English mother say *old man* so many times and with such affection, he thought Charbonneau's first name was Oldman. Achilles, all black except a white patch on the back of each hind leg, served faithfully as Meth's closest friend. After some convoluted conversation with his mother about Greek mythology, and over her protests that he failed to understand, Meth insisted on the name. To him, it felt comfortable—familiar, like the ozone at the gare.

Meth's mother finally accepted the name. His father never did.

Meth managed to twist the knob with his mittened hand while continuing to balance the firewood in his arms. He pushed the door open with his shoulder and left Achilles behind on the porch. The whole house welcomed him with the smell of fresh-baked bread. He stacked several pieces of firewood—a respectable load for his age and size—near the wood-burning stove before stepping back to take a breath. To his chagrin, the stack teetered, then toppled across the wooden floor.

Meth's father, François Moreau—a portly, obstreperous, and undignified excuse for a man—turned toward the noise, a half-smoked cigarette dangling from his unkempt face. He bellowed in slurred French, "Again? You make me sick. You are the pain of a filthy dog!"

It was a strange phrase. It made no sense to Meth. He'd had no time to think about it then, but he'd contemplated it innumerable times since. All that registered in the moment was "You make me sick. You filthy dog!" That's what he would hear endlessly for decades.

Meth cringed at the loud voice and cowered as François stumbled closer. He began to cry in anticipation. He wasn't sure what was coming but the cigarette burn on the back of his left hand assured him it would not be good. François grabbed Meth's left wrist and twisted it until he could see his perverted handiwork. He widened his stance to steady his drunken frame and pushed his face close to Meth's, spraying bits of sweat and spit with each insult. He pulled the glowing cigarette from his mouth and snubbed it out in Meth's still-healing wound.

Adelaide, Meth's soft-spoken and diminutive mother, witnessed her son's abuse from across the room. It was over before she could react. She reflexively covered her ears as the sound of sizzling flesh disappeared behind her son's tortured scream. Sadly, she was powerless to help; her attempts to do so in the past had only made things worse. She instinctively rushed toward her injured boy only to be stopped by François' glare and raised fist. Meth saw her eyes widen as a horrified expectation swept across her face. François opened his mouth but said nothing. Instead, he turned and stormed out of the house. On the porch, Achilles had begun barking when he heard Meth's cry. François kicked the pup so violently that he launched him over the porch railing toward the deep snow and sent him yelping across the yard.

Adelaide quickly gathered herself, altogether too practiced in doing so, and came to Meth's side. Her face was bruised from her own recent encounters with François. Her dress was modest and worn, her shoes still dusted with flour. She knelt and wrapped Meth's charred hand in her apron then moved back to her corner of the room to her spindly bentwood rocker, cradling him on her lap as they wept together. It seemed for a time there was nothing to say—nothing with meaning, nothing that had not been said too many times before.

"Prometheus," she finally whispered in her East-London accent, wrapping her arms a little tighter around his slender frame. She paused. Just saying his name brought comfort. "I'm sorry, Son," she said. "It's the alcohol. He wasn't always this way. He was kind and loving."

Meth endured a long pause, his right leg trembling, feeling his mother's tears against his face. She shuddered intermittently as she struggled to compose herself.

"I love you, Son."

She waited again, staring out the window.

"I hate him," Meth said in French.

"Love matters," she told him, seeming to remind herself in the process. "Choose to love."

"Pourquoi, Maman?"

"English, Prometheus. He's gone now. You can speak English."

English was a bond they shared exclusive of François. She comforted and encouraged her son in English, connecting him with that portion of his heritage and family. Though too young to understand or articulate it, Meth felt safe speaking English. It seemed like some invisible barrier between him and François; he never uttered a word of English in François' presence.

"Why is he so mean, Momma? Why does he hate me?"

Adelaide was accustomed to Meth's precocious questions, to his unusual maturity and intelligence. He had spoken early in life and had added to his bilingual vocabulary rapidly. She cradled his face in her hands as only a mother could and looked through his green eyes and deeply into his soul.

"I hate him, Momma. I hate him."

Failing a meaningful response, Adelaide pulled Meth close and embraced him in silence.

TIME PASSED. Snow melted. Achilles grew, as did Meth, though no one had called him by that name yet. A Cambridge flatmate would coin the nickname years later. To his mother, he was always Prometheus. To the monster he later refused to call father, he was *The Dog*.

Life on the southeast fringe of Bayeux, in the tiny community of Saint-Martin-des-Entrées, might have provided Meth a rich historical experience had he lived there longer or been less consumed with the primal need to simply survive. William the Conqueror, more infamously known as William the Bastard, became the first Norman King of England in 1066, the tale of his conquest famously depicted on the 900-year-old, seventy-meter Bayeux Tapestry. Meth never saw the tapestry as a child, but he later concluded that whatever was French in François had compelled him to repeatedly re-enact the battle with his English wife.

Meth would later learn, too, of the more recent history of his childhood haunts. On D-Day-plus-ten, Bayeux became the first town liberated in the Battle of Normandy. In the 21st Century it remained a central hub for visitors to the region. The walls of the Churchill Hotel were plastered with black-and-white glossies of liberating allies and grateful Normans, but no such liberators had come to Meth's home when he most needed them.

Despite ongoing abuse, Meth found times to laugh, especially when alone with Achilles. He drew from an unusual abundance of childhood resilience and optimism—an irrepressible optimism that somehow smiled through the cracks of hell—at least, that is, until his seventh birthday. Achilles presented opportunities for distraction. If Meth ever felt safe—if he ever felt happy, like a child should feel—it was with Achilles, as far from François as possible. Sometimes Meth almost forgot about the abuse, but such times came infrequently and with stark interruptions.

One summer day, six months after the most recent cigarette incident,

Meth laughed with his friends at his seventh birthday party. He and his mother were operating under the false notion that François was gone for the day—gone on another drunken stroll to the gare. He would drink himself to near oblivion then vegetate on the platform, watching the trains until he passed out on the bench. The whole town knew where he would be at noon. Adelaide spoke of better times, but Meth had never seen them. He never understood François' drinking or his obsession with trains. He was just grateful for a few hours with his friends, away from François.

Achilles, nearly grown but still rambunctious, enjoyed the kids and the party. When François was absent, the front door often remained ajar, giving Achilles free passage in and out. As Meth turned from his dog to unwrap presents, Achilles walked outside and disappeared beyond the partially open door. Before he could finish opening his first present, Meth froze as he heard his dog bark, then painfully yelp, then fall silent. He instantly recognized the French obscenities and the drunken voice of François.

"Damn dog!"

The door slammed open, shattering a pane of glass and silhouetting the slovenly and irascible François in the doorway. Despite the summer heat, he was wrapped in the same soiled and tattered overcoat he wore every day, a corked flask protruding, as always, from his pocket. He dropped his bloody axe on the threshold and staggered toward a terrified Meth, leaving crimson footprints on the unwaxed planks. He clenched his fist. For no apparent reason, he brutally struck his defenseless son, sending him sprawling across the room. Meth landed in a crumpled pile in the corner, too stunned to cry, bleeding from his right eyebrow. Blood trickled into the corner of his mouth. It tasted like the two-cent coin he'd once stashed under his tongue for fear François might see it and take it away.

François stared at Meth. Then he looked away, through the open door toward the unseen dog, then back at Meth. Without attempting to clarify whether he was talking about his son or the pet, he repeated, "Damn dog!"

François stumbled out the door, passing the body of the dog near the bottom of the steps on his way. Meth struggled to his feet and darted to the porch, hoping against the worst. Blood from his eye dripped onto the axe and trickled into the small puddle left on the porch by François' weapon. Achilles lay motionless, the ground stained red. Meth would never miss Le Soûlard, but he would fail in his attempts to forget him.

Meth slept little, and fitfully, that night. He could not bear the thought of parting with Achilles. He gave up on sleep around midnight. François had not come home; sometimes he didn't come home for days. Gambling his safety, Meth slipped quietly through the front door and down the porch steps, dragging the gray wool blanket from his bed. He wrapped his fallen comrade in the blanket and struggled to pull the bundle onto the porch. He curled himself around Achilles, as he had done in his bed the previous night, and slept in the warm summer air.

The sun woke Meth early but failed to dispel the darkness in his day. The only bright spot in his life had been extinguished. Meth's blood had mixed with Achilles' and was now an indelible stain on the porch slats, a daily reminder of what he'd lost.

Two hours into the day, Adelaide watched from the porch as Meth, his face bruised and eyebrow bandaged, attempted to dig a grave. He could barely wield the small spade, let alone swing a pickax into the hardpan. He moved to the corner of the garden where the soil was softer, but the task was still beyond his seven-year-old arms. He'd already refused his mother's help. There was nothing she could do but watch. The motionless form of Achilles, wrapped in the gray blanket now stained with blood, rested near the first attempt at a grave. A crude wooden marker leaned against the lifeless form, A. M. freshly scratched through the gray weathered surface of the board. He had wanted to carve Achilles Moreau deeply into the wood with a knife but he'd done the best he could with a sharp rock.

Meth glared at his mother on the porch. Only as an adult, looking back, would he see the pain in her face. He was too young to understand her limitations or the undeserved shame in her eyes. She'd tried twice to leave the porch and come to his aid only to be stopped by his haunting stare. When he finally conceded his inability to complete the morbid task, he left Achilles, the spade, and the would-be marker, and disappeared into Oldman's orchard. Later, when he returned, all three were gone. From a distant corner of the orchard he'd seen Charbonneau talking with Adelaide, but he never asked who had buried Achilles. Whoever had buried the dog had also buried a portion of Prometheus. Adelaide refused to salt her son's wounds by offering an answer to his unasked question. As it turned out, that etched chunk of wood would prove more a wedge in their relationship than a marker for Achilles' grave.

Meth had learned something on his seventh birthday, even if only by accident. Bleeding in the corner and on the porch, it was as if he'd forgotten to cry. In the moments that followed, his absence of tears had given him a sense of control—a control his mother and guests had seemed to notice and admire. An array of emotions had cascaded through his young mind, but he'd given none of them an outward display. He was too young to understand how anger and hatred had become his means of control that day, but he had practiced it again when he tried to bury Achilles the next morning. Rather than crying over the hard ground, he'd walked away determined to never cry again.

"Someday, Mother," he said, when he finally returned home from the orchard. "Someday I will kill him, just the way he killed Achilles."

The ominous declaration from Meth's seven-year-old lips carried an inescapable sense of determination. Goosebumps arose on Adelaide's arms as a worried look, filled with a mother's love and intuition, settled on her face. Young Meth walked past her on the porch and into the house, clearly communicating with his eyes that he did not wish to be touched or spoken to. She bowed her head and wept.

4

APOPLEXY

BACK ON the train—back in the present—Meth flinched as he realized he was rubbing his right brow. Rage, confusion and hatred all churned as if his seventh birthday had been yesterday—as if he were struggling to bury Achilles all over again. He could almost see the cigarette smoke, and smell it, mixed with the pungent stench of liquor that always accompanied François. He could smell the burning flesh from the tiny conflagration on his hand. His face tightened. He looked out the window and began kneading the muscles in his trembling right thigh.

"Bonjour, monsieur."

The bright, feminine greeting jolted Meth's from his darkness. He looked up to a petite thirty-something smiling back. She seemed the sort to smile at everyone. She smiled as much with her eyes as with her deep red lips. As rapidly as he had scanned upward from the floor, he had still managed to notice a few things: her tall heels, the crease in her slacks, her slender fingers, and the button-down collar of her blouse. When he finally got to her dark wavy hair—in that moment that seemed much longer than a moment—he noticed it bouncing on her shoulders with each bump of the train.

Initially Meth resented her smile. He just wanted to be left alone. *She is one of those*, he thought, using contractions no more in his thoughts than in his speech. *Everybody is wonderful. Life is grand.* He could do without her exuberance. At the same instant, he sensed something different about her. Her smile proclaimed she had experienced life's every challenge and come off conqueror, and that others could do the same. She had spoken only two words but had plucked some familiar chord or some long-forgotten emotion that Meth struggled to interpret.

19

The woman plopped into the aisle seat diagonally across the table from Meth—the seat he was accustomed to having empty. Before he could respond to her greeting or protest her intrusion, the conductor interrupted.

"Billet, monsieur?"

Meth extended his rail pass and passport. The conductor gave each a cursory glance and looked back.

"Prometheus?" he asked, confirming the name on the documents.

"Oui," Meth answered matter-of-factly, still looking out the window.

The conductor returned the papers and turned to the now seated smile. She proffered her ticket without waiting to be asked. He gave it the usual fleeting look, perforated it with the rectangular TGV punch, handed it back, and moved on.

With a curious expression, the woman politely echoed the conductor's question.

"Prometheus?"

Frustrated, Meth nodded without speaking or making eye contact. He hoped his cold response would end their exchange. One thing he liked less than talking to a stranger was talking about himself. He had dug deeply into his tiny reserve of congeniality to tolerate the cabin attendant with his breakfast. He knew she would quickly move on; she had no choice. But this one had claimed a seat, in his extended personal space no less, and offered no hint of being dissuaded.

"Interesting," she said in French. She watched, still smiling, like she already knew she could outwait his reluctance.

Hoping to bolster his isolation, Meth tapped a key on his laptop, bringing the screen to life. *She is not very tall*, he thought, as he fixed his eyes on the computer. *In fact, she is kind of a stub.* If he had said it out loud, it would have been offensive, but in his mind it was the opposite. To him, she had a perfect stature. In Meth's world, Stub was a term of endearment. He struggled to remember people's names—one of many challenges rooted in his refusal to engage the world socially—so he often used descriptive nicknames, even if only in his mind. He began typing as if still alone—wishing ambivalently that he was.

"Is that it?" she asked, continuing in French.

"Madame?"

He peered over his computer screen, catching her eyes squarely for the first time. They coaxed a strange tingling through his head before he forced himself to look away.

"Your name; it's fascinating. Does it mean something?"

Meth leaned back and again looked her top to bottom, unconcerned about whether she would notice. He turned toward the window where her image flashed repeatedly in the panes, like a wall poster under a strobe light. He liked her tailored crimson blouse, her tweed pantsuit and the loose-knit scarf she pulled from her shoulders. He looked back just in time to see the Prada label disappear under folds of fabric as she dropped it onto the table. It fanned wisps of Shalimar in his direction. She seemed so comfortable, so nonchalant. He paused and looked back at her, conflicted and a little less certain he wanted to be left alone. He especially liked her deep brown eyes and the tiny hint of a dimple in each cheek when she raised the corners of her mouth.

"¿Eres de España?" he finally asked, completely ignoring her inquiry about his name.

Meth grew up speaking mostly English and French, but he also conversed comfortably in Spanish, Italian, and German. He had spent several years with his grandfather in Geneva and had traveled throughout the languages and geography of Switzerland. He enjoyed languages—as much as Meth enjoyed anything, that is—and discerning the accents of the people he encountered. It was one of the few things that inclined him to engage with strangers. He made no claims as a linguist, but he had a knack for mapping an accent.

"Sí, señor," she bubbled. "Barcelona."

"Me gusta tu acento," he replied, assuming he had successfully diverted the conversation.

"Gracias, señor. And I like yours. Do you speak English?"

"You prefer English?"

"English intrigues me. It's odd. What happened to gender in the nouns, for example? And how did the adjectives end up ahead of the nouns instead of after them?"

Meth raised his brows.

"I don't *prefer* English," she said, "but I practice it when I travel." She shrugged, as if to flick away any need to apologize. "And I like American slang."

Meth turned back to his computer. "Why?" he muttered, shaking his head.

If she sensed his contempt for American slang, she let it pass. She neither softened her smile nor looked away. Her resilience intrigued him, though it also triggered suspicion. His work made him suspicious of everybody, of every circumstance and coincidence. *What is she after?*

"What about your name?" she persisted. She waited and watched until Meth slowly reestablished eye contact. Then she continued, "What does it mean?"

He rubbed his whiskers for a few seconds like a contemplative Santa with a difficult child on his lap. He took a deep breath and squirmed a bit.

"Really?" he asked, dreading the notion of a longer conversation.

Stub again offered what had already become her signature expression. Then she raised her brows slightly and pursed her lips, silently reiterating her query. In contrast to Meth, she was a talker. She apparently liked to talk, and to listen, to engage people and to know them, even if only for a few hours on a train. Completely undeterred by Meth's aloofness, she persisted.

"Yes. Really. I want to know."

Somewhere between embarrassment and resignation, Meth glanced around to see if others were listening. He looked out the window and began relinquishing tiny fragments of his past as if Stub wasn't there, as if he were talking to some specter floating alongside the train.

"It came from my mother's husband," he said, glancing back to measure her response. He gradually increased eye contact as he continued. "Some might call him my father," he said, shaking his head, "but not me." His expression hardened. He took an audible breath. "He was there," Meth admitted, momentarily nodding his head before again shaking it side-to-side, "but he was no father."

The tension in Meth's face increased. Stub sat silently, waiting. He resumed typing, not inclined to spill his secretes so easily.

"What does it mean?" she coaxed. Her tone was soft. The curiosity in her eyes now seemed more like concern.

Meth's only answer was a puzzled expression. He had failed to redirect her thoughts, but he'd managed to derail his own. He looked back at his computer, trying to remember where the conversation was headed.

"Your name?" she reminded.

"Are you always so persistent?"

She nodded, her smile returning as if her mission was to rescue the introverts. Unlike most extroverts Meth had encountered, Stub seemed less self-centered, more genuine. She didn't put out an air of superiority, as if introversion was a character flaw. Rather, she behaved as if life was simply more fun when people were friendly, and she was there to be a friend. It was not merely her persistence; it was her disarming affability. She seemed to genuinely care. And Meth found himself surprisingly willing to talk.

"It is not so much about what it means," he explained, "but what he did."

"Okay. So what'd he do?"

"In Greek mythology, Prometheus was a Titan. He created man from clay. Then he defied the gods and gave man fire."

"Ah, grandioso? How you say? . . . Uh, heady? Is that right? Heady stuff."

Meth nodded and offered his best attempt at a smile. She had conversed, to that point, like a native English-speaker—like an American, really. He'd become so comfortable with her English he was surprised when she hesitated.

"It all sounds wonderful and heroic, except Zeus became enraged and sentenced Prometheus to eternal torment."

He looked at Stub. She waited.

"Zeus bound him to a rock and sent an eagle to devour his liver. Because Prometheus was immortal, his liver regenerated overnight just to be eaten again the next day."

She cringed but remained silent.

"Why would a man name his son Prometheus?" Meth asked, more to himself than to Stub. The question had become rhetorical over the years. He actually liked his name, but he wondered what had rattled around in François' head when he chose it. "He never even explained it to me. I learned about Prometheus years later on my own."

For some reason Meth failed to understand, he kept talking, mostly looking at his computer, only occasionally making eye contact.

"The only mythology I recall from childhood was a vague reference to Achilles and his vulnerable heel. When a neighbor gave me a puppy with white patches on his legs, I named him Achilles. My mother tried to talk me out of it, but I insisted."

"Why did she object?"

"I never knew. I still do not know."

Meth's countenance saddened. He looked out the window. For just a moment, he forgot someone was listening.

"I loved that dog," he whispered.

After a long heavy silence, Meth remembered himself. He looked across the table just as a tear slipped from Stub's cheek to her chin to her lap.

"I'm sorry about your dog," she said without asking details.

Meth squirmed—inside, at least—wondering why he had revealed so much. And why did she care? Angry about his revelations, he returned to his computer. He banged away on his keyboard, ignoring her as if they had never spoken.

A cabin attendant broke the tension, offering drinks and snacks. As the attendant loaded their table, a hint of Stub's perfume floated again in Meth's direction. He drew it in like the first breath of spring. He stole a glance then turned his face to the sun and closed his eyes.

Free from the burden of conversation, the creases around Meth's eyes soon softened. Stub studied his face until his breathing slowed and deepened, until his clenched fist relaxed. Another tear trailed down her face and fell onto her hand. She pulled a notebook and a Waterman fountain pen from her small purse. She twisted the cap from her Perrier, releasing a gasp of carbon dioxide, and slowly filled her glass. For several minutes she watched bubbles zigzag to the surface. Then she looked intently at Prometheus and began to write.

TEENAGE PROMETHEUS laughed as he coaxed three other puppies aside in order to reach the smallest one. He slid his hand under the smiling two-week-old terrier-mix. She had more energy than the other three combined. She wriggled and licked his hand as he brought her close to his face. Then she licked his chin.

Next to Meth, wrapped around his arm and reaching to pet the pup, was Addison Ainsworth. Meth was nearly sixteen; she was a few years older but looked the same age. She smiled and kissed him on the cheek. Then she kissed the pup. She vibrated with enthusiasm.

"Get it," she said. "You have to get it."

"I can't. I don't have anyplace to put it. I couldn't take care of it."

"I'll help. We can do it."

They held the bustling little ball between them, laughing and exchanging looks until the storeowner gave them a look of his own. It was the third time that week they'd been in to play with the pups. He let them know he had a business to run. Addison shrugged and warped her eyebrows at Meth, as if to acknowledge the storeowner's point. She reached for a nearby display and grabbed a collar with a blue tag. She bounced over to the counter and winked at the middle-aged man in his dirty white shirt. He blushed as he took her money and invited them to come back anytime.

Meth and Addison returned the yet-to-be-named puppy to her siblings and walked hand-in-hand to Trockel, Ulmann & Freunde, Addison's favorite café. They'd been there many times. She'd called it unpretentious; Meth took that as code for affordable. They sat outside in the warm sun, talking more than eating. Addison—Adi, as she liked to be called—had never seen Meth so happy. After sharing a classroom with him for weeks, and without receiving any attention, she'd asked him to share a cup of coffee at the TU&F on Pembroke Street. He'd stumbled with his response until she finally said, "It's just coffee. Let's go." Her pragmatism had helped him through unnumbered moments of social awkwardness—*Let's go*, he'd hear her say in his head. The simple phrase had moved him forward. It's what she'd said the first time she'd held his hand and the first time they'd kissed. Sometimes she could say it with just a look.

"What's with the collar?" Meth finally asked after they were seated at the café.

The buckle-end and unstamped tag had dangled from her pocket and jingled as they walked. Now it reflected the sun into Meth's eyes. He knew the answer to his question; he was just making conversation—another talent Adi had helped him to develop.

"It's for Muffles."

"Muffles?"

"That puppy. We're going to get it, right?"

Meth thought about her pronouns and their implications. He started to drift until she snapped her fingers in front of his face. It was a nonverbal cue they'd adopted over the last eighteen months as she had helped him stay more fully in the present. Initially it irritated him. Now it just made him smile.

"I'm not owning a dog named Muffles."

"Muffles is a great name."

Meth offered an incredulous look. He'd stopped short of saying he wouldn't have a dog. He'd said that many times in the past—but he hadn't said it yet today. He let Adi assume she was making progress. Truman had tried several times to buy Meth a dog—he'd encouraged as strongly as a grandfather could—usually each spring. Meth assumed Adi and Truman had conspired in this latest effort. He was happier around dogs. He knew it. Truman and Adi had both noticed. But feeling happy around a new dog left him feeling guilty about Achilles, like he was being unfaithful to his fallen friend.

"I told you. I can't get a dog right now."

He became wistful, almost tearful. Adi watched intently. She knew about Achilles, though it had taken more than a year of friendship before Meth had told her. He'd told her about François and Adelaide as well. She knew Meth better than did anyone except Truman. She knew, and she loved him. He was young but very mature—mature enough to understand friendship. Adi loved him and he knew it.

The conversation had suddenly become too serious. It was time to move on. He smiled and squeezed her hand.

"If I ever get another dog, it won't be named Muffles."

A few days later, under the shade of an enormous English elm, Meth kicked off his shoes and stretched out on the grass. Adi pulled a blanket from her picnic basket and rolled it out like a red carpet. She loved old movies and quoted lines occasionally. She'd even dragged Meth to Nostalgia Night to see the old classic, *To Catch a Thief.* She arranged their food on the blanket and handed him a soft drink. She pulled the lid from their bucket of chicken and grinned.

"Do you want a leg or a breast?" she said, reenacting the question Francie (Grace Kelly) had asked John Robie (Cary Grant) during their picnic between Nice and Monte Carlo.

Meth opened his mouth, debating for a moment how to answer. Before he could say anything, Adi raised her index finger and lifted her eyebrows. He waited. She reached into her basket. Without a word, she placed a small wrapped box in front of him on the blanket. He looked at it for a long moment and wrinkled his forehead. He looked back at her, uncertainty deep in his expression. Meth didn't celebrate his birthday. She knew that, and she knew why. She'd only learned the exact date by accident when Truman let it slip. The forbidden day was near, but she'd chosen a different day for her gift. This was not a birthday present. There was no card.

"Please," she said quietly nodding her head, "open it."

He tugged at the paper until it fell away from the plain brown box. He held it to his ear and gave a quick shake. He looked at Adi. She smiled, listening, as the muffled metallic jingling escaped. He popped open the box and pulled out a collar too big for any pup, the blue tag now stamped APOLLO.

"Someday," she said.

THE TGV slowed near the Swiss border. Meth, calm again after his nap, tapped at his keyboard. He tried to convince himself he was again ensconced in his safe little world, but Stub still sat diagonally across the table, now reading Victor Hugo in English. He looked up occasionally, hoping she wouldn't speak; he had already exceeded his daily quota for conversation. Deeper, in places he seldom explored or acknowledged, he hoped she would resume their visit. His opposing feelings surprised him.

"What are you working on?" she asked, still looking at her book.

Meth looked up from his computer. He drew a breath and debated his answer. Had it been anyone else, he'd have offered no more than a disgruntled look. But Stub left him feeling somehow compelled to answer.

"I write," he said in a tone as conflicted as his emotions. He liked her unabashed style. He tried not to, but he couldn't help it. He even liked the way she gently pried information from him while seeming genuinely interested. She pushed just hard enough.

"That I figured," she said. "What are you writing *about?*"

"I write about a guy on a train—a writer—about what he sees, what he hears, what he experiences. I write on the train because there is so much to see, so much happening. It is good fodder for writing."

She closed her book and placed it on the table, giving her full attention to Meth.

"So many details go unnoticed," he continued, "like the woman behind you, quietly weeping as she repeatedly twists her diamond ring, or the guy over my left shoulder,"—he pointed with his jaw—"whose hands are excoriated by incessant washing as he tries to placate his OCD."

Meth knew plenty about implacable urges—insatiable, unrelenting, inescapable thoughts—but there was no room for that in this conversation. His two standard coping mechanisms, denial and sublimation, had served him often and, as far as he was concerned, they had served him well. He quickly moved on, offering another example of life waiting to be written.

"See that lump across the aisle," he whispered, "the one waving his gold Rolex around trying to make sure everyone sees it?"

"What about him?"

"The Rolex is fake. He is fake, a dim bulb, rubbing his last two neurons together, trying to get a synapse, trying to impress someone. Ironically, most people who care about Rolexes would know."

"You know, when you talk about other people that way, it makes me wonder what you're *not* saying about me."

Too judgmental, Meth thought, noticing a change in Stub's expression. *I should not have said that.* He had a habit of summing people up in a word, sometimes two—such as *lump* or *dim bulb*—and sometimes he let the words spill out. He had offended others by such slips. He wondered if he had offended Stub (noting, at the same time, the irony of referring to her as Stub).

If she was offended, she moved on quickly. Without waiting for a response from Meth, she snuck a glance at the Rolex and looked back.

"How do you know it's . . . as you say . . . fake?"

"Watch the second hand. It snaps second-by-second because it has a quartz movement. A real Rolex, in that model, has a mechanical movement with a smooth, sweeping second hand." Meth retreated again to his computer, like a turtle to its shell, and started typing. "Train rides provide lots of details."

Stub waited and then looked at the gold watch on Meth's wrist.

"Is yours a Rolex?"

Meth glanced at his Patek Philippe 1925 Grogan. Then he peeked at Stub's watch before answering.

"I would not wear a Rolex," he said, making no effort to conceal his disdain. "This is a Patek Philippe. But you already knew that."

She offered an inquisitive look.

"Anyone wearing a rose-gold Jaeger-LeCoultre with a diamond bezel would know," he said.

Stub looked down at her watch and back at Meth.

"Sí," she admitted. "But I've never seen a Patek like yours."

"It is very old," he said. He looked out the window, just as he had each time the conversation ventured too close to something meaningful. "My grandfather gave it to me."

"You were very close, no?"

Meth nodded. He waited for her to speak. He had earlier complimented her Catalan accent only as a go-to tactic for avoiding a real conversation. But the more she spoke, the more he liked it. He'd visited Barcelona with his grandfather, Truman Hamstead, and had enjoyed the dialects of the region. Her accent felt comfortable and inviting. He liked the way she paused at times to find the right word and the occasional uncertainty in her voice.

"Does he use contractions?" she asked.

"My grandfather?" Meth tone shifted from wistful to puzzled.

"Your character, when you write," she clarified. "Sorry. I jump topics sometimes. I try to force myself to use contractions in English, so I hear these things. Does your character use contractions? I notice that you don't."

"So I have been told," he said, as portions of the bahnhof began sliding past the window. "It is a personal quirk, but people do not usually ask me about it until they know me better."

Passengers began standing and arranging their luggage to depart.

"Well, I have quirks of my own," she said with a broadening smile. "I ask too many questions. And too soon."

Meth wanted their visit to continue but that concept was so foreign to him he followed his more comfortable path instead, like a horse turning toward the stable. Saying nothing, he closed his computer and shoved it into his bag. He sat, ready to disembark, and might have ended their conversation then and there had it not been for her irresistible gaze.

"Sometimes, particularly when I am concentrating on something, my sentences become mechanical—some say robotic. They say I sound like a book-on-tape. I do not know why I speak this way. It just feels comfortable for me."

"Have you published?"

"Not yet. I have an editor and a half dozen unfinished manuscripts, but they always hang up on the same problem."

"What's that?"

"The love story. Some call it the B story. I can never make it work. When the heroine expresses her love, the hero collapses somewhere between catatonia and apoplexy."

"Apoplexy?"

"Stroke."

"Why don't you just say stroke?"

"You sound like my editor," Meth shrugged, "only less frustrated."

He slung his scarf around his neck, grabbed his coat and satchel, and stood up. Unconcerned about social norms for ending a conversation, he stepped into the aisle and gave Stub a quick look as he began walking, still having never asked her name.

"*Adiós, señora*," he said over his shoulder as he faded away.

Then Meth did something unusual, something he was unaccustomed to doing. Near the end of the coach, before descending the stairs, he glanced back. No woman had ever caused him to look back. He wasn't sure what to expect, but he was curious. As disconnected as he was, even he could discern the perplexed expression on Stub's face as she stared out the window. He kept moving. His abrupt departure sprung from the same well as his unfinished novels. And his speech was not the only mechanical or disjointed aspect of his character.

PARIS TO Basel was a short trip—just three hours by TGV. It was only an hour further to Meth's home in Zurich, but he had an afternoon to burn, and he liked Basel. Further, he had business there. More particularly, he had research to do for future business. And he had not forgotten a TGV attendant by the name of Michaela Idoni.

Meth appreciated Basel for its culture, history, and art. The Centralbahnhof opened in 1854 and was sometimes touted as the world's first international rail station. It sat in the Dreiländereck (three countries' corner), where the borders and peoples of France, Germany, and Switzerland met. He checked into the Grand Hotel Les Trois Rois, little more than a stone's throw from the Marktplatz and only a kilometer from the twin spires of Basler Munster. And, when he left his hotel, he walked just around the corner to cross the Rhine on Mittlere Brucke, the oldest existing crossing between Lake Constance and the North Sea.

Along with its history, Basel was firmly established in the modern era and looking forward. For a full week each spring it played host to Baselworld, one of the largest international watch and jewelry exhibitions in the world. Meth had been told that Patek Philippe would invest upwards of two million euros for their temporary three-level exhibit. The expense was arguably justifiable when they displayed watches like the Sky Moon Tourbillon. Patented in 1801 by Abraham-Louis Breguet, a tourbillon movement countered the effects of gravity on a watch's accuracy by mounting the escapement and balance wheel in a cage that rotated approximately once each minute. The tourbillion mechanism in the Sky Moon consisted of sixty-nine parts and weighed just three tenths of one gram. The watch, valued at approximately one million euros, incorporated several additional features (or complications, as they are called by watch aficionados) such as a perpetual calendar, a minute repeater, moon phases and a sidereal time display. As much as Baselworld intrigued Meth, he'd never attended. It reminded him too much of Truman, who had worked for Patek for decades and loved their watches.

Meth took a long jaunt around town, once grabbing a taxi when he felt like a rest. Long walks were something he did to quiet the voices in his head—to stop François' mantra: *You make me sick. You filthy dog.* He hated the words, but sometimes he couldn't stop them, even after thirty years, particularly when he was alone and without an assignment. Sometimes walking helped. More often it didn't.

At the Kunstmuseum, he visited the Picasso collection and one of his personal favorites by Giovanni Segantini, a painting variously titled in German or Italian as *Two Cows Yoked* or *Cows at the Water Trough*. He particularly liked Segantini's colors and brush strokes and his depictions of the Swiss Alps. From the Kunstmuseum, Meth went to visit some of Claude Monet's Water Lilies series at the Fondation Beyeler. He still couldn't clear his head.

Meth endured an agitated longing that had waxed and waned for decades but never fully subsided. He could never placate it because he could never identify exactly what he lacked. The first dozen years of his current work—the only job he'd ever had—vented his childhood rage and gave him a measure of relief. But that was years ago. Now, it seemed, nothing helped. His mind refused to relinquish the demons. He would lay them aside, like a bad habit, determined to move on, but they'd eventually crawl back into his world.

Meth didn't like to admit it, but he had considered seeing a professional. *Get over it*, he'd imagined the psychiatrist saying. A self-diagnosed obsessive, Meth had tried that approach on his own. It didn't help, and he didn't need a professional to remind him. In recent months, the voices seemed worse. Anonymous women calmed the drumbeat of François' taunting for a day, maybe two, but never longer.

Meth paralleled the river walking back to his hotel after dark. He loitered briefly in front of three different nightspots, debating about the women inside. As he neared Mittlere Brucke, he thought about Michaela in her TGV uniform. He could see the Merian just across the Rhine. He knew she was waiting for him.

Cold January air rolled off the water and froze his breath. He closed the top button of his overcoat and shoved his chilled hands into his pockets. He felt a folded piece of paper between his fingers and pulled it out for a closer look. He teased open two folds to reveal flowing calligraphy in blue ink on a piece of lined paper with one torn edge. Brief as it was, it held his attention and stopped him under a bright streetlamp.

> Dear Prometheus,
> Thank you for sharing. I'm sorry about Achilles.
> Hélène

He stared at the note and wrinkled his forehead. He turned it over but found nothing new. He turned it back and read it again. He swallowed the stone that was rapidly swelling in his throat. He carefully folded the paper and secured it in his shirt pocket. He forgot about Michaela and turned toward his hotel.

Meth ate dinner alone, surprised by his frequent thoughts of the smile he now knew as Hélène.

After dinner, he sat in his hotel room, his computer open on his lap. He rarely gave a thought to people he passed or interacted with. In general, he exerted every effort to ignore them. He felt different about Hélène; her message had invaded his world. He could hear her accent and her occasionally misplaced words. She'd burrowed under his skin just enough to cause an itch, and every time he tried to scratch it he found himself unable to slide back into the shadowy isolation he had previously found so comfortable.

Incapable of dealing with his real issues, Meth turned to his writing. He contemplated his conversation with Hélène and considered making her a character in one of his stories, but he found himself hung up on the usual problem—the B story, what to do next—in life as well as in his novel.

He labored at his keyboard, staring intently at the last sentence of his most recent unfinished manuscript: I LOVE YOU, PIETRO. Unsatisfied, he rearranged the words: PIETRO, I LOVE YOU. Still frustrated, he inserted a different name: DIEGO, I LOVE YOU. Recognizing the futility of his tweaks, he decided on a different approach. He'd leave that sentence alone for now and work on the Italian protagonist's response instead. If he could just get something, anything, on the page, he would work backwards into a plausible transition. He hit the return key twice, ready to start a new paragraph, but nothing came. His creativity had abandoned him as quickly as he had abandoned Hélène on the train, her inviting smile and perfume still swirling in his head. Feeling as apoplectic as the character he'd described to her, he slammed the computer closed and tossed it across the bed.

Embarrassed, he wondered if he would ever see her again.

5

LE SOÛLARD

METH STRODE past the tired GLOBAL RESOURCES INC. placard in the hallway, through the outer office, and into his boss' inner sanctum over the protests of Alexia Traynor, the American secretary in the anteroom. He could have thanked Alex—that's what she called herself—for his breakfast on the train; she had purchased the ticket. But he had other things on his mind. He was no better at offering thank-yous than receiving them. He calmly pushed the door closed behind him, terminating her "Hey, you can't go in there righ—". It was one of Meth's not-so-endearing traits: he ended conversations when *he* was done, not when someone else was.

Meth sailed a slightly wrinkled newspaper over three piles of office clutter, landing it perfectly on a heavily-doodled desk blotter, the headline now facing the reluctant occupant of a worn-out swivel chair. Everything important was front page, above the fold: a picture of the distinctive Thoumieux sign and a headline, DISGRACED DIPLOMAT DEAD IN HOTEL, APPARENT SUICIDE. The article listed several people who had died as a consequence of her abuses of diplomatic immunity. It outlined several other offenses—the most publicized ones—committed after her diplomatic status had been revoked. And it highlighted her trial, conviction, and flight from justice. But the article was only a small chapter in her volume of bloody deeds; it covered only what the public knew. The file provided to Meth had been far more comprehensive.

Karl Morgan, a balding, corpulent, cigar-smoker in a sweaty white shirt and loose tie—an American who imported his young secretaries from the U.S.—read the headline before looking up. He quickly shoved the manila file he'd been reviewing under the blotter on his desk. When Meth looked at the still-protruding edge of the file, Karl covered it with a stack of similar-looking folders.

"Clean, quick, efficient," Meth said, wagging his finger. "No loose ends. No investigation. Have I ever let you down?"

In Karl's office, with the door closed, Meth's cold, unflappable demeanor took a break. It wasn't that his practiced façade cracked; rather, Karl's office was simply the place where Meth decided to relax. Karl had the privilege, if one could call it that, of being the only person to see an outward display of Meth's other side: anger, frustration, impatience, intolerance, and resignation, but mostly anger. He always had it, but Karl got to see it. Meth didn't care much for Karl's cigar smoke, but they'd long since come to an agreement that Karl could smoke what he wanted in his own office, and Meth would keep his mouth shut about it.

Karl didn't respond initially. Having been through it before, he'd learned to let Meth vent. There would be plenty of time to revisit the facts.

"Do not *ever* call me when I am on a job."

Meth knew it was an unreasonable demand when he said it. Things change. Contracts evolve, even at the last minute. That's why he'd answered the call in Paris. But sometimes—in Karl's office, that is—Meth still behaved like the hot-tempered teenager he was on the day he first walked in. An uninformed observer would never have guessed from Meth's behavior that Karl was his boss. But Karl was a patient man, and he liked Meth: anger, sharp tongue, and all. And it was clear to Meth, from years of their interactions, that Karl not so secretly enjoyed their verbal melees.

"Sit down," Karl finally barked. He knew how to handle Meth . . . and when. His eyes showed no anger; it was just the tone he used when he wanted to get Meth's attention. "I'll call you whenever and wherever the hell I want. I needed to make sure things were on schedule so I could reassure the client and collect the fee."

"I do not like the distraction," Meth persisted, his right eye twitching. "I am a professional. I—"

"I couldn't give a rat's furry little pimpled ass what you like," Karl snarled. "Sit down! You act like a professional in the field. Act like one now."

Meth scowled—invigorated by Karl's chutzpah and his willingness to stand toe-to-toe—then he turned and dropped into a tired leather armchair in the corner of the austere office. Karl concentrated more on business than on decorating his office or on keeping it clean. On the table next to Meth, an IBM Selectric with a missing K sat under two years of dust (Alex didn't dust). Meth swiped his finger through the dust before looking back at Karl. He wasn't ready to surrender, but he did acquiesce to a brief ceasefire. Karl took a long drag from his Padrón and tapped at the headline, the cigar between his fingers dropping ashes onto the paper.

"Ya know," he said, "sometimes you've got all the warmth and charm of a three-fingered prostate exam, but you still do good work."

Meth thought Karl read too many cheap American novels. His speech was part of the reason Meth disliked Americanisms. (*Oh, Hélène would love this guy,* he thought.) Despite himself, Meth picked up some of Karl's slang, like the *dim bulb* quip he'd used on the train the day before. Meth often expressed his disdain for Karl's choice of words and how he put them together but Karl was a pachyderm when it came to Meth's criticisms.

"How'd you feel about killing a woman?" Karl asked. "A young beautiful woman, at that?"

It was a strange question from Karl, who was generally all business. Female contracts were less common but gender was not a criterion for deciding on a target. Karl had never asked such a question. He might have predicted the answer.

"Woman, man, young, old, beautiful. What do I care?" Meth shrugged, his right shoulder elevating a bit higher than his left, a shrug so distinctive Karl had once recognized it from the opposite end of the bahnhof. "It is a job," Meth insisted. "A paycheck."

Meth had genuinely felt that way for the better part of twenty years— after he worked through his initial reservations—but he wasn't sure he felt that way anymore, not after his feelings in Paris. Still, he wasn't ready to admit his doubts to his goading American boss.

Karl was accustomed to Meth's staccato sentences, his lack of contractions, and his obtuse words. He'd once told a colleague—Srecko Knezevic, an operative who had come to Global directly from the Cobras, the Serbian Military Police Special Operations Battalion—that he had noticed Meth's verbal quirks became more prominent when he was uncertain about something. This seemed like just such a time.

"You sure?" Karl asked, on the verge of taunting.

"I am certain," Meth said, his intensity escalating. "Do I sound ambivalent?"

"You're never equivocal. Even when you're wrong, you're certain."

"I am not wrong!"

The room fell silent, so silent for so long that it was uncomfortable. They looked at each other like two cowboys waiting for someone to say, *Draw.*

"It makes no difference to me," Meth finally said. "You pay me; I do the job."

As if to demonstrate his point, Meth stood up and moved toward Karl's desk. He thumbed down vertically through the stack of manila folders as though he was about to grab one at random. He snatched the file from beneath the blotter—the file Karl had just stashed and covered. Karl reached to grab it, but he was too late. Meth dropped back into his seat before glancing at the name on the folder. When he read it, rage swept across his face. His right leg began to tremble. He resisted the urge to look back at Karl.

"You can't have it!" Karl barked. Meth offered no reply. Karl looked surprised by his silence, but he gave no quarter. "Listen, you arrogant bastard," he said, pulling another enormous drag from his cigar, "I know you like to think of yourself as some rogue assassin, but that's not how we do things here." Their eyes met. "And you know it."

"How long have you had this?"

Karl refused to answer.

Meth opened the folder and scanned the picture. He might not have recognized the face if he hadn't already seen the name. It was the first likeness of his father he had seen since he was a child. He remembered his mother taking a wedding picture from the mantel a few days after the infamous birthday party and shoving it into the wood-burning stove, frame and all. She must have cleared photos from the rest of the house as well because Meth had never seen another one as long as he lived there. He leaned back in his chair, the leather creaking around him. He glared at his boss. Meth had fantasized about killing his father for more than twenty-five years, always with an axe. Now he could pretend he had a legitimate path. In the heat of the moment he couldn't go beyond that thought. He tossed his go-to phrase at Karl with a strikingly flat affect: "Fine. I will take care of it."

"You *won't* take care of it!" Karl yelled. "You can't have it."

What Meth lacked in affect, Karl provided, and more. He was as animated as Meth had ever seen him. He threw his cigar across the room. It broke in half against a picture frame on the far wall and fell onto the stained linoleum tiles.

"It's not even finalized," Karl said.

Meth eyed his boss without budging.

"You know the rules, Meth, not to mention the laws, the treaties, and the less formal agreements. It's not yours to take. This isn't the Wild West. Act like the professional you claim to be."

"Your temerity is stunning," Meth blasted back.

"Oh, nice word. How long ya been waitin' to use that one? If I hadn't known you for twenty years, I'd be pissed off by now. You and your sesquipedalian speech; you think you're so chrysostomatic."

Meth fired a piercing stare.

"Yeah. Go look 'em up," Karl taunted, jutting his chin. "I can be a pretentious ass too. I can string together a bunch of words that people don't use. There's a reason they don't get used. Just because I have an accent and talk like a hick doesn't mean I didn't learn something at Princeton. You know, there's a rumor around here that you offed a bloke just for his profanities."

"I abhor billingsgate," Meth replied, leaning even more on obscurities, "but I have never killed a man for his parlance. He was a contract whose death just happened to coincide with a stir in his verbal cesspool."

"You've got your own verbal cesspool sometimes," Karl said.

Billingsgate was a word Meth liked but seldom found opportunity to use. He picked it up from Truman, his mother's father, a proper bloke steeped in English heritage. The word sprang from Billingsgate Market, constructed in 1850 on Lower Thames Street, shorthand slang—a euphemism—for the vulgarities spewing from the seafarers and fishmongers who made it their workplace. If Karl knew the etymology, he made no effort to say so, perhaps to avoid encouraging Meth's obnoxious habit.

"I never killed a man for his language," Meth reiterated, "and I do not appreciate your sardonic wisecracks. He died *while* he was swearing, not *because* of it."

"I know," Karl responded, as if trying to ratchet things down a notch. "I said it was a rumor." Karl smiled and lit another cigar. He took a long puff and sent a smoke ring across the room. Then he started to laugh. "Why don't you ease up a bit? Take a breath."

Karl and Meth would sometimes go at it for hours: thrust, croisé, parry, riposte. It was a verbal extension of Karl's fencing heyday. Yet, between their bouts, they seemed to care about one another. "Listen, Son," Karl would occasionally say in an unguarded moment. And when Karl's wife died in a car accident in Lugano, Meth swallowed his abhorrence of funerals and served as a pallbearer. As much as he antagonized Meth, Karl was the closest thing he had to a father. Alex never witnessed any affection between them, but Karl would occasionally tell her about Meth's soft spots—mostly for dogs and children—trying to convince her that Meth was more human than he seemed. Sometimes he'd even try to convince Meth.

As he shifted in the worn-out chair, Meth wanted to know why there was a contract on François—he could have turned a page and found the answer—but he refused to look or ask. He'd always refused to ask. Asking led to judgments and questions—Was the reason good enough? Did he agree? Was there an alternative?—none of which he wanted to answer. Questions were for someone else. He wanted no moral judgments, unless deciding *how* to end a human life is a moral judgment. Other contracts were terrorists, escaped murderers, international spies—already tried and convicted but somehow beyond the reach of traditional enforcement—but what could Le Soûlard have done? Meth wouldn't go there. That a file existed was enough for now.

"Listen," Karl said, his tone now more sincere. "I know—"

"You know nothing."

"Maybe he wasn't as bad as you remember," Karl said.

"Are you serious?!" Karl's suggestion was beyond Meth's pale. "Are you . . ." he trailed off, breathing deeply and sucking on his bottom lip. It was the first time Karl had seen him unable to plug in the right word. Then, just as quickly, he returned to full volume and vitriol. "Not bad? Maybe? And maybe Napoleon was not French. *I have the scars!*" Meth shook his head in disbelief. "He has a contract and you tell me he is not that bad?"

"He doesn't have a contract. Not yet. It's just a file."

"Just a file! That festering excuse for a human being . . ." Meth stopped. He looked at Karl and then through the window at the Zurich skyline. His placid air returned as suddenly as it had left, and he concluded as he began: "I will take care of it."

Before Karl could say more, Meth walked calmly out of the room, file in hand, pulling the door closed behind him. He even offered a nod to Alex as he passed, as if to suggest that everything was wonderful and she had somehow failed to hear the exchange through the door.

Alone in his office, Karl glared at that precarious stack of folders on his desk. It looked like an illustration from a Dr. Seuss book, files protruding in every direction, defying the laws of physics merely to remain upright. Karl felt certain Meth would not go after François—at least not right away, not without careful planning—but the situation still angered him. He lashed out at the stack of folders, sending an avalanche of paper across the floor. Then, with Meth gone, he managed to get in the last word: "Asshole."

6

THE CITADEL

T HE FUSE was short and burning fast. Meth had had blow-ups with Karl before—no big deal—but François' file had him ready to explode. He didn't go home. He went, instead, to his favorite gun range. He'd been there so many times over the years they gave him his choice of guns, no charge; they made plenty selling him ammo. Staff called him by name and spoke to him in English. His Browning sidearm was locked in his safe at home. That's what he'd shoot if he cared about precision. This trip was about pure aggression, about placating his adrenaline.

Meth took his favorite lane at the far left. The back and left walls met in the corner behind him, narrowing his exposure to ninety degrees. He didn't have to worry about anyone behind him. He began with .45 ACP, one hundred rounds, twenty meters, Colt 1911. It was comfortable and effective. *There is something special about a Colt 1911*, he thought. It just felt right in his hand. He fired fragments of anger downrange with each trigger pull, each hole in the target a bloody spot on François' tattered overcoat. He'd always imaged using an axe but this would suffice for the day.

He switched to a .357 magnum. He wasn't fond of the revolver but he was accurate. Another hundred rounds. *Where was François and why was there a file? What could he have done?* He pictured Le Soûlard draped over a bench at the gare watching the noon express speed by. He couldn't imagine him standing long enough, let alone having sufficient intelligence, to do something warranting Karl's attention. Just the idea that François had somehow crept back into Meth's life infuriated him.

By the time Meth got to the 9mm semiautomatic his wrist ached and he had to concentrate to avoid flinching. Still, he liked the sense of control and simplicity—point, squeeze, BAM, destroyed! He felt calmer with each shredded target, with each empty magazine. Halfway through a box of 9mm the inexpensive rental jammed, the spent casing stovepiped in the half-closed action. That never happened with his Browning. He cleared the gun and resumed only to have it malfunction again.

Shooters had taken notice of Meth's rapid fire and tight patterns. Some had gathered to watch, as if they could sense his anger (as well as his skill). He'd managed somehow to make generic gunshots sound angry. While clearing the weapon, he eyed his observers, like a viper about to strike, sending them all back to their respective lanes.

"Sorry, Meth," an employee said, delivering a replacement weapon, an FN Five-seveN. "These are on us." He plopped down two more boxes of ammo.

After fifty more rounds, Meth's right hand was too swollen to continue. He shot the last box left-handed. Each round sent a lancinating pain from the scar on his hand to his shoulder, reminding him of François, and of Newton's third law—every action has its equal and opposite reaction. Wincing in pain, he pushed through, determined François would never again control his actions. Strangely, the pain calmed him. Enduring the pain restored his sense of control.

Decompressed but still pensive, Meth chose to not go home. He had a weekend ahead, and he knew where to go. It was a place of solace for him made almost sacred by memories of the tender care Truman had shown him there after Adelaide's death. With his necessaries still in his Tusting satchel, he headed for the train; his first stop would be Lucerne.

In Lucerne, Meth bought a change of casual clothing at Manor and ate in a restaurant he liked above the store. The train—its sounds and vibrations, and the recollections of traveling with Truman—had proven therapeutic. It had picked up where the gun range left off, softening the sharp edges exposed by that file Meth still refused to read. He continued to unwind over dinner, then walked to Hotel des Balances and checked in to his favorite suite overlooking the Reuss.

Meth stuck his card key into the wall slot, bringing his room to life. He dropped his bag near the chaise lounge on his way to the king-sized bed. After emptying his pockets onto the table, he pulled off his clothes and stuffed them into a plastic bag. He checked a few boxes on the accompanying card and hung the bag on the knob outside his door. A call to the concierge assured the bag would receive its due attention before morning.

The backhanded benefit of Meth's week was his exhaustion; he was too tired to obsess over the events of the day. He hadn't slept in Paris two nights ago and he'd hardly slept in Basel the following night. He was going on sixty hours with virtually no rest. He still had questions about that file but the gun range and the train had settled the rage that might have otherwise kept him awake. He sprawled out on the down comforter on one side of the bed. Without bothering to turn out the lights, he grabbed the far corner of the comforter and wrapped himself in down. He didn't move again until morning.

Meth donned his new clothes before sunup, including a leather-trimmed Paul & Shark sweater. He arose fully rested, though still a bit sore in his right arm; it was a small price to pay for the release of anger. He hadn't slept so well in months. Getting away from Zurich and looking forward to the weekend had helped to clear his head. He began filling his pockets from the items on the table: his passport, wallet, and a handful of bills—euros mixed with Swiss francs. The only thing left on the table when room service tapped on his door was the half-folded note from Hélène.

He opened the door to a fresh smile. She delivered his meal and his bag of clothing, now laundered and folded. She carefully arranged his breakfast, moving dishes and food from her cart to his table. She poured orange juice and coffee. Meth was surprised by her unhurried attention to detail.

"Anything else, Meth?"

First name? English? He turned for a closer look just as she settled onto the corner of his bed and crossed her legs.

"Should I stay?"

He hadn't recognized her until she spoke. He still couldn't recall her name. He wondered if he'd ever known it. He thought this might be a good time to refresh his memory. He lifted his coffee, blew away the steam, and took sip. With a growing twinge of recollection, he took a step alongside the table toward her. He set his coffee back in the saucer, drawing his eyes to Hélène's note. *I'm sorry about Achilles*, he heard her saying. It jolted him. He picked up the note and slid it carefully into his shirt pocket.

"No, Ma'am," he said with a distant expression, as though he'd never met the woman now waiting on his bed. It was easier to pretend he'd never met her than to explain why he didn't want her. He took another step and dug the wad of bills from his pocket. He thumbed through and pulled out five francs. "Thank you for breakfast."

She offered a bewildered expression and showed herself slowly to the door.

For the second time in as many days, Meth had let a few lines of blue ink derail hours of distraction from his hateful life. He wondered why. He slid his freshly laundered clothes into his satchel and left for the bahnhof.

On the train, Meth left his computer in his bag. He looked out the window instead. He thought about the first time he was kicked out of school for fighting. He was ten. He'd cowered when his grandfather arrived to pick him up, but Truman proved himself kind and encouraging. Meth had felt more guilt than fear when Truman had to leave work again a few weeks later for the same reason. On his second visit, Truman had assured the headmaster it would never happen again. Meth had fretted the punishment that awaited him at home, but Truman didn't take him home or punish him. They drove to Chamonix, instead, and skied the rest of that Friday. The next day they drove through the Monte Blanc Tunnel and across the northwest corner of Italy to the coast of Monte Carlo. Meth loved Monte Carlo. On the Sunday trip home through Turin and Aix-les-Bains, Truman finally broached the subject Meth had waited for all weekend.

"Sometimes we feel we have to fight," Truman had said without introductory comments or qualifiers. He kept driving, kept looking ahead, as if consciously trying to minimize any sense of confrontation with his nervous grandson. "I'm proud of you, Son. You're making good progress. When you realize how much I love you, you won't feel the need to fight." That was the extent of Truman's counsel. At the time, Meth felt like he'd gotten away with something.

That wasn't Meth's last fight, but it was his last trip to the headmaster's office. He couldn't recall anyone ever having said they were proud of him. He couldn't bear the thought of disappointing Truman. The fights lessened over the next few years. As a boy, he'd thought of Truman's counsel in connection with his schoolyard brawls. Now he wondered about it in the context of his latest fracas with Karl. The boyhood fights stopped altogether after Meth's first trip to Murren. He was glad to be returning.

As his train approached Interlaken, Meth envied the calm waters of Brienzersee. He found himself equally enthralled a few minutes later by the rushing, boisterous rapids of the river Weisse Lutschine. He disembarked in Lauterbrunnen near the base of the 300-meter Staubbach Falls, one of the tallest unbroken falls in Europe. His love of water—calm or raging—came from his grandfather. Truman had convinced him it was a metaphor for life—placid at rest, powerful in motion. Of late he'd felt less like the water and more like the rocks at the bottom of the falls.

Meth listened to the water and watched it move: endlessly, relentlessly. When J. R. R. Tolkien hiked from Interlaken to the Lauterbrunnen in 1911, the landscape inspired his fictional valley of Rivendell. Meth found the area no less inspiring. On previous trips with Truman, he had visited nearby Trummelbach Falls, a series of ten waterfalls crashing 20,000 liters per second—sometimes more depending on the weather—from the glaciers of Eiger, Monch and Jungfrau, through the stone corkscrew to the river below. It was much too loud for conversation. Truman would just sit for long stretches and adsorb the majesty of the experience. Young Meth had learned to do the same. Now he was back. He sat and watched and listened for an hour. It filled his senses and drowned out everything else.

Meth had once found Murren intriguing because James Bond, *On Her*

Majesty's Secret Service, had skied from the restaurant on Schilthorn peak—Blofeld's hideout—to safety in Murren. Meth, too, found it a place of safety and escape, partly because of the effort it took to get there, more so because of pleasant memories. The trip from Zurich to Murren was not mere geography for Meth, not just scenery. His obsessive mind, more than most, connected places to feelings and memories. And nothing had made him feel as secure as Murren and Truman.

The next brief leg of his journey was by cable car. The clunk and jerk of the funicular had fallen victim to the cable in 2006. Now he floated silently, ascending 700 meters in one and a half kilometers. If he closed his eyes, he had no sense of movement except for the changing pressure in his ears. He missed the nostalgia and texture of the funicular, but what he really missed was a time when he could enjoy James Bond or a Tolkien novel.

The cable car stopped at the tiny Grutschalp station; in fact, the tiny station was the entirety of Grutschalp. Meth took a few steps across the platform and into a quaint narrow-gauge train for the last four kilometers to Murren. The air at altitude was cold and as crisp as a fresh apple. The train clung to the steep mountainside. The terrace in places was barely wide enough for the tracks. Alone in the small train car, with no one to complain or feel chilled, he opened the window. He drew in the invigorating midday air and floated his visible breath across the aisle. It reminded him of Karl blowing cigar smoke across his office. He quickly expelled the thought; Karl wasn't welcome, not in Murren.

As Meth traveled, the weight of Zurich fell from his mind, like ice from the side of the train. He felt a hint of the warmth and promise he'd enjoyed on previous visits. He imagined Truman sitting next to him, wrapping a firm and reliable arm around his young shoulders, assuring him life would be better in Geneva than it had been in Saint-Martin-des-Entrées. *I was so naïve*, Meth thought.

A few minutes later in Murren, Meth inched the zipper of his new sweater a little closer to his chin. He walked across the icy street and into Hotel Eiger, where he took the only vacancy, a three-bedroom suite on the top floor. He wasn't certain, but he thought he'd stayed there before. His balcony commanded an impressive view of the Eiger, Monch, and Jungfrau. He thought of Murren as his personal citadel. Things were quiet in Murren, even in the restless depths of his mind, and it had been that way since his first trip at age twelve. That's why he had come. He settled into a marginally comfortable steel chair on the balcony; the comfort of Murren eclipsed any discomfort from his chair. He was glad to be back.

Meth's phone buzzed against his hip. He pulled it from his pocket. It was Karl, of course; nobody else called. He silenced it and set it on the table, frustrated by the intrusion. Then came a shorter buzz, a text: BRING THE FILE BACK! He glanced at the message and slammed the phone back down on the table. He refused to respond but resisted the urge to launch the phone into the deep drifts below. It buzzed again. Meth chewed his bottom lip. Without looking, he turned off the phone. He wondered why he hadn't done so earlier. *Habit, I suppose.*

He looked back at the icy granite peaks and remembered Truman's tale of the pious monk standing resolutely between the ogre and the virtuous young maiden (the jungfrau). Truman's messages of right and wrong sounded so simple then. Now truth and right seemed complex and gray, but the safety of Murren had not changed. For the first time in over a decade, Meth had come again to his citadel.

He sat on the balcony for hours, thanks, in part, to the warmth of his new sweater. There were no cars below. People arrived and departed on an electric train too quiet to be heard. Then, if they wanted to move from one area of the tiny hamlet to another, they walked. While the world hustled from place to place, missing the very essence of life, Murren held sway against the rush. Meth was no longer angry. He wasn't hungry. He had nowhere to go. And, with his phone turned off, he was content. It was a strange feeling for him, being content. He liked it. He emptied his mind and reveled in the solitude and silence.

Sunset came early in January, especially in the Western Alps, and the temperature plummeted. Meth pulled a thin mattress from the hideaway bed he found in a closet. He laid it on the balcony. Then he gathered comforters from every bed he could find. He stacked them atop the mattress and climbed into the pile.

Meth's makeshift bed reminded him of winter nights in Saint-Martin-des-Entrées after François had disappeared. When he lost the companionship of Achilles and the dog's competition for his pillow and blanket, he would sometimes escape his nightmares in the security of his mother's feather bed. She had always slept with the windows open, even in the winter. As he reflected on those cold nights, he wondered, too, about the day she had buried Achilles—something he hadn't thought of in months, maybe a year—and why she had never shown him the grave or what she had done with the wooden marker he'd tried so hard to carve.

SATURDAY MORNING found a dusting of snow on Meth's balcony and bed. He'd enjoyed two consecutive nights of sound rest—one in anticipation of being in Murren, the other a consequence of arriving. He kicked off the comforters and hustled to the Keurig machine. He'd awakened from a dream of the afternoon Achilles first learned to fetch. There wasn't much learning really; he'd accomplished the task rather instinctively, but he wasn't very good at it. Rather than returning the stick and dropping it at Meth's feet, or holding it still for him to grab, Achilles had trotted around the yard, just out of reach, until Meth gave up and sat down to catch his breath. Then Achilles would lie down and chew the stick into pieces, all the while whipping his stubby tail from side to side and offering a mischievous grin. After a few minutes, as if to encourage his faithful master to keep playing, Achilles would cautiously approach, drop the masticated fragments of wood, and lick Meth's face.

Meth pulled his mug from the brewer and sipped his breakfast. Memories of Achilles in Saint-Martin-des-Entrées and the smell of fresh coffee brought images of his mother's final days and of Truman's visit to their home. Meth still recalled bits of a conversation he'd overheard all those years ago:

"We should tell him," Truman had said.

"We promised," Adelaide protested. "The day we buried Achilles, we promised."

"We made a mistake. He should know."

Meth recalled their words as if they had been uttered that very morning—as if he had heard Truman and Adelaide conversing while the Keurig dripped its lifeblood into his mug—but he had heard only fragments. His mother's voice had been weak and plaintive, and the conversation had transpired on the other side of a partially closed door. It had never made sense to him because he'd never seen his grandfather in the days surrounding Achilles' death. He couldn't imagine how Truman could have been involved. Meth had been too young and too distracted by his mother's illness to ask questions at that time. As he got older, he'd been reluctant to ask about a conversation that had not been intended for him. Now he had no one to ask.

METH GATHERED his few belongings on Sunday morning and checked out of his hotel just before noon. He had decided to take the long way home, partly for the scenery and added relaxation of a longer ride, partly because he didn't want to go home at all. Never having taken a vacation, he hadn't realized the stress of his job while he was immersed in it. Now, after being away for a couple of days and feeling the tension build in contemplation of returning, he was keenly aware. When he got to Lauterbrunnen, instead of heading toward Interlaken, he took the train up the hill to Kleine Scheidegg. He switched trains there and went down the other side, to Grindelwald, where he stopped for lunch and a short walk.

Snow covered much of the landscape in January. Years before, when he'd visited in the summer, he had admired how the residents kept every blade of grass neatly manicured and every building in perfect repair. He'd never seen a piece of equipment, or even a piece of firewood, out of place. He'd certainly never seen a piece of trash on the ground. The area and the people that cared for it appealed to his sense of order and reminded him of Truman.

EVERYTHING HAD been in order in Truman's tiny home when Meth first arrived. Truman had lived alone for twenty years after his wife died. He'd had simple, inexpensive tastes. The furniture was comfortable and clean, not fancy. Nothing in the home was fancy, but it was calm and inviting. When Meth was a little older, he learned the modest accommodations were rented. He wondered what Truman had done with his income over the years but concluded his grandfather's contentment was not entangled with the trappings of wealth and gave it no further thought.

Just days after his arrival in Truman's home, Meth glimpsed a sliver of his future and his past. On a narrow mantle above an electric fire sat a row of framed photos: some were of people and places he recognized, while most were of events long preceding his birth. One in particular caught his attention. He reached high and brought it down for a closer look. He'd never seen the wedding photo before—it was the first picture of François he'd seen since Adelaide had shoved similar images into the fire—but he recognized Adelaide and François. His mother looked full of the promise of life. François was thin, clean-shaven, and smiling.

"They were happy and in love," Truman said, as he entered the room behind Meth.

Startled, Meth dropped the picture. Glass shattered across the floor. He began to tremble. Truman must have seen the terror in his grandson's face. He offered a warm smile as he carefully approached. He knelt in front of Meth and rested a gentle hand on each of his grandson's shoulders.

"It's just a piece of glass, Son. It's easily fixed."

He pulled Meth into a warm embrace. He held him for a few moments then gently pushed him back to arm's length. He looked him in the eye and smiled again as if to promise the first had not been an accident or a trap. Meth saw the concern in Truman's face. He saw the pain of his past reflected in Truman's eyes. And he saw what he believed to be a promise of the future—what he saw in his mother's face in the photo—hope.

"I love you," Truman said with a crack in his voice. He waited, struggling to maintain his composure. If Meth didn't appreciate the gravity of these first days in his new home, Truman apparently did. A life hung in the balance. "Don't worry, Son. I won't leave you."

METH DIDN'T want to leave Grindelwald. *Why go back?* He didn't need the job. And he couldn't shake the ambivalence he felt about Brigitte. But he still struggled with some irresistible sense of duty.

Back on the train, Meth reluctantly reengaged. He pulled his phone from his pocket, hit the ON button, and placed it on the table. Knowing what would happen, he looked away. After silently booting-up, the little fiend began vibrating. It vomited one rattle after another. Meth had violated one of Karl's rules; he knew there would be consequences. He caught himself counting, stopping at eleven—short buzzes for texts, longer ones for missed calls. He refused to pick it up, or even to look. He wasn't ready to surrender his weekend. Leaving Interlaken, he had one hour to Bern and another to Zurich; he'd hold out till Bern.

Apprehension stole Meth's appetite. Normally he would have stopped in Confiserie Eichenberger in the Bern bahnhof. He'd been there enough times to be called by name. When his phone buzzed yet again in front of the cafe, he just kept walking. He found his seat on the train for the last leg of his trip and finally looked at his phone.

Every voice message and text had come from Karl, except one from Alex on Karl's behalf. They began matter-of-factly, demanding but businesslike. Over a period of twelve hours they had degenerated into belligerent obscenities. Then they had stopped altogether. *He must have given up*, Meth thought.

By the time he finished listening and reading, Meth was infuriated. He knew it was a power struggle. He didn't need the file; he wasn't even willing to look at it. And Karl didn't need it; he had all the information and could easily reproduce it. There was, of course, the issue of where the file might end up, but they both knew Meth was not careless. Regardless of Karl's motives or methods, he'd only succeeded in making Meth more defiant.

The weekend was over. That was sure. Meth's emotional barometer had been up and down like a skier at Chamonix. When he got to bed, he rolled back and forth incessantly, twisting his Egyptian cotton sheets into knots. He punched his pillows, trying to make a comfortable spot, but no sleep came. He thought incessantly of François and the file. Should he kill him? Should he wait for a contract? Did it really matter? His anger overwhelmed the solace of Murren. It was as if he'd never gone, except that the quietness had accessed memories he hadn't thought of in years. He wondered about that secret between Truman and Adelaide. And now he kept seeing his mother's face on a lifeless body in Hotel Thoumieux. Despite his best efforts to leave his past in the past, he'd thought more about his mother in the last week than he had in the last quarter century.

Meth dragged himself from bed and paced, his bare feet slapping the hardwood, bouncing echoes off the door at the end of the hall. The only other sound in the house came from the grandfather clock in the entryway. He kept pacing, sometimes unintentionally synchronizing with the clock, until he felt too tired to continue. Convinced his thoughts were under control, he returned to bed but still found no rest. When the antique clock struck 2:00 a.m., he threw the blankets on the floor and sat up. *What is the point? I might as well get up.*

After a lukewarm shower and a slightly warmer cup of coffee, Meth had a place to go. He hoped it would lead him to answers, but the train didn't leave for several hours. He'd walk off the wait. He pulled his scarf around his neck and turned up the collar of his jacket behind it. He glanced at his Patek and pulled the door securely behind him. In times when he couldn't forget about François he could sometimes walk himself to exhaustion then sleep.

He passed the twin towers of Grossmunster and crossed the Limmat River on Munsterbrucke. He wandered street-to-street seeing nothing new; he'd traversed virtually every street in town at one time or another. It wasn't about what he would see, or hope to see; he was simply dissipating nervous energy by being in motion. The opposite of being at peace in Murren, Meth now played hide-n-seek with his thoughts through the predawn streets of Zurich.

He ignored the blue-green copper spire of Fraumunster; he'd seen it too many times. He'd been inside at least a dozen times, mostly to admire Marc Chagall's stained glass depiction of the Crucifixion of Christ. He liked Fraumunster for the art, not the religion. He never found comfort in religion, troubled most by the crucifix that had dangled from François' neck as he doused himself with alcohol and abused his wife and son. Meth could still see flashes of light bouncing from that golden cross on his seventh birthday. He'd heard his mother read Bible stories: love, patience, forgiveness, and something about the kindnesses one should show to little children. As young as he was, he had understood enough to cringe at the contradictions. His ideas of religion were all tainted by twisted and confusing memories, like the beating he received when he spilled his Vittel during Christmas dinner. Where was *that* taught in the Bible?

Meth also liked Chagall for the irony—the Crucifixion of Christ by an artist raised in Jewish orthodoxy. But it all hit painfully close to home when Meth learned of Chagall's disturbing 1912 oil-on-canvas titled *The Drunkard*.

Meth climbed the long string of stone steps to Lindenhof Square and walked past its enormous chessboard. Later in the day, old men would push around near-life-sized pawns and bishops while overlooking the placid river. He sometimes watched them play for hours, admiring their apparent comfort with life and the world around them, but he'd never played; he couldn't get himself that comfortable.

As Meth circled back toward the bahnhofstrasse, he passed a bakery on Bleicherweg and inhaled the yeasty smell of fresh-baked bread. The aroma snatched him into the arms of his mother, only to be interrupted by the smells of François. He hated that every pleasant recollection was defiled. He wanted something pure in his life, something that would wrench him out of the past and plant him firmly in the present.

The only building with signs of life at that time of the morning, other than the bakeries, was the street-level office of David Wright, a publisher and once Cambridge classmate of Meth. It seemed David was always in his office.

On a warm summer morning about ten years earlier, David had seen Meth walk by. He'd rushed into the street and called out at 4:00 a.m. They hadn't seen each other in nearly a decade, but Meth recognized him immediately when he turned around. David was a wiry, nervous Englishman who talked fast and long—sometimes in a single three-minute sentence strung together with a smattering of conjunctions. His editorial prowess cowered in the corner when he spoke. He abhorred run-on sentences in print, but he talked like he'd never met a period. That, and his frequent shoulder jerks, had long ago earned him Meth's moniker, Twitch, though Meth had never said it aloud.

WRIGHT NOW PUBLISHING, in gold letters (German and English), arched across David's large office window. He'd never explained to Meth why he'd chosen Zurich. He didn't even speak German. And Meth, true to form, had never asked. It was as if Meth had filled every nook of his mind with important details relating to work—to the contracts, that is—and had no room for anything else. Either that, or he just wasn't interested enough to ask.

Writing was David's passion—his dream—ever since Cambridge. Meth's presence in composition classes was more for hobby than career. David and Meth were never close friends, but they now shared an alma mater and occasionally exchanged an early morning wave. Whenever he'd had the chance, David would ask Meth about his writing. He'd offered editorial suggestions when Meth was willing to share, and he'd always promised a path to publication.

Nearing the end of his endless night, Meth couldn't endure a conversation. When he saw David at his desk in his dimly lit office, he slid down the adjacent alley and traipsed into the fading shadows.

The sun finally peeked between the steeples and reflected off the river as Meth turned into the bahnhof. On a normal day, he could run twenty kilometers, hardly breaking a sweat, but the sleepless night and long walk had left him exhausted. Moving slower than usual, he made his way down the platform, ignoring others around him, and stepped into his car. He dropped his Tusting into the adjacent seat and placed his computer on the table, leaving it unopened. Despite fatigue, he remained agitated and restless, staring out the window as the bahnhof disappeared behind him. A few minutes later, as the train rolled through Gleisfeld, Meth's sleepless night overtook him. He finally closed his eyes.

7

NEMESIS

SEVENTEEN-YEAR-OLD METH—slender, fit, and clean-shaven—strolled through the Grand Library at the University of Cambridge and out into the courtyard, all the time chatting and laughing with his Vietnamese classmate, Duc Pham. Meth wore a navy blazer and tie, and he carried just two books: chemistry and philosophy. In his other hand, he caressed the fingers of Addison Ainsworth—Adi—a sophomore from nearby Lowestoft, England. They'd met soon after arriving in Cambridge.

Over the previous two years, Adi had eased Meth into two things: a more relaxed pattern of speech, including the use of contractions, and a relationship. He'd traveled with her to the theater in London and once to his home in Geneva. They'd traveled together enough that she had teased him about his favorite seat in the Cambridge train station. He'd even traveled to her home, to meet her parents. In Lowestoft, Adi's English Setter, Bubbles, had bobbed around Meth like he was family.

Meth had come close to getting a dog, especially when Adi had dragged him to the pet store to play with the pups. But he couldn't bear the thought of losing another friend. It was easier to not care than to care and lose; that's what he'd told himself. On his bedside table he kept a dog collar with a blue tag stamped APOLLO, a gift Adi had given him more than a year ago in hopes of moving him forward. At night, it rested next to the Patek Philippe Truman had given him for the same reason.

Duc had taught Meth the value of a good, albeit immature, practical joke, including the classic dribble glass. There was something childlike in Duc that made it funny. At least it made Adi and Duc laugh. Adi, Meth, and Duc, it seemed, were inseparable.

Meth's favorite subjects were chemistry—organic and inorganic—and math. He found their intersections particularly intriguing, such as the derivation of Avogadro's number. It mathematically correlated the weight of any substance with its atomic mass—one mole contained 6.022×10^{23} atoms or molecules and equaled the atomic mass of the substance in grams. To Meth, the number offered a perfect symmetry. It had imprinted on his brain the day he first heard it. That such a complex concept could be reduced to a mathematical formula gave him a sense of order and comfort. He wished he could reduce other complexities, like human motives and relationships, to a formula on a page—to something he could understand and predict.

Meth's eyes were bright, his smile broad—both were a legacy of his time with Truman. He strutted across campus with an optimistic bounce in his step, greeting fellow students as they passed. Some called him Prometheus; others—mostly those who also knew Duc and Adi—called him Meth. Duc had coined the nickname when he struggled to pronounce Prometheus, and others had picked up on it quickly.

Meth enjoyed a resurgence of his humanity at Cambridge. François had faded away after the birthday party, never to be seen or heard of again. Two years later, when Meth was nine, Adelaide had grown increasingly ill. Truman had gone to Saint-Martin-des-Entrées and tenderly cared for his dying daughter and his only grandson. He'd tried to go sooner but she wouldn't allow it. She had proven fiercely independent, just like Meth on the day he'd tried so hard to bury Achilles and refused his mother's help. The doctors had called her illness cancer. Meth, as a child, had thought otherwise. He'd felt certain it was François' vile poison—his hatred and abuse—that had killed her from the inside out.

Truman, two decades a widower, had left Bayeux with Meth, whom he had always insisted on calling *Son*, and a mahogany casket. He knew then that Meth was wounded, doubly so with his mother's death, and he had determined to be as much a father as possible. On the train to Geneva he'd done something Meth could not recall François having ever done. He had rested his kind hand gently on Meth's arm, without anger or inflicting pain, and conveyed an eternity of comfort and reassurance with a soft touch.

"It will be well," Truman had said, in his proper English voice, as they crossed the border into Switzerland. Meth had struggled but came almost to believe him.

In the security and serenity of Truman's Geneva home, Meth had flourished. Emotionally, his confidence had soared; academically, he'd shocked his teachers. The beatings had been replaced with sailing a rented boat on Lake Geneva and skiing at Verbier and Chamonix. Truman had taken him repeatedly to London, insisting he have an understanding and appreciation of English history, culture, and tradition. He'd introduced

Meth to art in some of Europe's most renowned galleries. He'd given Meth everything he needed to excel, most importantly love and stability. His home had been safe, his encouragement constant. Meth had come to feel invincible with Truman at his side.

When Truman called his lifelong friend, Sir David Kipling, the University Vice-Chancellor at Cambridge had taken the call on friendship; Cambridge had accepted Meth on merit. In the right environment Meth had proved his brilliance. At age fifteen, he'd become the institution's youngest student since fourteen-year-old William Pitt the Younger in 1773. At Cambridge, Meth thrived.

Approaching the lecture hall with Adi and Duc, Meth encountered Kipling, an engaging middle-aged man who usually smiled but now wore a solemn expression. Meth sensed what was coming, and there was a long silence before either spoke. Kipling rested his hand on Meth's shoulder and began speaking as they turned and started back across campus. They left Duc and Adi near the lecture hall looking at each other and wondering. By the time Meth arrived at the university offices several minutes later, he had only partially processed the doleful news. He and Kipling continued their exchange across a large oak desk surrounded by walls of books and leaded glass windows that extended from the low radiators to the three-meter ceiling.

"Master Moreau, Truman has long been a friend of the University of Cambridge. The Hamstead name garners great respect in these halls."

Meth sat silently, nodding acknowledgment, struggling between anger and devastation. A heart attack—at least that's what someone had told Kipling—took Truman suddenly. His friends and colleagues at Patek Philippe had found him hunched over his bench, parts of a watch still in his hand. Despite his age, he'd been active and in good health. When Adelaide died over a period of several months, Meth had had an opportunity to prepare himself. No one can prepare fully for their mother's death, but Adelaide's passing was not a surprise. Truman's death now came unexpectedly. He had been there for Meth; now he was gone—no time to ease into the idea or prepare for it. The news sent Meth reeling. He felt disoriented, almost confused, as if he could see and feel the darkness circling from his past. He felt betrayed and powerless and angry. Forgetting Adi and Duc, he felt totally alone.

"Your grandfather and I were dear friends," Kipling added. "I loved him. I wanted to inform you in person."

Meth blinked and shook his head slightly, as if to reshuffle his dark thoughts of the future in hope of a better outcome. He felt as wounded as he did on his seventh birthday, but this time it was an invisible enemy from which he could not escape. He lost all perspective. Pain—horrible psychic, emotional, spiritual pain—consumed everything good in his mind. He couldn't imagine things getting any better tomorrow. Truman would still be dead. Another source of love would still be gone. He couldn't conceive of a reason to live.

Kipling kept talking, but Meth heard almost nothing. Kipling's formality and his accent reminded Meth of Truman. As a child and young adult, Truman had spent much of his life on the outskirts of London. Then, for decades, he'd bounced back and forth between London and Geneva. He'd been comfortable in both cultures and languages, but his accent and his English manners were indelible. And Kipling's words only jackhammered Truman's absence more deeply into Meth's already wounded soul.

"Thank you," Meth said matter-of-factly as he stood and turned for the door, determined to make an expeditious departure. By the time he left Hélène on the train years later, he had mastered his unfettered escape. This was his earliest version.

"Your studies, Master Moreau?" Kipling offered concern in his voice. "You have done so well. Your grandfather's promises of your potential have all been exceeded. In just a few weeks you will graduate, and before your eighteenth birthday." He waited for a response, but none came. "Will you still attend medical school?"

Without bothering to answer, Meth moved across the sculpted rug toward the door of the large academic office, the campus visible through the broad windows. Shadows from the muntins marched across Meth's face like dark omens of his future rolling out ahead of him. When he finally spoke, he used the chopped brevity that had marked his speech as a freshman. The social skills and contractions he'd refined during his years at Cambridge had disappeared in a moment. They'd died as quickly as Truman. He felt like the universe had conspired against him, and he surrendered.

"I must go now," he said. He had to escape. He couldn't stand to be in that room another moment. He wanted to grab every heavy object within reach and throw them through the windows. He wanted to scream. He wanted to cry. "There is much for me to do," he said in a cold, distant tone.

"Master Moreau," Kipling began again, only to be interrupted.

"Hamstead."

"Sir?"

"My name is no longer Moreau. I am Prometheus Hamstead."

He might have changed his name earlier had Truman not dissuaded him. "Wait until you're an adult," Truman had said. "Maybe you'll change your mind." Meth couldn't imagine why he'd change his mind or why Truman would have thought that. But now, with Truman's death, he could finally break fully from François and honor Truman's name at the same time. Everything would be different when he left Kipling's office. Everything.

METH WANDERED the campus until the other students disappeared. Darkness consumed the sun and its shadows. His world became black and white, but mostly black. He forgot about Adi and Duc. Loneliness overwhelmed him. He'd loved Achilles until François butchered him with an axe. He had loved his mother until cancer consumed her. And he'd loved Truman. His affectionate and patient grandfather had reconnected Meth with life and hope, but it had now become all too clear: love leads to pain; hope to disappointment. He saw no future, no hope, no reason to care. He was determined to never care again.

Committed to a clean getaway, Meth headed down Regent Street on his way to the rail station. He didn't say goodbye to Adi or Duc. He carried Apollo's collar in his pocket, determined to never fill it. He would do what he had learned from others; he would simply disappear. He dragged his bag to the counter and bought a ticket but the train wouldn't leave for an hour. He made his way to a bench near the platform, to that perfect seat Adi had teased him about. He thought about killing time in Costa Coffee around the corner. He'd eaten there many times. He hadn't eaten since breakfast but he wasn't hungry. He was tired. He was angry. He was devastated. But he wasn't hungry. He just wanted to sit and be alone.

Meth saw just one other person in the station. She sat facing away from him, her dirty blond hair dangling over the back of his favorite bench. He turned to find a different seat.

"Where are you going?" came a question from the bench.

He recognized Adi's voice. He shuddered. He looked right, then left, contemplating an exit before he turned toward her. She was still seated, craning her neck to see him over her shoulder.

"Come here," she said with a kind, firm tone.

Meth had heard the tone before. It said: *I care, but you'd better listen.* It was the tone she'd used as a freshman—when they first met—when she first dragged him for coffee at Trockel, Ulmann & Freunde. He'd loved her tone; it had helped him venture into the world.

He inched toward her, a lump growing in his throat. He hadn't cried in more than ten years, but he felt like he might. He bit the inside of his lower lip to keep it from quivering. She patted the bench seat with her open palm and looked down at her hand. He dutifully took a seat next to her. He was glad to sit next to her; it made it easier to avoid eye contact.

"How did you know?" he asked.

"Kipling's secretary. I was worried." She looked away and quietly began to sob as if she could feel the expanse of Meth's pain. She brushed away a tear and swallowed hard. "When you weren't in your flat, I came here."

"Nothing to worry about," he said, as if discussing the weather.

Meth's words and demeanor belied the emotions he struggled to control. He feared if he let a single drop of emotion escape it would open a crack and breach the levee. He desperately wanted her touch, but he couldn't risk showing it. He felt her hand on his—first on top, then underneath, palm-to-palm, then interlocking fingers. He couldn't speak. In his anguish and turmoil, he twisted her concern into pity and snatched his hand away. He felt his anger swell. It swept his sorrow aside and overpowered everything else. He rose and started for the other side of the station.

"Where are you going?" she asked. "Talk to me."

He kept walking. She jumped to her feet and followed.

"I love you, Meth."

"Don't love me!" he yelled over his shoulder, still walking away. He found himself again struggling to use contractions, like he was slipping back into the darkness of Saint-Martin-des-Entrées. And now, having tasted something better, he hated François all the more. "Do not ever love me. I don't want it."

"I know you love me."

"I do not love anyone."

At the end of the platform, Meth turned around. Adi froze a few feet away, her eyes open wide and her brows drawn together. Meth couldn't discern whether she was frightened or concerned. It didn't matter. He glared at her, overwhelmed with grief, determined to conceal his pain. He pushed his right hand into his pocket and pulled out Apollo's collar.

"Take it," he said, throwing it at her feet.

She looked as devastated as he felt. There was nothing more to say. He left her there looking at the collar and crying, and stormed into the darkness. He circled back to the station forty minutes later and boarded at the furthest end of the platform. When the train rolled out of Cambridge, Meth pretended to not notice Adi sitting in his favorite spot, weeping.

TEN DAYS after leaving Cambridge, in a dark suit and tie, Meth held vigil at his grandfather's grave as the minister concluded services. He'd hardly eaten since leaving Cambridge. He still wasn't hungry. Death had swallowed his appetite and his plans for the future.

Eight years earlier, when Adelaide died, Truman had secured two adjacent plots in the Cimetière des Rois (Cemetery of Kings). Some of the trees in the Geneva cemetery seemed as old as John Calvin's grave; he had arrived in 1564. While at Cambridge, Meth had studied Calvin's teachings. After his hellish childhood with François, and after walking away from his mother's Christianity in his early teens, Meth thought a cemetery was the appropriate place for the champion of predestination.

He stood on the ugly artificial turf morticians use in their vain attempts to dress-up an open grave. *Looks like the same stuff I stood on eight years ago*, he thought, watching Truman take his final rest next to his only daughter. In his mind, Meth could still see Truman's handprint on the polished top of Adelaide's casket. Already detaching, he consciously opted not to leave a similar print on Truman's.

When he'd buried his mother, Meth's only fellow mourner had been his grandfather. This time, in a crowd, he felt more alone. The mourners all seemed to know each other, hugging and weeping. He'd marched off to Cambridge too young for them to have really known him. Duc and Adi had made him more vulnerable by teaching him to feel. It seemed, for a time, he'd conquered his resentment of François, but Truman's death left him resenting both life and the pleasures that had set him up to be injured again. He'd left his friends behind with no intention to return. Bitterness left him determined to show no emotion and to never again invest himself in anyone who could hurt him by leaving. A professional might call it attachment disorder—in fact, that's what Meth would call it in his more sanguine moments—but he still liked to think of it as some form of independence, like the day he'd decided not to cry. If he didn't care about anything, losing it couldn't hurt him.

As the rest of the crowd moved away from the grave, a distinguished elderly man pushed against the flow. "Are you Prometheus?" he asked in French.

"*Oui*," Meth responded, "but I prefer English."

"As you wish, sir. I am Weldon Andrew, the curator for the Patek Philippe museum here in Geneva."

"Not today," Meth said.

"I knew your grandfather very well. I loved him."

"Everyone loved him," Meth said, a twinge of envy in his voice. He could not imagine a crowd attending *his* funeral. Off the top of his head, he couldn't think of a single person inclined to eulogize him. What was more, he didn't care. *Cremate my body and dump the ashes in Lake Geneva*, he thought. *There is no need for all this fuss and formality.*

"I don't wish to intrude," Weldon continued, "but I need to speak with you about your grandfather. If you—"

"Not today."

"Yes, sir. I—"

"Not today!" he snapped as he turned and walked away, leaving Weldon mid-sentence.

Only a few steps later, two men approached, both in dark suits. In the sea of suits, Meth mistook them for mourners.

"Monsieur Moreau?"

"Hamstead," Meth abruptly responded. He rolled his eyes, not wanting to explain.

"Prometheus?" Suit One asked in another effort to confirm his identity. Young and slender, Suit One did all the talking. Suit Two was fiftyish, thick in the middle, and quiet. He continually scanned the environment, like a sentry on watch, allowing Suit One to concentrate on the conversation.

"Yes, Prometheus Hamstead. Who are you?" Without waiting for an answer, Meth continued, "And why are you irritating me at my grandfather's funeral?"

Suit Two continued his surveillance without responding or changing expression. He seemed every bit the professional until his head jerked slightly and tracked back the other direction, his eyes fixed on the youngest and shapeliest mourner, her black skirt well above her knees. Catching himself, he lit a smoke and resumed his lookout.

Undeterred, Suit One continued: "My name's of no consequence."

"It is if I ask," Meth demanded, his tone sharpening.

"I represent Mr. Karl Morgan from Zurich."

"I do not know Karl Morgan . . . or anyone in Zurich."

"*Oui, monsieur—*"

"English! If you intend to converse with me, do so in English."

"Yes, sir, my apologies. Karl Morgan wishes to offer you a job."

"I need no job. I am returning to Cambridge."

Meth had no intention of returning, but he hoped his declaration would end their exchange. His mind was spinning with grief, anger, and resentment. Truman had sacrificed everything to support him at Cambridge. Now Meth had no plans for the future and no resources. He desperately needed a job, but he had no intention of revealing that to strangers. *And what is so urgent that they need to talk to me now?*

With a tiny hint of compassion—just enough to catch Meth's attention—Suit One explained: "Sir, medical school is expensive. And you have no scholarship to Harvard."

Meth studied Suit One intently, then Suit Two, and then he looked back at the grave. He wondered whom they were and why they were talking to him, but he felt asking questions would only encourage them. They were seeking him out. As he saw it, that gave him the upper hand, and he didn't want to give it up. He remained silent.

"Yes, Mr. Hamstead," the man continued, "we know about you and your circumstances. And, if I may be so bold, you should not reject this offer before you hear it."

Sensing a glint of interest, Suit One offered a face-saving conclusion by simply passing a business card. Meth eyed the card and slipped it into his pocket as the three silently dispersed.

SIX WEEKS after his grandfather's funeral, Meth stepped off an elevator in a Zurich office building. He looked a bit disheveled. He felt worse than he looked. The same two suits he had encountered in Geneva flanked him. They'd met him in the ground-level lobby and escorted him to his destination. He had already nicknamed them Mutt and Jeff: Mutt on his right, Jeff on his left. As young as he was, Meth was well-read. He knew how passé and derisive the nicknames were. He liked them anyway, and he never intended to say them out loud. Mutt pointed across the hall and followed Meth past a shiny GLOBAL RESOURCES INC. wall placard and into an outer office.

"Please, come in," an American voice invited from the next room. The suits found their chairs in the anteroom, one on either side of an empty desk, the secretary conspicuously absent. Meth continued through the open door and into the office. Later, he would learn that the secretary was always absent for these discussions. The figure attached to the voice came around his desk and warmly shook Meth's hand.

"Karl Morgan," he said as he pushed the door closed.

Headquarters would change little over the next twenty years. Even the leather chair in the corner—a little less worn, a little less faded—endured Meth's visits from this first day to the present. Karl, ten kilograms lighter—still in his pre-jowls years—and with a bit more hair, smoked a smaller cigar and offered a clean-cut, professional look. His voice was a half-octave higher, his chords having endured several thousand fewer cigars. He also spoke with a less jaded tone. The only adornment on the far wall of his office was his épée and a dusty trophy from the United States Southeast Regional Junior Fencing Competition.

"It's a pleasure to meet you, Mr. Hamstead."

There was a long pause. If Karl was waiting for a response, an expressionless Meth disappointed him.

"I'm sorry about your grandfather."

Silence.

"Please, have a seat."

Meth sat down but his demeanor remained at attention. Karl made a one-sided labor at conversation. Meth offered an occasional one- or two-word jab.

"How are you getting along in Zurich?"

"Fine."

"Need anything?"

"No."

Meth's standoffish style demanded determination from a would-be acquaintance. If Karl hadn't vetted Meth personally, and already decided he wanted him, he would have cut bait and saved himself the headache. In fact, if he hadn't been certain of where the conversation would end, he wouldn't have started. Other candidates were preapproved and fully committed before ever meeting Karl. But Karl knew Meth was different, and he knew why. He'd had a personal interest in Meth for years. Now he put his neck on the line just to have this conversation in advance of a commitment. Soon—and none too soon for Meth—the discussion evolved to the business of the day.

Meth had spent the last several weeks coming to a realization of his desperate financial circumstance. The long path from Truman's funeral to Karl's office had left him ready to entertain any offer. He wouldn't admit his predicament, but his tired appearance and wrinkled clothes offered an interested observer—someone like Karl—a generous clue. Too angry to mourn and too injured to revisit his past, Meth had refused even to see his former home in Geneva or to make any attempt to settle Truman's meager estate. From what he knew, the estate was more than likely in the red and not worth the emotional price he would pay to settle it. *Let the dead bury the dead*, he thought, wresting a verse from his theological studies. Walking away from his past, he'd decided to go forward with an eye only for himself.

Karl's presentation was smooth and well-rehearsed. He pressed the key buttons: mystique, respect, travel, wealth. Knowing Meth's situation, he focused more than usual on money. He would normally focus more on women, but he also knew about recent developments with Adi, and he left the opportunities for debauchery almost untouched. To Meth it sounded like a sampling of the seven deadly sins. Karl said little about killing. *Dispatch* was his euphemism, but he mostly talked about *contracts*.

"We get a file—a dossier, as they say in French—with all the information: why, where, when, though they leave plenty of latitude on where and when. The client, usually a government agency, pays when the target's dispatched. We do the research, check out all the details, all that crap. We decide how. Later, you'll decide on your own. Most important, you were never there. You'll have weeks, sometimes months, between contracts. Stay proficient; otherwise, your time's your own. Just keep your phone on."

Karl's polish could not overshadow his passion. He left no doubt that he believed in the value and rightness of his cause. The world was a safer place with him and his organization in it. Global Resources Inc. was a generic-sounding front. NEMESIS—Nonmilitary Evaluation, Monitoring and Enforcement of Selective Interdiction Strategies—was the real business and had its origins in post-war Europe: first tracking down and dispatching war criminals; years later, cold war spies; then, more recently, terrorists.

"The name's too damn long," Karl said. "You've heard me say it once. Don't expect to hear it again."

The name of the organization, the players, and the techniques they utilized, had all shifted over the decades, with a resurgence of American involvement and financial support following 9/11. Karl had arrived in Zurich three years earlier. The attack on the World Trade Center and the Pentagon had galvanized his loyalty to NEMESIS, whose name was seldom spoken and never appeared in print. Stealth, precision and timing were key, the less conspicuous the better.

"There are two cardinal rules," Karl said after nearly an hour of explanation. "One,"—he held up his index finger—"never speak of NEMESIS. Two,"—unfolding a second finger—"when you're in, you're in—no one leaves."

If it all sounded like cloak-and-dagger vigilantism in the morning, Karl had made it seem more palatable by the end of the day.

"These people are international criminals," he'd said more than once. "Most have been tried and convicted by at least one jurisdiction; some by several. Their existence jeopardizes lives. Even if re-incarcerated, they still exert deadly influence."

Meth wasn't so easily convinced. He asked questions until Karl grunted and turned red. They talked about international borders, extradition, identity changes, electronic tracking, and a myriad of other topics. Karl had an answer for everything. Meth could tell he'd given the spiel many times, and none of Meth's questions were new to him.

"Look," Karl said as the sun disappeared behind the Zurich skyline, sounding more than a bit exasperated, "I know you have questions. Everybody has questions. I had the same questions. The short of it is this: you don't need to know the source of the contracts or the reasons they have to die. It's simple. We give you a pile of money and you use that brilliant Cambridge mind of yours to complete the task. It sounds gruesome, but we'll train you. You'll have no difficulty getting up to speed."

It wasn't Karl's best hour—this was the beginning of his prickly relationship with Meth—but something clicked. They finally seemed to understand one another.

Though he hated the world (a sentiment rekindled by Truman's sudden death), Meth had initially been repulsed by the notion of being an assassin—another word Karl refused to use—or *operative*. At one point he'd taken a break to walk the streets of Zurich and process Karl's pitch. It was difficult, as young as he was, to not be intrigued by prestige and wealth. His brilliance and Cambridge education didn't protect him from teenage concepts about life and success. Karl made it all sound so easy, so heroic, all for the good of society. Maybe medical school could wait. Cutting ties, as Karl had described, would be easy. He had no ties to cut; there were no relatives. Even Duc and Adi had been left without an expectation of seeing him again. And he could channel all his rage. He could take a bloody swipe at a world that had treated him so horribly. That's what appealed to him the most. Plus, he could get paid for it.

"I have to think. I have—"

"Take a break, Meth," Karl said, coming around the desk and opening the door. "Take some time." He handed Meth a business card as generic as the Global sign in the hall. "Call me when you're ready. We'll put you up in a nice place." He pointed across the room. "Jeff will take you."

How ironic, Meth thought. He almost laughed. Suit Two—Jeff—was gone. Mutt was still waiting in the outer office, and *his* name was Jeff. Meth smirked and followed Jeff to the elevator.

Meth thought about it for two months. He took long walks around Zurich and weekend trips around Switzerland. He was grateful Karl had put him up in a posh hotel and funded a new wardrobe. Nice meals, cash as needed; it was a taste of the good life. He wasn't naïve enough to miss the intent of Karl's generosity, but he was still grateful. And he was tempted to make it permanent. He needed the money—the more the better—but what he *wanted* was revenge. His initial revulsion gradually morphed into acceptance—he could even call it a patriotic duty—then opportunity. As he saw it, the worst that could happen to him was death, and he wanted that anyway.

METH RETURNED to the office on a cold autumn day, teetering on the best way to verbalize his decision. Karl must have sensed his change in mood. He stood and handed Meth a fat envelope and a pair of car keys on a chain.

"Here," Karl said. "Perhaps this will help you make up your mind."

Meth's mind was already made up, but he decided to take all he could get. He took the envelope and keys, glancing at the prancing horse on the yellow background of the Ferrari keychain. He opened the envelope and flipped through a large stack of bills, like an old-style mobster he'd seen in a movie.

"Why me?" he asked. "Why now?" He'd contemplated the question for two full months, but this was the first time he'd spit it out.

"We research these things," Karl responded. "We don't just go out and hire any asshole off the street. We know how smart you are: your early acceptance at Cambridge, honors program, scholarship, all of it. We know these things. We know you had run-ins with the law after your mother died. We know the teacher who identified your potential and worked with your grandfather to secure your spot at Cambridge when you were still too young to drive. Hell, you're *still* too young to drive in most of Europe."

As benign as Karl's language was, he occasionally triggered Meth's tic, but it was too subtle for Karl to notice, too infrequent for Meth to care. He thought about the irony of his age and the car he'd just been offered as an incentive. He bounced the keys in his hand.

"None of that answers my questions."

"We know about your childhood and your father. I know you think so highly of him that you recently changed your last name."

"Oh? Really?" Meth felt defensive and couldn't resist taking a shot at Karl. "Your *Suit* did not seem to know when he assailed me at my grandfather's funeral."

"Touché," Karl conceded, a remnant of his fencing experience showing itself. "You got me. Can we move on now?" They glared at each other in silence.

Meth felt the tension, but he still had no answer. He pushed for a third time, demanding to know why they had approached *him*. Of all people, why him?

Karl's smile was a distant memory. Any hint of civility that might have floated in the air earlier had now evaporated. He hesitated for an instant and began pacing.

"Because your father beat you and your mother died and you felt abandoned." Karl's tone was cold. He paced and sucked long drags from his cigar. He looked fleetingly in Meth's direction. "Now your grandfather's dead. Everyone you loved, or who loved you, is dead. You have no family. You have no friends. Despite your grandfather's best efforts and all your progress in recent years, you have no meaningful connections to anyone, not even Addison." Meth winced. "We've seen your psychological profile. We know. You live a calm, inconspicuous life except for your moments of rage."

Karl stopped pacing and looked out the window for an uncomfortably long time. He hadn't seen Meth cringe with the mention of Adi's name. He couldn't have known how deeply he'd driven the knife. He turned to Meth.

"We can show you how to control the rage. With control, you become the perfect operative. Does *that* answer your questions?"

"Assassin, you mean."

"Call it what you want. Did I answer your questions?"

Meth offered a smugly satisfied grin, more pleased with the emotion he'd extracted from Karl than the answers he'd heard. In some sick way, Karl's growling and expletives reassured Meth and helped him crush the rising thoughts of Adi.

"Yes," he said, fully realizing Karl had only set the questions back a step. Now Meth wondered why they were aware of his family in the first place and why they were looking in Cambridge, but he decided not to ask. He'd explore that later.

"Are you interested or not?"

Meth looked at the large envelope in his hand. He held it in his upturned palm and raised his irregular brow. He'd played plenty of poker at Cambridge; he sensed an opportunity.

"Do you have another one of these?" he tested.

Without hesitating, Karl reached into his desk, pulled out another identical envelope, and tossed it across the room. Another bundle was nothing to him, it seemed. It wasn't his money. If Karl felt he had won the day, Meth felt the same and left the rest of his questions unasked. He opened the envelope, checked its contents, and accepted what seemed like a fortune in exchange for the soul his father had convinced him was worthless.

"Yes," he said. "I am interested."

8

JUST A JOB

METH'S TRAIN jerked to a stop in Geneva, snapping him from sleep. He shook his head a few times, reorienting in time and place. His weekend in Murren was a distant memory, his dreams of Cambridge and Adi abruptly interrupted. He stood, shoved his still unopened computer back into his bag, and pressed the slotted leather straps over their brass studs. He exited the train and trekked down the platform slower than usual. His mind was on other things, most notably his mother.

By the time he arrived at Cimetière des Rois, Meth's mind was clear and painfully reconnected with the present. He stepped from the taxi without speaking and dropped the fare and a generous tip into the driver's hand. Despite his antisocial tendencies, Meth was generous with tips. It stemmed from seeing a beleaguered Adelaide wait tables in Saint-Martin-des-Entrées after François disappeared. Sometimes Meth had waited alone at a corner table for her to finish her shift. The whole town had seen her waiting tables; some had left generous tips. He'd seen how their kindnesses had lightened his mother's burden. Meth had later learned from his grandfather that Adelaide had persistently refused his help. "It's my mess," she had said. "I'll clean it up." Meth ultimately came to understand she had viewed life through the undeserved guilt and distorted perspective of an abused woman.

Meth walked a few dozen meters down Rue des Rois and turned into the cemetery near the chapel, one hand in his pocket, the other wrapped around the satchel strap that hung from his shoulder. A mild gust unfurled two flags from their respective poles, each snapping softly. One bore the familiar white cross of Switzerland, the other—the flag of Geneva—waved the Imperial Eagle and the Key of St. Peter, as it had since the 15th century.

The eagle turned repeatedly in the wind as if to chaperone Meth's visit.

The sun forced a slight squint until Meth donned the Ray-Bans he had pulled from his pocket. It was even warmer in Geneva than it had been in Paris a week earlier. January felt like spring. He dropped his bag near a pair of headstones and panned the sky, pausing briefly on the one dark cloud that threatened the otherwise perfect weather. He noted a few people in the distance, weaving in and out of the shade that fell from the trees. He was essentially alone, but he still felt exposed; he found himself more vigilant than usual.

Most of the headstones were old—some very old and covered with moss or vines—like the tomb of Charles Pictet de Rochemont who had prepared the declaration of Switzerland's permanent neutrality. He was interred in 1824. Two nearby graves were so new they still had temporary wooden crosses facing mounds of fresh earth and piles of wilting flowers. The newest graves shot a chill through Meth. Despite his best efforts to be impervious, they reminded him of why he hated cemeteries. He saw himself—first as a young child, then as a teenager—standing near an open grave. He winced in pain then quickly refocused and moved on.

Fixing on the headstones in front of him, Meth began to whisper, haltingly at first, not sure whether he was addressing himself or the graves. Though not inclined to admit it, he was angry about being there, embarrassed and feeling vulnerable by the very act. *It is so cliché*, he thought, *so pathetic. I am talking to the dead. Not even to the dead, I am talking to a grave.* He hadn't yet spoken aloud, but he looked around again as if to make sure no one could eavesdrop on his thoughts.

"Eighteen years, Mother. I have not been here in eighteen years, not since I buried Grandfather."

He looked at the adjacent stone with his grandfather's name on it. Truman had prearranged the simple marker. This was the first time Meth had seen it.

"I hate it here. Talking to the dead? I must be out of my mind."

He started pacing. His volume gradually increased as his timbre softened. He unconsciously pulled the sunglasses from his face each time he paced north, away from the low southern January sun, and replaced them each time he reversed course. A small path of trampled grass soon appeared across the two graves. More confident he was alone, he became more comfortable with his audience and topic. He was finally talking about things that mattered, even if to no one but himself.

"You are so fortunate," he said, again surveying the vicinity. He watched a young woman place flowers on a distant grave. Her beagle tugged at his short leash, trying to reach the birds that seemed to know exactly how close they could venture without being harmed. He looked again at the black eagle on the Geneva flag waving at the gate. He turned back to his mother's headstone and read the inscription: CHOOSE TO LOVE. He could still remember her saying it.

"How could you feel that way? François had no love. He was a drunken monster."

François' file had probed every old wound. He continued pacing, speaking as much to the sky as to the headstones. In those minutes that stretched into an hour, he said more than he would normally say in a week. He'd hoped his visit might quell the recent thoughts of his mother. He'd tried to put them out of his mind. Failing that, he'd decided to challenge the thoughts head-on, person-to-headstone. It sounded silly in his mind. It felt silly as he spoke. He wasn't much given to spiritual notions, but he wondered if she might be out there somewhere, floating around in the ether, listening. If she was, she wasn't answering. The more he spoke, the faster he paced and the angrier he became. His demeanor darkened.

"I hate him. I hate his voice in my head."

Meth wasn't psychotic. He knew the voices were mere echoes of his past. But they were intrusive—sometimes destructive—and he couldn't forget them. Sometimes he'd even argue with them. He wanted to forget. He'd tried. The dark side of his brilliance was his memory. Sometimes he'd hear Adelaide, sometimes Truman, but mostly François. Meth's mother had spoken of God's promise to a wayward Israel, that he would remember their sins no more. Apparently, God could forget. Meth knew the verse in Jeremiah. He'd read it as a child; he'd studied it at Cambridge. In contrast to the prevailing dogma about the great miracle of God's omniscience, Meth had come to wonder if the godliest of gifts might be an ability to forget. He'd tried, but he couldn't.

Meth studied his dark shadow on the grass. *Should I kill him?* He looked back to his mother's headstone. He'd considered every scenario. He'd asked every question the night before and again in the morning as he tromped through Zurich. He'd asked them yet again as he walked around Geneva for two hours before waving down the taxi that had driven him to the cemetery. His answers had vacillated. He felt like a cartoon figure with an angel hovering over one shoulder and a demon dancing on the other, each with Meth's face and a contrasting portion of his affect. Neither character offered peace, the sweetness of revenge on one side and the bitterness of leaving it unresolved on the other.

Meth knew he was prohibited from acting. He'd heard Karl say it was not yet a contract; it was just a file. And if it had been a contract, his involvement was still prohibited. The folder was an excuse, a vain attempt to legitimize his actions. *Besides, who can stop me? Karl? François? And what is Karl going to do? Turn me over to the police?* Meth wondered why. *What could that miserable inebriate have done to warrant a file?* All the same questions stormed through his mind again and again. He had refused to look through the folder. He wasn't willing to admit it, but he was afraid the answer might thwart his plans. *After all, it is just a job.* If Meth had offered his soul for lucre in Karl's office as a teenager, he now fully intended to consummate the deal.

"I am ending the blackness, Mother," he said, his right thigh now trembling. "I am going to look him in the face and kill him, just the way he killed Achilles."

Meth wanted to be done—to have the debate settled—but his mind never worked that way. He perseverated over and over and over again. He would consider every angle: rationalizing, ruminating, and recriminating. He would persuade himself he was justified and then condemn himself yet again. He knew well how to condemn himself. François had taught him that much. He hoped his mother might moderate the debate or, better yet, settle it. He didn't really believe that could happen, but he hoped. His feelings about guidance from the great beyond were as muddled and fleeting as a schizophrenic on the Metro. He began to regret having come at all.

An eye for an eye, he thought, still trying to convince himself. He had stopped his mental Rolodex on a convenient passage—one that served his purpose. Though agnostic—still debating on atheism—he was familiar with several sacred texts and could quote hundreds—literally, hundreds—of pages. Several ran through his mind in rapid succession: *Love your neighbor as yourself*, from the Torah; *Thou shalt love thy neighbor as thyself*, from the New Testament. The passages cut deep, triggering more anger than pain. The god of the Jews had demanded Abraham kill his long-awaited and beloved son—Meth knew the story well—and the god of the Christians had stood away while his only-begotten son was beaten, spat upon, and crucified. Neither scenario offered encouragement to the son of an abusive father.

The passages continued their march through Meth's head. *The ideal soul is incapable of ill will*, from the Bhagavad Gita. Like Mohandas Gandhi, Meth had memorized the entire Gita while at Cambridge. He could see in his mind the passages and pages as he had read them in the Wren Library at Trinity College. He continued his silent recitations: *Spend of your substance out of Love . . . practice regular charity*, from the Qur'an; *When ye are in the service of your fellow beings ye are only in the service of your God*, from the Book of Mormon. When his mother's favorite verse rolled into the queue, he unconsciously said it aloud. It spilled out onto the grass between him and the headstone:

"Turn the other cheek."

He flinched. *Maybe she is here*, he thought, then quickly pushed it aside. Neither his distain for organized religion nor his questions about god precluded contemplations of the hereafter, but he remained ambivalent at best. He was glad he didn't have to say it out loud or explain it to Karl. Then, in a flash, he saw Brigitte's auburn hair fanned out on the floor.

The pendulum had made its way to the angel's shoulder. Meth decided to return the file and to forget about François—maybe walk away from NEMESIS altogether. It might not resolve his resentment, but, unlike the abuse he suffered as a child, it would be *his* decision and he could live with it. Then, as he picked up his bag and repositioned his Ray-Bans, he saw a young boy laughing and rolling around on the grass with his dog. He saw himself and his black puppy.

"I'm sorry about Achilles."

It startled him. Hélène's voice was so unmistakable he turned, but he found himself as alone as the day he'd walked into Oldman's orchard. Then, just as abruptly as the pendulum had swung one way, it swung back. Death had won.

The lone dark cloud still hanging in the sky began to claim its portion of the day, speckling headstones and raising that first-drops-of-rain aroma from the soil. *Petrichor*, Meth thought, as he inhaled. It was a scent he normally relished and an obscure word he seldom used. Now, even petrichor failed to distract him. He looked again at the inscription on his mother's stone, glad she could not speak, knowing what she would say— what he did not want to hear. He shook his head in disbelief and walked away, darkly determined that his personal version of patricide would somehow be just.

9

HERCULES

METH STOMPED through his house, no shirt or shoes, carrying a short-handled axe. The honed edge intermittently caught sunlight through a window and shot a streak across his mostly bare walls. *Pink in Abstraction*, a Christian Nesvadba oil-on-canvas, hung alone on the east wall of his bedroom. He'd purchased it on a bright spring day in Vienna. It buoyed his mood when he stopped long enough to look at it. This was not one of those times.

His residence was neat and well lit. Except for his few pieces of art, it was quite Spartan. The moldings were darkly stained, mostly oak, the walls off-white, except in the den where they were paneled with imported cherry wood and hidden behind shelves of books.

Meth's house was quiet most of the time. He liked it quiet, except when the voices became unrelenting. On those days, if he stayed home, he blasted Gustav Mahler's *Symphony No. 2* so loudly the Nesvadba vibrated with each crescendo. Meth had once viewed the original 232-page manuscript of the symphony, complete with Mahler's detailed notes to the conductor. He stole some comfort in the fact that the creator had exerted such effort to control the performance of his work.

American businessman Gilbert Kaplan had purchased Mahler's manuscript in Zurich in 1982. He became so obsessed with the opus he dedicated his life to learning how to conduct it, and did so over 100 times. Kaplan's purchase price was not disclosed but his estate would later sell the manuscript at Sotheby's in London for £4,546,250. Meth appreciated Kaplan because he'd made the manuscript available in facsimile form, one of the few books in Meth's den that occasionally made it off the shelf. Sometimes he would pull it out and follow the music as it played. Even in his darkest hours, Meth realized the irony of rejecting Christianity while finding some modicum of refuge in Mahler's alternatively named *Resurrection*. He liked it despite the title.

Meth had hoped to find peace—or, at least, answers—at Cimetière des Rois. He was sadly disappointed. The dead souls he'd gone to see didn't talk back. All he'd found was a path to destruction. His determination to kill François had only encouraged the voices. From his infrequent words, no one would have suspected the incessant dialogue in his head. Over the years, he'd argued about his choice to leave Cambridge: I should have finished my degree; Who needs a degree?; I could have been a doctor; The world doesn't need another doctor; I needed the money; You don't need it anymore; I could have been somebody; *You filthy dog.* Sometimes it would go on for hours. He'd similarly debated his abandonment of religion and his decision to never own another dog. Sometimes the voices sounded like the erudite debates he'd attended at university. They used those arcane words he liked. Though the voices were often his, the sentences seemed to flow from some outside source. He'd collect the obscure words and use them as his own. That was the only aspect of the voices that appealed to him.

He pulled the price tag from his axe and tossed both onto the bed. He stuffed a few more items into his leather overnight bag. He looked at the axe, Mahler's ninety-minute symphony still blasting from the hall. He picked it up, sheathed it, and dropped it into his bag. He scanned the room, drew in a deep breath, and studied the ceiling for a few moments—as if the answers to his questions might be written there—before exhaling. He shunned his doubts, reminding himself he'd already decided. It was time to act.

Meth moved back across the hall and punched a button in the den to silence the music. Mahler still echoed through the house as Meth returned to the bedroom. He latched his bag and locked the door as he left, wondering if he'd ever return.

AS METH found his usual spot on the afternoon train, a woman in a brown fedora scrambled past, dragging an enormous bag. With a muffled grunt, she hefted the luggage, only to find the lower racks full and the upper rack out of reach. Surprising himself, Meth rushed to her aid.

"Danke, Herr," she said to his back.

"Ja, Ma'am," he replied without looking. He slid the unusually heavy bag into position on the top rack.

"Prometheus?" she asked, sounding uncertain as to whether she recognized his gravelly voice.

Meth turned to Hélène's signature smile. As cold and distant as he'd been during their previous encounter, and as abruptly as he'd left her on the train, he was surprised by her smile and friendly tone. Without waiting for a response, she reached out and rested her hand on his forearm. Meth looked at her fingers, then slowly traced up her arm and shoulder to her face. A tingling spread from her touch, like ripples across a pond. A warm and intensely pleasant sensation marched along behind the tingling. The hair on his arm and neck stood up.

Meth's mind raced. He wondered why her touch was so different, so inviting. Why did it grab him so deeply and immediately? He couldn't understand, but he wanted to find out. He had to force himself to speak.

"German today?" he asked, trying to remain as nonchalant as possible.

"Hey, I live in Zurich."

"Do you still prefer English on the train?"

"Not a preference; just a habit. I like English."

Meth couldn't help but return her smile.

"Why such a heavy bag, Hercules?" he said, pointing to her suitcase. He was surprised by his flippant tone. It sounded more like something he'd have said to Adi on one of their picnics.

"Just a few necessities," she teased as they moved to their seats. "Actually, my name's Hélène, not that you ever bothered to ask."

Her charisma bubbled. Her comment could have stung, but it didn't. She'd made it sound inviting. Meth couldn't understand it. He couldn't even describe it. He already knew her name; he couldn't forget that. It was emblazoned in his mind, in blue ink and beautiful script. Her note sat atop his bedside table. He'd read it at least a dozen times since Basel, but he'd hidden it in a drawer earlier that morning when he packed his axe. The contrast was irreconcilable. If there was a hint of anything good in his life, he'd pushed it aside so he could butcher François. A slave to habit, Meth tried to resist his attraction to Hélène, but he so enjoyed the way he felt in her presence he almost forgot where he was going, and why.

"You can call me Hercules if you like," she said. She shrugged and raised her brows. "I *am* freakishly strong."

Scenery began rolling past the windows as she asked about his presence in Zurich.

"I live here," he said, "in Altstadt. You?"

"Wollishofen. I have a meeting in Geneva this evening, then a weekend near the lake. Care to join me?"

Meth's expression changed. Not many things surprised him, but Hélène was making a habit of it. At the mention of Lake Geneva, the dark specter that had driven his trip thus far faded behind memories of sailing the lake with Truman. He enjoyed thinking about something less ominous than death. He reveled in the way Hélène spoke and the way she gently touched him. She seemed like a window into another world, complete with emotions and a glimmer of hope. Before he spoke, however, his excitement gave way to self-discipline—or habit—and he bolstered his calm expression, afraid he might give too much away.

"Join you?" he finally said, sounding incredulous.

"You don't think it's coincidence we meet on this train," she said, her Catalan accent peeking out, leaving it unclear whether she was asking a question or making a statement. "I don't believe in coincidence."

"You do not even know me."

"Yes, I do. You talk funny sometimes. You wear a fancy watch and you're a writer. How am I doing?"

"You *were* listening."

"I always listen." She nodded then winked. "And I watch. You like a table for your computer and you like facing the front of the train."

"I like to move forward," Meth admitted, surprised by his candor. "I do not like looking back."

"But you *did* look back," she teased.

An inquisitive expression swept across Meth's face.

"On the train, when you were leaving," she said. "I saw you."

He offered no response. He tried, but he had nothing. He wasn't sure whether he was embarrassed, irritated, or intrigued. He finally conceded a slight nod.

"I'm not suggesting anything heavy or emotional," she said, "just a fun weekend in Geneva—good food, casual conversation, separate rooms—if you're interested. Perhaps you can tell me more about Achilles." She doffed her hat and scarf and dropped them onto the table.

Meth recalled his feelings in Basel after leaving her on the train, how he had only met her and yet already missed her. He had determined then, and a few times since—every time he'd read her note—to not let another opportunity go unanswered.

"So," she said, "what are your plans for the weekend?"

"Geneva . . . I guess . . . near the lake."

"What about your *other* plans?"

"They can wait," he said, looking a bit more solemn. He quickly pushed the original purpose of his trip into the shadows. "I have time."

Hélène reached across the table and wrapped her tiny hand around three of his fingers.

"Smile, Prometheus. We'll have fun."

"Meth."

"Pardon?"

"I go by Meth; like Beth, but with an M. My Cambridge flatmate had a hard time saying Prometheus. So he shortened it to Meth."

"Like the drug?" She cringed. "That's odd."

"It was different then. Nobody used meth: amphetamines, yes, but not meth. Duc called me Meth. It stuck."

"Who's Duc?"

"My Vietnamese flatmate, Duc Pham. He said his parents named him Duc because they loved John Wayne. He pronounced it *Duke*, but he spelled it D-U-C. I was never sure whether he was joking or serious. He joked a lot."

Hélène listened, leaning closer.

"He was the most jovial person I have ever met. I only saw a serious expression once, when he talked about his parents escaping Vietnam on a boat." Meth became increasingly somber. "When he spoke of it, the veins in his neck and forehead bulged. You could see the hatred in his eyes."

As he described Duc, Meth fully transformed into a different time and place, almost into a different body. He became silent. Hélène felt the trembling in his hand. She looked down, then back into his distant eyes.

"Meth," she said. No response. "Meth!" she said a little louder, shaking his hand in hers and snapping the willowy fingers of her other hand in front of his face.

Almost startled, Meth returned to himself. He thought momentarily of Adi and how she used to snap her fingers the same way. Then he returned to his story.

"Within moments he would return to normal. That transition always intrigued me." Meth continued, failing any insight into his own behaviors. "How could he snap back and forth that way? How could he be so happy when he had experienced such hatred?"

"Hey," Hélène said, showing her palms, "can we lighten the mood? Let's talk about something more pleasant."

She shuffled her hat and scarf to the seat beside her as Meth recovered from his brief trip to Cambridge. He was surprised she didn't ask him more about his college years, but he was glad. He felt like he'd already volunteered too much.

"Now, about this weekend," she said with enthusiasm, "I think we can have a lot of fun."

Meth felt something in her tone. He liked it. But he didn't know what it was and he didn't know what to do with it, so he retreated to his comfort zone. He broke their pleasing eye contact and looked out the window. The passing scenery didn't look back or require his interaction. When he looked at Hélène, he felt compelled to reveal more than he wanted to say. If he refused to speak, he feared she would extract his secrets through his gaze.

Undeterred, Hélène gently hooked Meth's chin between her thumb and the crook of her index finger and turned him back to the conversation. She looked perplexed or concerned, like she could sense his discomfort.

"You in?" she said.

Her assertiveness surprised him, but he liked it. He offered a cautious nod.

"Good."

She smiled and leaned back in her seat, like she'd just won some hotly contested debate.

"I like you, Meth. You make me smile . . . in some angry sort of way." She chucked as she said it.

Meth leaned back, too, strangely relieved. He wondered who she was and why she cared, but he let those judgments pass and lost himself in the moment. Hélène put her hat and scarf back on the table as if she'd only been moving them from place to place to keep her hands busy. She excused herself to the bathroom. He turned his head and watched until she disappeared down the aisle behind him. He looked back at her scarf and remembered the day they met. He scanned the aisle again, feeling a bit uncertain. He pulled the scarf close and drew a slow, deep breath through his nose. The scent gathered feelings from their first encounter and connected them with the present, and with a painful longing to continue. He lost himself into some other world for a several minutes. He wondered about the future.

Meth's contemplations had taken longer than he realized. As he pushed the scarf back across the table, Hélène dropped into the seat next to him.

"Do you like it?" she asked with a playful grin.

Like what? he almost said, as if to pretend he didn't know what she was talking about. He felt like six-year-old Prometheus when François caught him in the gelato. Though vulnerable and embarrassed, he shrugged nonchalantly as if to suggest he had nothing to hide.

"I like it a lot," he said.

"It's Shalimar. Guerlain's been making it since 1925. It's all I wear. Pricey, but worth it, don't you think?"

"Definitely worth it," Meth said, breathing a little easier.

WHEN LAKE Geneva came into view, the conversation between Meth and Hélène had taken as many turns as the train and had gained as much momentum. Their route pressed along the north edge of the lake, through perfectly manicured orchards, until it curled south along the lake's west end. Remnants of lunch rested on the far corner of the table. Their dialogue was more relaxed. Meth even shared recollections of his childhood on the lake.

"So, you lived in Geneva?" Hélène asked.

"For about five years, with my mother's father. He raised me after she died."

"The grandfather that gave you the watch?"

"Truman Hamstead. He worked at Patek. They loved him. Everyone loved him. He was just one of those people. And when he retired—"

"The watch was a retirement gift?"

"No. They offered him a watch but he declined. He asked them to make a donation to the university in my mother's name . . . for cancer research."

"She had cancer?"

"It was his way of doing something. He *had* to do something. He had to make a difference for the next person."

"So, where'd the watch come from?"

"Truman's grandfather, Ivory Hamstead. He also worked at Patek. The family moved back and forth between Geneva and London over the years. My mother was born in London but spent much of her life in Geneva."

Meth had a way of drifting off topic. Sometimes he used it as a defense mechanism when things got too personal. Sometimes he just drifted because he was unaccustomed to conversation. When he wandered from the watch to his family, to London, to Geneva, and on, Hélène smiled and realigned his focus.

"What about the watch?" she asked.

"It was almost new when Ivory received it as a retirement gift."

"Almost? Why almost?"

"He was left-handed."

"So?"

Meth unbuckled the leather strap and passed his gold watch to Hélène. Not quite square, not quite round, the Grogan had four corners with bulging sides, like a square pillow trying to hold too much stuffing. Just below the left-handed stem was a button. It activated the chronometer and sent the additional hands sweeping across the dial. She examined it for a few moments, turning it over twice before looking back.

"It's upside down or backwards . . . or something." She looked at it again, then back at Meth, her head askance. "The stem's on the wrong side."

Meth smiled. Hélène's eyes brightened, seeing a side of him almost hidden and definitely out of practice. He felt encouraged. For the first time since they'd met, he wanted to share more.

"It is not backwards," he said. "It is built for a left-handed person, like Ivory. It is the only Patek ever made for a left-hander. That is why they gave him this one instead of a new one, and why it meant so much to him."

Rolling the watch in her hand, Hélène noted an inscription. She squinted to read it.

"This inscription is—"

"I know," Meth interrupted. "It is too worn to read, but it still means a lot to me. *He* meant a lot to me."

She looked carefully at the watch, focusing again on the inscription. She opened her mouth as if she was about to read it, but stopped and handed it back instead.

"Are you left-handed?" she asked as he repositioned it on his wrist.

"No, but I wear it anyway. Someday I will buy a new one so I can retire this to a secure place."

The train rolled slowly into the gare in Geneva just as the sun disappeared. It seemed everybody was in a hurry. Meth and Hélène looked at each other and relaxed in their seats until the aisle cleared.

"Come on, Hercules," he teased, reaching for her heavy bag.

Her eyes widened, as if she'd just witnessed a hint of Meth escaping his shell, as if a couple of hours on a train had changed who he was. She looked as if she couldn't believe he'd just made a joke.

"Carry my bag anytime," she said.

Meth felt different in Geneva than he had three hours earlier in Zurich. If Hélène had sensed it, he had experienced it. He felt like she'd unwound his intensity. He looked forward to the weekend. He felt awkward, like he didn't deserve her company or, if he enjoyed it too much, it would disappear. He looked at her and surprised himself when he again smiled.

They stepped off the train together and started down the platform. When Meth's phone rang, he hardly broke stride. He noted the caller ID and braced himself.

"Bonjour . . . Oui . . . Genève."

Meth reflexively answered his phone in the language of his location. He began the day speaking German in Zurich; now, in Geneva, he toggled to French. Most exchanges with Karl eventually ended up in English. Karl spoke in a cool, professional tone—all business. Meth had already decided this was not the time or place to settle the feud over François' file. He remained civil. After a long gap and a change in tone, he offered his standard response: "I will take care of it."

He disconnected and dropped the phone back into his pocket.

"Problem?" Hélène asked, noting the change in his countenance. "You need to go?"

"No. Just a little business." He tried to smile.

"You want to talk about it?"

"No. Not now." He was curt, his tone saying more than his words. "I will take care of it while you are in your meeting."

Hélène recoiled half a step from the tension in Meth's words. She relinquished his arm.

He grew quiet and pensive, almost sullen. Anyone listening to his end of the call might have connected the dots—as easily as a child with a crayon— and concluded that the caller was no friend. Hélène's disappointed look suggested her conclusion: that *business* was not good for Meth. Any softening of his defenses that had occurred during their train-ride was now gone. Without speaking further, they continued through the gare, out to the street, and into a taxi.

"Le Richemond, s'il vous plaît," she requested, and the taxi sped away.

10

I AM WILLING

METH REMAINED silent in the taxi, his mind rolling faster than the car. He retraced his steps since leaving Zurich and planned every move he would take for the next twelve hours. When Karl called, Meth's mind engaged another gear. His transformation into *dispatch* mode was abrupt and dramatic, as abrupt and dramatic as his shift back to baseline when a job was done—when his leg stopped trembling. Between those two transition points, Meth's only thoughts were about his target and his task: their habits, idiosyncrasies, geography, weather, extenuating circumstances, egress, and escape. Suddenly he had no time for Hélène. She sat on his left; he looked out the window to his right. He'd forgotten about her and all that was good during their train ride.

Meth's mind backtracked to a gun range in Zurich nearly twenty years earlier. It was the first time he'd fired a gun, or even held one. He'd lived in Geneva for several years before college, and he knew guns were more prevalent and more accepted in Switzerland than in neighboring countries—Swiss firearms laws were more similar to laws in the U.S. than in other parts of the E.U.—but Truman was not a gun owner or enthusiast.

Meth's first trip to the range came as part of his NEMESIS training. Firearms proficiency was mandatory. It came naturally to him. Within two weeks he could rapidly fire ten rounds from his 9 mm Browning Dual Mode, or BDM, punching a five-centimeter pattern through a target ten meters downrange. One hundred rounds, three times a week; Meth had no difficulty with the task.

At the range, Meth met Srecko Knezevic, the most senior active operative and one of Karl's contemporaries. Srecko was a founding member of the Serbian Military Special Operations Battalion when it was formed in 1978. The Cobras, as they were called, were charged with various responsibilities, including counter-terrorism. Srecko was so highly regarded among the Cobras they offered him a command when the unit became part of the newly formed Serbian Special Brigade in 2006. He stayed at NEMESIS but accepted the Special Brigade's gift of a Zastava CZ 99 semiautomatic pistol, which replaced his long-trusted M57 sidearm.

Srecko proved to be the only operative who consistently outperformed Meth on the range. At twenty meters, Srecko could quickly empty his .40 S&W with each of the ten holes in the target touching the others. And he could do so with either hand, another reason he liked the ambidextrous CZ 99. Over the years, he was the only truly ambidextrous shooter Meth would meet. Meth liked his cool, focused manner—no fanfare, nothing superfluous, just business. He was surprised when Srecko went out of his way to offer tips on marksmanship. He never saw the stone-faced Serbian offer help to others.

Meth carried his weapon everywhere for about six months. NEMESIS left that decision to individuals. Young Meth enjoyed a sense of invincibility when he first carried a gun. He liked the adrenaline rush. He hoped he would encounter François, and he imagined scenarios in which he could justifiably empty his fifteen-round magazine, plus one from the chamber, into the thief who had stolen his childhood. After a few weeks, his sense of invulnerability gave way to the simple discomfort of wearing the weapon. It was heavy and uncomfortable, not worth the trouble. Except for those frequent trips to the range, the BDM moved from his belt (or sometimes his underarm holster) to a small gun safe in his den.

Some of Meth's colleagues, like Srecko, effected their contracts with firearms. Meth chose otherwise. He didn't like revolvers, and he didn't like retrieving the spent cartridges from a semi-automatic. More to the point, he didn't like the noise—even with a suppressor—or the blood or the investigation. With gunshot wounds, there was always an investigation.

Meth returned to the present when his taxi stopped at Hotel Le Richemond. He'd enjoyed the conversation on the train but after the phone call he was glad he and Hélène had agreed to separate rooms. His contemplations of a night together hadn't included Karl. Now he had work to do. He'd already planned a thousand moves and contingencies, like a grandmaster at a chessboard. Hélène must have sensed a need to leave things alone; she hadn't spoken since the call. At the desk, the clerk provided key cards and directions to the elevator. As Hélène's heels clicked across the marble floor to the elevator, she finally spoke.

"Sure you don't want to talk?" she asked, as if she already knew the answer, as if she was just being polite. When the elevator doors closed, she offered a smile, but Meth didn't budge.

"No . . . I, I mean, I would like to . . . but *no*."

His hesitation surprised him. *I have no time for this.* He straightened his spine and pushed his shoulders back.

"We can talk tomorrow," he said.

They decided to go their separate ways—her to her meeting, him to his business—before reuniting for a nightcap. (He'd already decided to make things appear as normal as possible and to construct a tight timeline in case he needed an alibi.) Meth dragged her heavy bag from the elevator to her door. She could have handled it herself—she had done so many times—but he pulled it along until they stopped at her door.

"Thank you, Meth," she said, grabbing his arm.

He looked at her momentarily then quickly away. He could tell she wanted to say more.

"I can cancel my meeting," she said.

Meth looked down the hall, his solemn expression stifling her effort. He began to lean away, toward his room, but she pulled him back. She gripped his arm until he finally returned eye contact. He saw an anguish there as deep as the realms of Iblis. It sent a chill down his back.

"Don't go," she said.

"I have to."

He could feel her eyes on his back as he walked to his room. He wanted to turn around, but he needed every moment to plan and every faculty focused. He wondered why she cared. He thought about calling Karl and requesting reassignment, but that seemed unmanly, unprofessional, and un-Meth. He quickly dismissed it. When the door of his room snapped shut behind him, it closed on all his doubts. He could again concentrate on the task at hand.

Meth didn't like surprises, and he didn't like to rush. He didn't like phone calls that came without a detailed file. He didn't like doing research online in hotel rooms because of the electronic trail it left behind. He had a VPN (virtual private network), but he didn't trust it. His modus operandi was to leave no trail. More particularly, because some trails were inevitable, he preferred to leave no reason to look. An evening taxi to the outskirts of Geneva could pose problems should there be an investigation, and, thanks to Karl's last-minute phone call, there wasn't time to walk. This job precluded several of Meth's preferences. Last-minute contracts compounded the difficulty of his work, but he didn't ask Karl about the urgency. He didn't care. Two things he *was* grateful for: the early January sunset and the unseasonably warm weather.

At least Meth knew the target and the location—that is to say, he knew who the man was and where he lived. They had never met, but Meth knew his face from news stories (mostly print, since Meth seldom watched television).

As much as Meth hated busses—with their lights, people, and

cameras—they were better than a taxi with a face-to-mirror conversation and a receipt; some drivers generated a receipt even when paid with cash. Meth learned the bus would travel the several kilometers from downtown Geneva to within 200 meters of the lakefront Genthod estate, but he would only ride a portion of that route. He'd walk two kilometers before boarding, to obscure the origin of his trip, and exit two stops before his destination, walking the last kilometer in the dark. He preferred to walk the full distance, but time was an enemy on this job.

The target, Jean René DeBarto, regularly sold his influence as a Geneva Councilman. That was just one of his virtues. Meth knew he was on the list. He'd once glanced at the file in Karl's office. He hadn't studied it in detail or committed it to memory, as was his standard practice, since he had no reason to think it would be his. In his brief perusal, however, he'd gleaned and captured more information than most people would gather from a weeklong cram session. He could see the satellite images of the residence in his mind, with red dots marking the location of the security cameras. He could see the fan-shaped highlights in front of those cameras, showing their fields of view, and the black corners that were safe from each lens. Karl had told Meth to expect DeBarto to arrive home sometime after a two-hour council meeting that was scheduled to begin at 6:00 p.m. There was no Mrs. DeBarto, at least not anymore, and anyone reading a newspaper in recent years knew why. The women on his arm changed frequently and never got any older.

Pressed for time and still formulating his plan, Meth grabbed the plastic send-out laundry bag from a shelf in his room. He wrapped it around a handful of cured meats from the mini bar and stuffed the bundle into his front pocket. He filled his other front pocket with a small coil of parachute cord, an occupational staple he kept in his travel bag. He donned an inconspicuously dark gray sweater and rolled out the side door of the hotel carrying an unopened black umbrella in his gloved hands. He left the axe in his room. That was for another mark on another day. It might as well have had a name on it.

Meth walked into the dark and boarded a bus on Boulevard Georges-Favon, not far from the Patek Philippe Museum. He disembarked in Bellevue and walked the last kilometer into Genthod on a less-traveled, less-lit road. From the road, he walked a paved path and then a boardwalk to the edge of Lake Geneva. The gravel along the waterfront allowed him to approach the backyard of the estate beyond the tips of the largely symbolic fences without leaving footprints. He hugged the cedar-slat fence along the east boundary of DeBarto's property until he came to the corner of the house.

A dog, chained in the backyard, began to growl and show his teeth. He pulled at his chain, staring Meth in the eye, and huffed out a few quiet barks. Almost immediately the neighbor's light came on. Meth heard a door open and footsteps on the deck next door. He crouched in the shadows and waited. He watched slits of light track across the grass as the neighbor fanned a flashlight back and forth on the other side of the fence. The dog looked toward the light, sniffed a few samples of what must have been a familiar scent, and became quiet. Meth continued to wait, his hyperflexed knees screaming for him to stand up. Finally, after several minutes, the neighbor's deck door closed and the light went off. Meth tipped onto his side, slowly restored his knees to a more anatomic position, and waited for the pain to subside.

He inched closer, keeping his eyes lower than the dog's. He pulled the plastic bundle from his pocket and unfolded the layers of cured meat from his hotel room. He extended his arm toward the Irish Setter that now seemed more like a pet than a protector: no barking, just a wagging tail. Meth moved closer. He extended his other hand, letting the dog first sniff, then lick, then wag more confidently. Only a novice would think this house was secure. Rather than hiring professionals, DeBarto had shelled out cash to charlatans who had convinced him he was safe. The Geneva Council might have insisted on better security if he had not offended or abused each of them at one time or another through the years.

Pulling off his right shoe, Meth tied it to one end of his parachute cord and threw it over the small branch of a tree—a tree that any competent security consultant would have cut down. The only hint of disturbance from his shoe was a white-tailed eagle that launched from the limb and circled wide over the lake. Meth payed out line until the shoe came again into reach. He untied it and put it back on his foot. With one smart tug on the cord, the branch cracked and came to rest on the eaves directly in front of the camera that was trained on the small dock in the backyard. He released one end of the cord, retracted it from the branch, and returned it to his pocket, leaving no evidence of his presence. As if sensing the disturbance had concluded, the eagle returned and settled onto a sturdy branch and watched as Meth turned his attention back to the dog.

To Meth, the dog looked like his name should be *Red*. He spoke to him and tousled his hair and ears to keep him calm. He traced Red's chain back to its source, calmly interacting with the dog as he worked. He unscrewed the lawn auger several twists and pulled up on it until the surrounding turf began to lift. Then he gave it one mighty heave in the direction of the lake, intentionally bending the auger and leaving a short trail of soft soil across the grass in the direction of the water. Red was in no hurry to go anywhere. He stayed close to Meth, enjoying the continued attention as he became an unwitting ally.

Meth pulled the plastic bag from his pocket, stripped as naked as a liar before god, and stuffed his clothes into the bag as it started to rain. He eyed the dense clouds, grateful the night was warmer and darker than usual. Knowing light would spill from the house into the backyard when DeBarto came home, he positioned his bag under a bush near the fence and covered it with his now-opened black umbrella. Then he led the dog toward the dock, dragging the chain and auger to leave a trail.

Meth heard a car roll up and a garage door open. He hastened his step and, for the first time, gently tugged on the chain to encourage the dog's reluctant approach to the lake. He walked to the end of the dock, leading Red along the side of the structure to leave paw prints in the soft ground toward the lake. He descended the three-step ladder at the end of the dock. As Meth touched the water, a thousand icy knives marched across his body. For an instant, he was unable to overcome the halting effect on his respiration. He continued to reel in the chain as his breathing settled (though it did not return to normal). He grabbed Red's collar, pulled him close, and gently muzzled a single yelp with his hand. As the dog struggled, Meth spoke softly and comforted him. He wrapped one end of the chain twice around the dog's neck and dallied the other around a dock-post, tangling the auger and chain into an ununravelable mess. Then he waited, shivering and holding Red's snout above water.

DeBarto entered his house from the garage and flipped a panel of switches. The wall of windows lit up like Piccadilly Circus. Through the windows, Meth watched DeBarto's every move. The east edge of the property, with Meth's bag of clothes, remained in the shadows. True to his reputation, DeBarto overflowed a large glass with dark liquor and took a pull from the bottle, like he might decompose if he waited too long for his next drink. Had Meth been a connoisseur, he might have recognized, even from a distance, the distinctive bottle of Louis XIII de Rémy Martin French cognac. As it was, he could have read the label and still not have appreciated its multi-thousand-franc price. DeBarto could afford it, but, knowing his ethics and lifestyle, it was more likely a gift—a bribe. He downed the first glass without a breath and filled it again. He sipped the second glass as he moved toward the window and squinted through the accumulating raindrops, trying to focus on the new small hole in his lawn. Realizing what should have been there, he swung open the large glass doors and called out: "Jamaïque." He called twice more, appearing unenthused about venturing into the rain to look for his dog.

Meth loosened his grip on Red's nose, allowing one small yelp to escape. DeBarto lifted his head and turned toward the sound, finally stepping out into the rain. Slipping and catching himself, he dropped his cognac, shattering the glass across the deck.

How lucky is that? Meth thought as his mark steadied himself and stepped onto the lawn. *Nothing like the trappings of alcohol to authenticate the scene of a drowning.*

As DeBarto neared the lake he called out again to his dog. Meth released his grip and sent Red around the corner of the dock toward the bank. DeBarto waded into the water to rescue his pet. He tugged at the chain. When it refused to yield, he waded deeper into the water and the shadows to investigate. Meth silently slipped under the water and around the dock. In one powerful motion, he hoisted DeBarto's ankle with one hand as he slammed his other hand into the middle of the councilman's back, forcing him under before he could gasp or yell. Forty years and as many kilograms closer to good health, Meth found DeBarto's struggles easily surmountable. One deep breath of cold water rendered Jean René limp. Another minute underwater finished the job.

If Red sensed what had just taken place, he showed no indication. There had been no effort to protect his master. Meth didn't have to dig too deep to conjure reasons for the dog's behavior.

Pulling slack from the chain, Meth wrapped it twice around the dead man's leg and once around his neck, assuring there was sufficient length remaining to allow Red's safe, albeit wet, rest onshore. He again comforted the dog before taking care of himself. He climbed the ladder and retraced his steps on the dock, leaving DeBarto's footprints alone in the soft soil; his own prints disappeared under the rain on the dock. He quickly dressed and casually strolled from the yard to the gravel path. He left as he had arrived, unnoticed and unflapped.

One thing surprised Meth as he made his way back to town: the doubts he had first encountered in Paris now resurfaced in Geneva.

METH DRAGGED himself into the lobby of the hotel, resenting the need to be there. He'd only surfaced because he'd promised, and for his alibi. He wanted a quick exit. Hélène, by contrast, arrived smiling and energetic. She found him slumped in an overstuffed chair, twisting a glass of sparkling water in one hand and massaging his trembling right thigh with the other. He stared out a dark window without acknowledging her approach.

"Ready for that nightcap?" she asked, looking at his trembling leg.

He looked up but showed no interest. The enthusiasm in her face dropped a notch. Meth's emotional black hole sucked every good feeling into the dark abyss and gave nothing in return.

"Did you finish your business?" she asked.

He nodded. "The rest of the weekend is free," he mumbled as he looked away.

"Your leg okay?"

"It just does that sometimes."

"You seem so serious, like the day we met. Is something wrong?"

"I am ready for bed," he said without addressing her question.

"Something stronger than Pellegrino perhaps?"

"No. No alcohol. I am ready for bed."

Hélène's brows elevated. Her head drew back on her shoulders as if to dodge a passing bullet.

"Fine," she said, her tone biting back. "You . . . you know . . . you don't have to be here."

She turned toward the elevator and took a step.

"Wait," he whispered, not sure what to say next. "It is personal. I cannot talk about it. I want to . . . " He trailed off. That was the best he could offer. She turned back.

Meth's expression softened. He tried to decide whether he was angry or impressed. Most people just walked away from his rudeness—as she was about to do. He'd found it an effective way to clear a room. Until now, Karl was the only person who'd called him on it.

If Hélène was curios or disappointed, she resisted probing further. She stood her ground, appearing more concerned than offended. She lowered herself carefully into a chair.

"Tomorrow?" she asked. "We still do something tomorrow, no?"

"Sure." Meth stood up. "Just not tonight."

He cringed as he walked away, thinking of François' abrupt and dismissive interactions with Adelaide—the few, that is, that were not physically abusive. He hated himself for straying into behaviors he so abhorred, but he couldn't stop himself, at least not immediately. He was done for the night; done talking, done interacting or making any attempt at it, done with the world. He hoped he wasn't done with Hélène, but at that moment he couldn't force himself to behave any better.

"Buenas noches, Meth," she said to his back from across the room.

"Good night," he mumbled without turning or slowing down.

In his room, Meth folded the parachute cord he had used earlier and carefully tucked it back into its designated spot, right beneath the axe. He sat motionless for over an hour, studying a snag in the drapes and the flicker of light that struggled through it. His Ferrari—the Berlinetta that had replaced his 456 signing bonus—gathered dust in his garage. He'd driven it less than a thousand kilometers. His €3,200 custom front door opened and closed like any other door and failed any longer to catch his attention. He couldn't recall the last time he'd seen a movie or listened to a concert or watched a ballet. His weekend in Murren had reminded him of feelings he'd once enjoyed but hadn't experienced in more than a decade. What, after all, was he working for? He'd accumulated a pile of money but couldn't buy what he really needed. He didn't even know what he really needed.

He thought about the Irish Setter he'd left shivering in the night. He hoped Red was still safe. When his leg finally quieted, he could at least attempt to sleep. He pulled off his clothes and flopped onto the bed.

METH SMILED at Hélène when he arrived in the lobby. He held a piece of lined paper with a torn edge and blue ink. He'd found it peeking from under his door.

> I hope you are feeling better.
> Meet me in the lobby at 8:00.
> Breakfast is on me.
> H.

He'd slept little. He was still tired, but his leg had stopped trembling. If she was willing to give him another shot, he was willing to try. He'd felt something on the train, and he wanted more. He liked that she had pushed back last night. He hadn't liked it at the time, but he respected her confidence. His pride wouldn't allow him to admit it, and his naiveté wouldn't enable him to articulate it, but he knew he needed to change and he knew he needed someone to push him in the right direction, whatever that direction was. And she knew, it seemed to Meth, just where to push and how hard and in which direction. He'd bristled, but he wanted her help.

Hélène seemed cautious at first, perhaps hesitant. She offered a warm traditional greeting, touching her cheek to his, first on the right, then the left. Her embrace raced through him as it had on the train. *How does she do that?*

They enjoyed breakfast near the lake. Sunlight from above and reflecting off the water flooded through the windows. They watched Jet d'Eau erupt at the point where Lake Geneva emptied into the Rhône, heaving 500 liters per second 140 meters into the air. For Meth, Hélène proved more captivating than the fountain. She wore bright flattering clothes and read *Anglo Swiss*, an English-language morning paper. As their server poured coffee, Hélène sat up suddenly and turned the headline toward Meth: COUNCILMAN DROWNS IN LAKE GENEVA.

"What happened?" he asked between casual sips.

"He was trying to save his dog. Got tangled in the chain."

"How is the dog?" he asked, sounding more interested.

"The dog's fine."

"Hercules?"

"Yes."

"I know you have plans, but may I offer a suggestion?"

"Sí. Of course. What?"

He reminded her of their conversation on the train, that his mother and grandfather were both buried in Geneva. That was his excuse. He wanted to get out of Geneva, but not for the reasons he'd shared. The memory he really wanted to escape was that of Jean René DeBarto. He suggested a quick train ride to Lausanne where they could still spend the weekend on the lake. Hélène readily agreed.

"I love Lausanne," she said. "I attended University there. We can stay at Château d'Ouchy, on the lake, and have lunch at Bleu Lézard. They have the best water in Switzerland, in cute little Bleu Lézard bottles." She grabbed him by the arm. "Let's go."

It was a common phrase—Let's go—but it had been Adi's. He wondered where Adi was and what had become of her. He wondered what might have happened if he'd given their relationship a fighting chance. He wondered the same about Hélène. He didn't know why she'd gone out of her way to suggest separate rooms for the weekend, but he was glad. He'd had plenty of sex; it never helped, at least not for long. He was ready to explore a relationship instead.

On the way to the gare, Meth and Hélène walked through the Plaine de Plainpalais flea market. Meth and Truman had visited the same flea market more than twenty years earlier. Truman was big on building memories. When he discovered a 1700 edition of William Denham's *The Artificial Clock-Maker*, he bought it for Meth as a memento of their day together. Meth never knew exactly how much it cost, but he saw Truman drop a handful of bills on the table as the vender slid the book into a bag. Young Meth had expressed concern about the cost. "It's an inexpensive memory," Truman had said as he handed the gift to his grandson. Meth still displayed his leather-bound horology text on a shelf near a picture of his grandfather.

While Meth and Hélène meandered between and around the tables, he thought about how much Truman's gift had meant to him. Perhaps he could do something similar. When Hélène moved on ahead, he stopped and bought her a Mercator map of Lake Geneva. The seventeenth century map measured 48 x 36 centimeters and had one vertical crease. Because it had been folded before, Meth allowed the vender to refold it and coax it into a Mylar sleeve, and then a flat paper bag. He dropped ninety euros into the vendor's weathered hand and quickly slipped the map into his bag before Hélène turned around.

Twenty minutes later, on the train to Lausanne, Meth revealed his surprise.

"For you," he said as he slid the brown paper across the table. "A memory."

Her face brightened. She grabbed his hand and thanked him repeatedly even before she opened it. She gently extracted the map from its covering and laid it flat on the table. She seemed completely mesmerized. Meth watched her finger carefully trace the border of the lake, then wipe away a tear that had fallen onto the map. He looked up to see another tear on her cheek.

"I was so lonely during my last year at university. I contemplated leaving school. My brother Olin had just started college in Madrid. He left his studies and spent a week with me in Lausanne. I knew it was hard for him, but he came to help. We drove all the way around the lake." She traced their route on the map as she spoke. "He promised me I could do it. I told him I was fine and tried to send him back to Madrid, but he wouldn't go. The next day he took me on the ferry from Ouchy to Evian. We had a long talk over lunch in France, and he made me promise not to quit. 'If it's worth starting, it's worth finishing,' he said."

She paused and swallowed hard, still looking at the map.

"If he hadn't come, I wouldn't have graduated. I don't know where I'd be now."

Meth studied her face as she spoke. He saw her love for her brother and a dark shadow of the pain she'd shown the night before.

"Where's Olin now?" he said.

She looked up from the map and struggled to answer.

"He died a week later," she said, her voice tender and quiet.

Meth wanted to ask but waited. It just didn't seem like the right time.

She squeezed his hand and looked again at the map. "It's perfect. It's . . . it's a perfect gift, Meth. Thank you."

BY THE time they entered the Bleu Lézard, the mood had lightened. Hélène was smiling again. She gripped Meth's arm with one hand and embraced several staff members with the other. She greeted them each by name, touching cheeks and kissing the air, sometimes speaking French, sometimes English.

"This is my new friend, Prometheus," she said at each encounter.

Her friends greeted Meth with smiles and hugs, like they already knew him. If he was good enough for Hélène, he was good enough for them. Their warmth and affection impressed him. Such friendships were so foreign to Meth they almost seemed contrived. But he felt welcome and, as the afternoon wore on, increasingly comfortable.

Two blue, teardrop-shaped bottles of sparking water soon arrived at their table. Each had a rubber-gasketed glass stopper and the Bleu Lézard logo. After a taste, Meth had to admit how good it was.

"Don't drink too much," she said. "I need you in your right mind."

He smiled, almost laughed.

"Tell me about Achilles."

His head spun around like a Charlie McCarthy doll. Nobody had taken him down that road. His mind raced. He felt the tension build. His initial reaction was to tell her it was none of her business and then leave. That's how he'd come to deal with uncomfortable issues; but, as she'd told him the night before, *You don't have to be here.* He was afraid if he left he'd never see her again.

"Tell me your favorite memory," she said.

Her request reframed his thoughts. Every memory of Achilles didn't have to be blood and sorrow. There were good times he seldom leaned on. He pondered for a moment and took another drink from one of the blue bottles.

"He had a funny walk," Meth began, his smile returning. "I think his right hind leg was shorter than the others. Sometimes he would fall down if he ran too fast and turned left. He was only six months old, but he was big, and it got worse as he got older." Meth started to laugh. He could see it all in his mind. "I would get him to chase me through the orchard. Then I would turn left around a tree and watch him roll through the weeds. I fell down laughing. Achilles ran over and jumped on me and barked until we were both out of breath."

He took another drink as Hélène laughed along with him.

"He tried to lick my ears. When I pushed him away, he got frustrated. He grabbed my pant leg—I was only six—and dragged me across the orchard until he tore a hole in my pants. My mother pretended to scold me, but she could not keep a straight face. All my pant legs had patches and repairs where she had sewn them up."

Meth stopped for a breath. He saw an encouraging happiness in Hélène's eyes, as deep as the pain he'd seen the night before.

"I have not thought about that in years," he said. He hadn't laughed like that in years either, but he didn't say that part out loud. "That silly dog made me laugh all the time."

"You're you again."

"Pardon?" He leaned closer. "What do y—"

"You're you. You're back. I missed you. I don't know who you were last night, but this is the Meth I wanted to spend the weekend with."

"Sometimes I check out," he admitted.

"Well," she said, as if accepting his challenge, "I'm here to check you back in."

Her mastery of English surprised Meth: her vocabulary, her tone, and her nuanced timing, her sometimes-playful sarcasm, even her sometimes American-sounding accent. Occasionally she'd slide in a Spanish word or struggle to find the right syntax, but she would most often hit the mark precisely.

She leaned over and kissed him on the cheek.

Meth sat spellbound for an eternity of seconds, surprised by the emotions he labored to conceal. Her kiss filled his chest with lighter, more invigorating air, then it sank into his bones and his soul.

"I have to tell you what I'm feeling," she said, hesitating. Her timing left him wondering if she could read his mind. "You don't have to say anything at all." She waited, struggling, it seemed, to interpret his expression. "Are you okay with that?"

Meth offered a halting nod. He was still digesting his own feelings. He didn't know how to make room for hers too. She rested her hand on his and began.

"I don't know what happened to the boy with the dog. Maybe someday you can tell me. Someone injured him. And when his wound healed, it scarred right over the wonderful person he was—the person you still are inside. I get glimpses. I saw it the day we met. I know he's in there. I'm going help you find him."

"Why?"

"What?"

"Why? Why do you care? I am the rudest, most impatient person I know. *I* have a hard time caring about me; why would you?"

She paused and took an audible breath. She followed Meth's lead, bypassing her glass and drinking straight from one of the blue bottles.

"I don't know," she said. "Maybe it's a mistake. I'm just guessing. There's something in you that reminds me of me. I think you're actually happy somewhere deep inside; you've just forgotten. But I have to admit it, I'm afraid."

"Of what?" Meth asked, like he was still the boy in the orchard, bereft of adult insight.

"Of my feelings."

If Meth was an assassin-savant, as Karl occasionally suggested, his emotional quotient rested at the opposite end of the spectrum. Hélène, however, seemed unfazed by his brevity. She accepted his naïve but sincere efforts.

"I'm surprised by my feelings," she continued. "It makes me nervous to feel so much so soon. I . . . I'm not sure what to do, especially when you're so cold at times. I feel to keep going, to . . . to trust you, yes?"

Her pauses were telling—at least they would have been to anybody but Meth.

"I do not do well with feelings," he said, his fear masquerading as indifference. The silence loomed long and painful, like a jury taunting a defendant. Even Meth sensed the ominous consequence of his comment. Hélène slowly dropped her head in disappointment.

"I *am* willing," he finally said. "I think I can trust . . . well . . . if it is you."

He stretched his other hand across the table, his gesture far more powerful than his awkward admission. He wasn't sure where trust would take him. He hadn't trusted anyone since Truman, but he couldn't let her go without an effort.

She tenderly stroked his fingers before gripping his hand. A tear welled in her eye. She blinked it away before it escaped, then she leaned over and gave him another kiss on the cheek.

"I won't let you down," she promised, her voice cracking.

"Hercules?"

"Hercules," she confirmed, seeming to realize his one-word question and her one-word answer meant something more to Meth than a simple nickname. She looked through his eyes as if she could see the pain corroding his soul and the fragility of his ego and the significance of his commitment, even if only a commitment to be willing.

Meth maintained eye contact longer than he had previously been able to endure. He managed a thin smile. They slid back from the table and started for the door, Hélène ahead and Meth a half step behind her. Then she stopped abruptly and turned back, not realizing he was so close.

"And one more thing," she said as she turned.

Meth walked smack into her. Face-to-face, literally and emotionally, she put him at ease with her broad smile.

"Can we work on the contractions?" she said.

He hesitated. "I will try."

She wrinkled her forehead.

"I'll try."

11

CIRCUMSTANCES AND FEELINGS

METH SAUNTERED into the outer offices of Global Resources Inc. on Monday morning carrying a newspaper and a manila envelope. Karl saw him through the open door and invited him in. Meth extended his expense report to Alex as he rolled past her desk. Instead of his usual nod in her direction, or no acknowledgment at all, he said hello. She smiled and took the envelope.

"Thank you," she said, surprise obvious in her voice and expression.

Meth and his boss spoke as if Karl's heated messages had never been sent. Meth politely handed him the newspaper.

"You don't have to make news," Karl said.

"It was not me; it was *him*. A Geneva councilman is news."

"Anyway, you're good at what you do. You've got a gift."

"Some gift."

"Nice touch saving the dog."

"Dogs are innocent," Meth said, "like children."

"How 'bout François?" Karl seemed reluctant to disrupt their newfound civility, but he had no choice. "I need the file back."

Meth thought of his visit to the Cimetière des Rois and the axe still packed in his overnight bag. He thought of Hélène, of the feelings she had managed to extract from him. But he still wasn't ready to change his mind. As far as he was concerned, killing François was a fait accompli. Karl could have the file back. It made no difference. It was just a file. *How can I stand an axe in the dog-killer's head and make it look like an accident?* That was Meth's preoccupation. "I will bring it back," he said, attempting to placate Karl.

"Sorry I busted your balls last week."

"My balls are just fine," Meth smirked, "certainly better than average."

Absent the antagonism of their last visit, Meth and Karl seemed more like colleagues than enemies. Karl thanked him again for taking a contract on such short notice and without the usual preparation. Meth acknowledged with a simple nod. Karl apologized for an unusually demanding schedule and asked if Meth could take a job in London the following week, promising a three-month break to follow. Meth nodded again. Their exchange was nothing if not efficient. Karl handed him the file.

"Wait a minute," Karl said as Meth made his way to the door. Karl grabbed one of those fat envelopes from his desk. "For Geneva," he said, launching it across the room. Meth caught the envelope with his usual dexterity and nodded his best version of a thank-you. "This one's for Paris," Karl added, tossing another envelope. "You left without it last time."

Meth caught the second as deftly as the first and shoved both into his pocket. He waved politely to Alex as he passed through the outer office and disappeared into the hallway.

BY THE time Meth got home, he'd already dismissed thoughts of work. He'd made room for thoughts of Hélène instead. The more he thought of her, the less he cared about François. He hadn't forgiven the abuse, not by a long shot, but he found his mind occupied with something more pleasant than retribution. He leaned back in his leather chair and perched his feet on his cherry-wood desk. He eyed the three-hundred-year-old horology text leaning against his grandfather's picture and thought of his recent visit to the Geneva flea market. The sun poured through an array of beveled glass windows, each acting as a small prism, filling his den with color. He examined the tiny rainbows around the room as he moved the phone from one ear to the other, speaking with an uncharacteristic lilt.

"So, leave on Wednesday, lunch in Paris, and take the afternoon Eurostar to London." He moved the phone again from his right ear to his left. "Be home the first of the week." In between pauses, Meth gave his usual succinct answers: "Yes . . . Yes . . . Interested?"

"Okay," he said, after another long pause. "The LaSalle in an hour . . . Right."

Hélène had caught Meth by surprise on the train. He hadn't had time or reason to be nervous. Now he was meeting her for a planned get-together and he felt more like a college kid than an assassin looking back on his mid-thirties. He crossed the hall to his bedroom and expended his nervous energy fumbling through his closet. He pulled out a fresh Hilditch & Key shirt and dropped the launderer's bright blue tag into the wastebasket. It kept a dozen brothers company. The only thing in his wastebasket was the last two weeks' worth of tags. He tucked the tail of his shirt into his black jeans and finished with a tweed blazer.

Meth saw a different man in the mirror: less anger, a glint of anticipation and the beginnings of a smile. He wanted things to go well. He wanted more of the feelings he'd experienced with Hélène. He wanted something other than death and hatred.

METH CONNECTED with Hélène at The LaSalle, a glass cube situated within the historic Schiffbau Hall. It welcomed light from every direction, the sun streaming through the windows and dancing on the tables. She drank wine; he nursed his usual Pellegrino. Hélène drenched an enormous shrimp in cocktail sauce and took a bite far too large to chew. She sputtered as she tried to speak.

"Let me understand," she coughed. "You'd rather spend a day on a train than an hour on a plane?"

"It is never an hour," Meth contested, launching a soliloquy on his favorite pet peeve. "With the numbskulls in security and the glacial pace of boarding, a thirty-minute flight always gouges at least three hours out of your day."

"But . . ." Hélène tried to respond but her mouth was too full.

"Train travel is just more civilized," Meth insisted, now adding gestures to every concept. Since Hélène couldn't speak, he just kept talking. "Stepping onto a train is like stepping back in time, when people enjoyed the journey as much as the destination. Travel today is too rushed. There are too many distractions, too many demands and interruptions. I enjoy the space on a train, the food, even the smell of ozone from the sparks in the bahnhof."

Meth shot a smile in Hélène's direction as she continued chewing. He started to laugh.

"Is that shrimp good?"

She nodded and quickly abandoned another attempt to speak.

"When I contemplate flying," he continued, "I see endless security lines, crowded planes, and slovenly attired travelers, all staking their little claims on seats and overhead storage before sitting down to fight for the armrest. I can almost hear the banal blather from the cockpit."

Deepening his voice and slurring his words to imitate a pilot on a blaring speaker, Meth continued, "You are no longer people. You are cattle and we are in charge. Enjoy your disgusting microwaved horse meat."

Hélène coughed a bit, trying not to laugh while taking a sip of wine. She hadn't seen this side of her new friend.

"Humor, Meth?" she finally managed to articulate. "Really?"

He shrugged. "Air travel is a load of bollocks."

"Why are you always so negative about things? You have a great smile. You should use it more often. People like a smile, you know."

They looked at each other. Hélène grinned.

"What do you really enjoy?" she said.

He shrugged again. Off the top of his head he couldn't think of anything he really enjoyed. *I enjoy you*, he thought, but he felt unable to say it out loud. Unfazed and unfinished, he continued his rant.

"I hate what planes and airports have become. Besides, my best writing comes on the train. It is not like I am wasting my time."

"Okay, okay," Hélène conceded, still catching her breath. "I get it. We go by train. One question . . . " She caught Meth's eye. "Can I sit next to you instead of across the table?"

She continued to smile, but Meth looked serious, almost frightened. He turned away and then back. "Of course," he finally promised.

She noticed his consternation but remained silent. She waited. Her eyes invited an explanation. She had a gift, it seemed, for waiting.

"No one has ever spoken to me the way you do," he whispered. "No one touches me like you . . . but . . . you have hardly touched me." Hélène opened her mouth. Before she spoke, Meth continued. "I have been with a lot of women, Herc, but I have never felt the way you make me feel. Truth is, I rarely feel anything when I am with a woman."

"¡Qué susto! Meth," she said, almost choking again, this time on emotion rather than shrimp. She swirled her wine, tipped the last drops into her mouth, and swallowed. "I wasn't expecting that, uh . . . how you say? . . . vulnerability. Not yet."

She pushed her empty glass out of the way. She reached across the table and rested her hand on his forearm with an ineffable air of sincerity. She paused just long enough to ease the tension.

"In the future," she said with a playful tone, "you might drop that 'I've been with a lot of women' stuff when we're having a relationship moment. Otherwise, it was a great compliment."

"How do you know these things?"

"What things?" she said, as a server poured more wine and lowered a collection of pastel macaroons in front of her. Hélène slid the macaroons toward Meth. He waved them off and continued his questions.

"How do you know what to say? What I am feeling?"

"I've been there," she said rather matter-of-factly, like she could read his mind and knew his past. She said it like it was a normal thing, like anyone could do it if they really tried. Her hand hovered back and forth across the macaroons, finally settling on green.

"I like the pistachio," she said, lifting it and taking a bite. As serious as her message was, her actions balanced the mood and kept things comfortable.

"Where?" Meth said.

"¿Qué?"

"You said you have been there. Where have you been?"

"Where you are."

"What do you mean? How do you know where I am or what I am dealing with?"

"Listen," she said, seeming about ready to take another bite. She waved her macaroon around like some kind of visual aid. She picked it up and moved it toward her mouth, then she started to speak and put it down again without taking a bite. "I learned it a long time ago. No one taught me. I just learned it the hard way—the long, painful way."

"When Olin died?"

"That was part of it, but there was more."

"What?"

"I learned that experiences consist of two things."

Uh-oh, here it comes, he thought, always leery of oversimplifications. Though he often saw things in black and white, he resented others who tried to force life into neat little boxes. Because this was Hélène, he put his skepticism on pause and leaned a little closer.

"First circumstances, then feelings," she said. "Circumstances prepare us for the feelings."

She looked fragile, like she was reliving the horrible circumstances that had taught her so much. She spoke slowly, sometimes starting and restarting, searching for the correct English. Her struggle added emphasis and sincerity.

"Circumstances take us to the feelings; and the feelings craft our souls."

Meth sipped his Pellegrino, not fully understanding but nodding anyway. He wanted her to continue.

"If you stop feeling, you stop growing. You stop living . . . or loving." His skepticism softened a bit when she admitted, "*Your* circumstances are different from mine. Everybody's circumstances are different. But our *feelings* can be the same."

Her acknowledgment brushed a tender spot with Meth. He'd always felt so alone, confident that no one could understand him because they lacked his experiences—or, in the context of the current conversation, his circumstances. He wondered what her circumstances were. The glimmer of empathy surprised him.

Hélène kept talking, almost fading into the background, as Meth's mind raced. *Could she really know? Could anyone really know?* He relived a thousand childhood horrors in a moment. He reengaged just as she suggested that some people might arrive at their defining moments vicariously, by watching a good movie or reading a well-written book, like *Les Misérables*, or by seeing a loved one pass through their own crucible.

"Once we get there, regardless of our path"—she promised—"many of our feelings are the same. That's what makes us alike. That's how I know. I've been there, Meth—not your circumstances, but the feelings."

He slowly nodded. He wasn't fully convinced but he was willing to consider it.

"Now," she continued, "what is this bollocks you said? I don't know bollocks." She took a sip of wine.

Meth started to laugh. "Testicles," he said.

She coughed into her glass and started laughing. She put her glass down and wiped her face. She laughed so hard tears streamed down her cheeks. Meth tried twice to explain, but he too was laughing so hard he couldn't speak. He thought wine might come out of Hélène's nose.

"How is air travel a load of testicles?" she finally said, trying to catch her breath.

Still laughing, Meth pieced together a response.

"It's not literal. It's an old English phrase. It means *nonsense* or *useless*. Think of it as something obnoxious and absurd."

"Strange words," she said, offering a perplexed grin and shaking her head. "A load of testicles . . . useless? . . . obnoxious? A woman made this phrase, no?"

FROM THE LaSalle, Hélène waved goodbye to Meth and strolled alone down the bahnhofstrasse, passing high-end shops—Louis Vuitton, Tiffany & Co., Prada, Cartier, Beldona, Giorgio Armani—without slowing down or looking in a window. She turned toward the Patek Philippe store and approached the locked door without slowing down. She'd been there enough times to know what would happen. The plain-clothed security guard opened the tinted-glass door from inside, like she was Ali Baba and had just said, *Open Sesame*. She walked through without breaking stride.

"Guten Tag," the guard said as she entered.

"Guten Tag, Frédéric." She patted his still-folded arms as she passed.

"Fräulein Ingebretzen," the store manager said, bouncing to his feet and bolting around the showcase to greet her. Gert Kroner had purchased more diamonds from Hélène than from all his other suppliers combined. When they first met, he owned one store in Baden-Baden. She had just finished a Master of Science degree in geology at the University of Copenhagen and was starting her new business. Now he had five stores. She supplied them all. He hadn't purchased diamonds from anyone else in nearly a decade. His business was a major contributor to Hélène's financial success.

They continued their conversation in German as they drifted into the private showroom and closed the door.

12

ONE MILLION CARATS

WHERE'S THE monster bag?" Meth asked, as he slid Hélène's average-sized suitcase onto the rack.

"That was business," she said, smiling. "This is pleasure. I travel light."

Meth realized just how little he knew about her. As much as she liked to talk and pry information from others, she spoke little about herself unless asked.

"What *is* your business?"

She offered one of her you-can-do-better-than-that looks.

"What's your business?" he said.

"Does that feel strange?"

"Definitely." He nodded. "But I'm working on it."

"I import gemstones." She raised a brow and grinned. "I make people's dreams come true."

"So what was in the bag, a million carats of diamonds?"

"Don't be silly," she chuckled. "That would be two hundred kilos, five carats per gram."

Meth was impressed with her quick math until she admitted she'd actually calculated it once.

She offered a coy smile. "My bag was more like two-hundred-and-fifty thousand."

"Well, next time I'll be more careful."

Meth assumed she was joking about the gems. On the other hand, whatever she did do for a living, she seemed to have more than adequate resources. Her watch, her clothes, her choice of restaurants and hotels; he knew she didn't need him for his money. Based on her open and independent attitude, he concluded she didn't need him at all. Surprisingly, though, he was beginning to feel like he might need her.

Before settling into their seats, Hélène had already convinced him she was indeed a broker of wholesale gemstones. And, by the time they left the bahnhof, he'd learned she had never married. It was shaping up to be a revealing conversation. She seemed wistful when divulging she'd had no children. They quickly moved to other topics.

"I thought you were going to sit next to me," he said as he reflexively drew his laptop and opened it on the table.

"I will, as long as you don't spend your time looking at that computer. I'll sit here for now so I can see your face, so I can tell what you're thinking." She waited for Meth's attention. "I like your face."

She dropped her hat, scarf and thin leather gloves on the table and slid out of her gray tailored blazer. Her turtleneck sweater and slacks were quite warm enough for the train.

"Tell me about your writing," she said as she wiggled her tiny frame back and forth into a comfortable position.

She seemed oblivious to how attractive Meth found her. Part of his hesitancy with eye contact was his apprehension that she might discern just how much he cared. He wanted to open up and let things flow, just to see where they ended up, but he couldn't yet part with that much control, or venture that far from his well-worn path.

The scenery accelerated past the windows as they spoke. Within minutes, a loud American tourist with a beer-belly rumbled down the aisle looking for a place to homestead. Meth preemptively moved his bag from the floor to the adjacent seat. Then he stretched his legs under the table and plopped his feet next to Hélène. Normally, he would have done these things already, but Hélène's presence disrupted his unconscious—or sometimes conscious—checklist.

Hélène was unable to see the passenger approaching from behind, but she noticed Meth's activity and looked inquisitive. A moment later she saw *and* heard. He smacked his lips, jawing an enormous wad of bubble gum, intermittently blowing then popping bubbles. He looked around like he thought the other passengers should applaud. He dragged an overstuffed San Francisco 49ers bag and wore a matching 49ers jersey and do-rag. The rag covered his mostly-bald head. A tiny braid of his last few hopeful locks trailed down his neck, like a tiny mouse tail (not big enough to be a rat tail). He paused next to Hélène long enough for his odor to catch up. When he saw the seats around the table unavailable, he moved on. Hélène eyed Meth in silence.

"He thinks he's on a plane," Meth quipped, just loudly enough for her to hear, convinced he could coax a laugh.

She winked but offered no comment.

"The guy's on a two-carbon diet," Meth said.

"What is this two-carbon diet?" she said, like she was still learning English.

Meth came up with the term at Cambridge when he learned that ethanol—the type of alcohol humans love to consume—was a two-carbon molecule, a carbohydrate with no nutritional value. He gave her more explanation than she needed and more chemistry than she cared to consider.

"That's why some alcoholics are undernourished and overweight," he said, thinking of François.

As the tourist faded down the aisle, Meth turned to his computer. He was having a meaningful conversation with Hélène and enjoying it, but he always fondled his computer on the train. It was engrained in his routine. He raised a finger, about to strike a key, as he had done on a thousand previous trains, when she asked about his avocation. He pushed the computer aside.

"A lot of people write on trains," he said. "Watch sometime. You will notice. There are all kinds of writers. You can almost tell what they are writing just by watching or listening. There are *angry thumpers*, typing loudly enough to keep you awake. They type like the whole world should hear them and surmise how important they must be. There are *frustrated pokers* who cannot make up their minds. They mostly stare at the screen. The *tentative tappers* play with the keyboard slowly and timidly like it might bite at any moment. I fail to appreciate how they ever accomplish anything of value. I used to call them *pensive pickers*, but that had a rather unsavory connotation. I avoid the common *hunter-pecker* description for the same reason."

Hélène wasn't accustomed to Meth opening up without her prodding. She seemed surprised to hear him offer more than half a sentence without her encouragement.

"You've put a lot of thought into this, haven't you?" she said.

"No, just a little observation. It is obvious once you notice. There are *manic flappers* who type absurdly fast to impress everyone around them and then spend more time riding the delete key than getting meaningful words into a sentence. You can tell whether a person is a real writer, enthralled by a burst of creative energy, or some schmo just plunking out his tedious job. Sometimes I wonder if being a good typist might be an ironic disadvantage. After all, the *one-finger stabbers* seem the most contemplative and deliberate. They never delete. They get it right the first time. They are definitely the tortoise to the flapper's hare."

"What are you?"

"Depends on the day, the mood, the company. It all makes a difference. I get my computer open when I am with you but I enjoy your company too much to write. Then, in the evening, sometimes through the night, when I think about you, it pours out onto the proverbial page. Not many people write on an *actual* page anymore."

Hélène leaned back and stretched to prop her boots on the opposite seat. She twiddled her pen between her fingers like a cigar and took a big puff. She smiled and started to laugh.

"I'm your muuuse," she said with drawn-out U, trying her best to look smug. Then she laughed again.

Meth rolled his eyes and offered a crooked grin.

"More than that," he said.

He sat speechless, queuing words and phrases, testing them before he spoke. She waited, seemingly comfortable to let the silence thicken.

"You are a prism," he finally said, thinking of the beveled windows and colorful rainbows in his den, "dividing the blare of white light into its intriguing component colors. I see things differently when I'm with you. I *feel* differently when I'm with you."

Meth forgot about himself as he spoke. He wasn't looking around to see if others were listening. He still spoke rather mechanically—too precisely to feel natural, and mostly without contractions—but his hateful, sometimes homicidal persona faded as he focused on Hélène and spoke freely.

Neither Meth nor Hélène had much to say after that—at least, not for a while. They sipped Perrier and enjoyed the rhythm of the train rolling through Switzerland toward France. Meth was surprised that she seemed as comfortable in silence as she did driving a conversation. She moved around the table and snuggled next to him, holding his arm, resting her head on his shoulder. He typed intermittently, trying not to bounce her head too much. When he spoke again, she responded just enough to encourage him to continue. Then she listened.

"Writing fiction is liberating. It reminds me of a sculpting class I took in school." He shifted a bit to get comfortable and took a drink. "You can craft your sculpture any way you wish. You can mold and morph the clay, doing and redoing things until they suit you. If you are not pleased, you can cut it off and try again. And, with few exceptions, nobody can tell you whether it is right or wrong." He looked at Hélène until she looked back. "What a contrast to medicine. I shadowed a physician in preparation for medical school. Patients don't give their doctors that latitude. They want things right the first time, every time, and they want it now."

Hélène nodded, making no attempt to interrupt.

"Fiction is like sculpting. I can create any problem. Then I can craft the solution. If I don't like it, I delete it and start again. It's a profound contrast to life."

"What's life?" she asked.

Meth leaned forward and craned his head back toward his left shoulder to make eye contact. "Are you really asking me that existential question?"

"No. No," she clarified. "Para usted. For you. What's *your* life? What do you do?"

"Well, I told you about my mother and Le Soûlard, even Achilles." He answered as if he were checking off a list in his head: places, people, sometimes experiences, but almost never feelings. "I talked about my grandfather and Cambridge. I regret leaving." He stopped, like a criminal having just spilled a detail during an interrogation.

"Why did you leave?"

There it was. He had painted himself into a corner. Still thinking about what he did *not* want to say, he took a moment to register her question, or pretend to register it. He had anticipated it, but it still unnerved him. *Dangerous territory*, he thought.

"Another day," he said.

"No, no, no . . . you don't get off that easy. You grill me and I, as you say . . . ah . . . spill my guts. Now *you* have to answer."

"Truman died."

He let his sad declaration fester until it had drained most of the energy from her face.

"I just gave up. I left school. I couldn't go back. My whole world changed."

Meth just stopped and stared out the window. Hélène let him go for a while and then redirected the conversation in a less painful direction. Landscapes changed. She napped intermittently, coddled by rhythmic wheels on rails. Meth, on the other hand, sat wide-awake. He struggled to put his finger on the intangibles that made her so different. He wondered if *intangible* was the right word. He definitely *felt* something. He wanted to call it *je ne sais quoi*, but that sounded too cliché and too French. In his typical, rational, logical, dogmatic process of thinking through things, he concluded that since he couldn't touch it—whatever *it* was—*intangible* was the right word. Then he wondered how much time he had wasted thinking himself through the process. He was glad his thoughts weren't broadcast for critique.

"READY FOR lunch?" Meth asked, as the train rolled slowly into Gare de Lyon. Hélène had started to rouse a few kilometers earlier when the train began to decelerate. Now she sat up, stretched her back and shoulders, and gathered her things from the table and the adjacent seat.

"I want to immerse you in something special," he said.

"Lunch?" she asked, as if wondering how special lunch could be.

"Much more."

He grabbed their bags and trundled down the stairs. He reached through the open door and dropped one bag on the platform. With his now-free hand, he reached back and helped her off the train. Together they strolled down the platform, through Hall One, and toward the main entrance. Meth paused at the base of a broad steel staircase that appeared a century older than anything around it. The cast iron risers were dark with age, and the stone treads were worn smooth, the portions nearest the railing slightly carved by innumerable leather soles. The staircase, unnoticed by most travelers, appeared too grand for the gare. As he took his first step, Meth let his hand slide from the newel post to the brass railing. Hélène grabbed the smaller bag, took his arm, and followed.

Not far away, in the dark shadow of the TGV status board, a blond, forty-year-old man with hollow cheeks and a bent nose leaned against a pillar and watched Hélène and Meth make their way up the stairs. He nervously shifted a toothpick from one side of his mouth to the other and then back. He ducked quickly behind the pillar when Meth looked in his direction. It had been Meth, after all, who had bent his nose in a bar fight. Several years earlier, Meth had trailed a contract into a bar where Lars got in the way; at least, that's the way Meth told the story. For now, Lars kept his distance and watched.

On the landing at the top of the stairs, Meth and Hélène encountered an antique revolving door. Above it, in the half-circle transom, glowed a distinctive neon sign: arching across the top of the sign, in double blue lines, Le Train Bleu; horizontally across the bottom, in single red scroll, Restaurant. With a push on the polished brass bars, they passed through the wood-framed revolving door and into another world.

High above the waxed parquet floor, forty-one paintings adorned the walls and ceiling—most depicting landscapes traversed by trains of the Paris-Lyon-Mediterranean Company that had built the restaurant. Since opening in 1901, it had welcomed guests such as Coco Chanel, Brigitte Bardot, and Salvador Dali. In addition to standard tables surrounded by traditional chairs, there were smaller, shorter tables scattered among overstuffed red leather seats where people gathered when they were more interested in socializing than in a full formal meal. Windows on the inner wall overlooked the train platforms, allowing just enough noise from the travelers below to remind diners where they were; from the quality of the food, they might have thought themselves in downtown Paris. The swirls of cigarette and cigar smoke, along with the occasional smoldering pipe—a smell loved by some, hated by others, including Meth—had fallen victim to laws prohibiting smoking in the restaurant. But the smell of fresh coffee and old leather still transported guests to an earlier era.

The maître d' greeted Meth and Hélène and showed them to a small table with red leather chairs. She draped her scarf and jacket over a large brass hook near the table and plunked her fedora on top.

"I can see why you like this place," she said. "I can't believe I've never been here. I've never even heard of it."

Lunch evolved into an experience—a memory, really—like eating a meal in an old movie or imagining one's favorite place and suddenly being there. Neither of them was particularly hungry, but their midday was free and their surroundings encouraged a luxurious embrace. They sampled foie gras on monogrammed plates, a fan of asparagus tips extending from one side, rich brown drops of balsamic vinegar drizzled half way around the other. For two hours they pushed cheeses, baguettes, and alternating fragments of their lives across the table at one another before sharing a crème brûlée. They sipped espresso and began to feel like something more than friends.

"Merci, madame, monsieur," the server said when he finally brought the check. "S'il vous plaît venez à nouveau."

Meth slid several bills into the leather check-holder and dropped it onto the table.

"Expensive lunch," Hélène commented.

"Inexpensive memory," he answered. He bobbed his finger toward a nearby table and struggled to speak. "That's where my grandfather gave me the watch." Another long pause. "I was fourteen. He called me Primo. We sat right over there. We ate lamb. Grandfather ordered crêpe Suzette for dessert. While we waited, he gave me the watch."

Hélène noticed Meth's fingers running over his Patek as he spoke.

"He loved you deeply."

Meth nodded. He stood and took her hand.

"It's okay to say it, you know."

Meth let her comment pass. He couldn't say it. Truman's death had wrenched his soul, and he'd felt betrayed by the sudden loss. He'd loved his mother, despite his childhood resentment of how she'd allowed François' abuse and how she had abandoned him in death. As an adult, he could walk his mind through reality—he knew she couldn't control François or the cancer—but his heart struggled to catch up with the reasonable or rational. He still felt abandoned, no matter the circumstance. Truman's death had only reinforced his detachment. But Hercules now had him wondering about his feelings. And feeling meant risk. Would she leave too?

"We need to grab the Metro to Gare de Nord," he said. "We can talk on the way to London."

They moved through the revolving door and down the stone stairs to the main hall. To Meth, moving back into the real world felt like descending into Milton's paradise lost. He was glad he was with Hélène.

LARS EMERGED from his hole. He followed Meth and the woman on Meth's arm onto the Metro and across town. He trailed them through Gare de Nord to the Eurostar. He saw them talking and laughing, but he kept too far away to hear their words. He followed them onto the train, occasionally speaking on a cell phone or taking notes. He mostly napped on the train. After all, there was nowhere for them to go. In Waterloo Station, he continued behind them, just out of eyeshot, from the train to the tube.

Meth and Hélène exited the tube station onto the London sidewalk just across the street from Piccadilly Circus. Though mid-afternoon, the Piccadilly lights flashed brighter than the beleaguered British sun. It struggled, as always, through those British clouds. Hélène and Meth spotted their destination and stepped off the curb just as Lars topped the stairs and appeared on the sidewalk behind them. He watched them cross the busy street, holding hands, and disappear into Le Méridien Piccadilly Hotel.

JUST BEING in the neighborhood flooded Meth with memories. Around the corner from their hotel, on Savile Row, H. Huntsman & Sons boasted one-hundred-and-sixty years of experience in making hand-cut, hand-tailored apparel. Equidistant in the opposite direction, on Jermyn Street, Edward Bates Ltd had served as London's haberdashery for over a century, though their display of a stuffed cat wearing an appropriately sized top hat and smoking a cigarette was a tad on the creepy side. Jermyn Street was also home to Hilditch & Key, established in 1899, and touted by some as the finest shirt maker in the world.

Meth liked Le Méridien Piccadilly, if for no other reason than its location. As a teenager, he'd occasionally taken the train from Cambridge to indulge his affinity for fine clothes. He couldn't buy much as a student, but most of that signing bonus from Karl got spent in London. Even now his sartorial style and most of his clothing came from Savile Row and Jermyn Street. And that Tusting satchel that rarely left Meth's side came from Fortnum & Mason, a presence in St. James Square since 1707.

Hélène liked the hotel for other reasons. When she was a young girl, her father took her to the London landmark—then known simply as the Piccadilly Hotel—to eat at the Carver's Table. Her father always requested the end-cut from the prime rib. Sometimes he requested a second helping and asked them to cut off the other end. Her fondness as a child was for the desserts. The restaurant eventually disappeared, but the hotel and her memories endured.

Neither Meth nor Hélène realized that the other had stayed in the hotel until they walked through the doors together and began sharing memories. It was the first time she'd spoken to Meth about her parents. Her father was Norwegian, her mother Catalonian. There had been a generational shift in nomenclature; while her mother was Catalonian, she was Catalan. Her parents had enjoyed twenty-four years of storybook romance until Olin's death. For inexplicable reasons, they had grieved very differently: she had wanted to be at the cemetery, near his grave, and he had wanted to be anywhere else. He had hated the cemetery (Meth understood that).

According to Hélène, it had only made him think of death. They had tried to understand one another's perspectives, but each was too wounded to help the other heal. Hélène had been devastated when they finally separated, but her faith in love was equally renewed when they found their way back together a year later.

"They're still together in Barcelona," she boasted with a smile.

Meth wondered about Olin's death. She'd mentioned it before but seemed reluctant to offer details. He teetered between the risks of causing pain by asking and causing offense by the appearance of not caring enough to ask. Based on his personal feelings about death and peoples' past questions to him, he left it alone.

After an hour of chatting in the lobby, they finally approached the desk. The hotel clerk slid key cards to their separate rooms across the marble counter and gestured toward the elevator.

"Would you like assistance with your bags?" he asked.

"No, thank you," Meth responded. "We do not have much luggage."

Hélène gently nudged Meth without speaking. He picked up her cue and tried again: "I mean, we're fine."

Somehow Hélène managed her coaching without causing offense. Her tone convinced Meth she was genuine; Adi had done the same thing at Cambridge. Meth and Hélène decided to drop their bags and walk off their long ride.

LARS, STILL skulking in the shadows, followed Meth and Hélène down Regent Street. They zigzagged over to Charing Cross, sometimes holding hands, and took Northumberland Avenue to the Thames, crossing on the Hungerford Bridge. When they arrived at the Eye a few minutes later, Lars took a thirty-minute break. The enormous Ferris wheel took a full half-hour to complete one revolution and, like the Eurostar, once they got on, there was no place for them to go until they got off. He relaxed on a bench, tendering surveillance to the never-blinking eyes of the gold-gilded eagle atop the Royal Air Force Memorial directly across the river. Meth and Hélène viewed Big Ben, the House of Parliament and Westminster Abbey, all from one hundred and thirty-five meters above the South Bank, while the eagle viewed them.

Lars picked them up again as they exited the Eye and headed back to their hotel. They stopped at The Sherlock Holmes on Northumberland for some haddock and mushy peas. Lars sat in a corner and nursed a pint of dark Guinness, smiling far less than Meth or Hélène.

HÉLÈNE LOOKED a bit unkempt—her hair mussed, in casual clothes—when she looked up and saw Meth. She'd shuffled from the elevator into the lounge a little after midnight, just in time to encounter

Meth entering the other side of the lobby from the street. He wore the tight, agitated expression she'd seen in Geneva. He saw her eyes widen. He wasn't sure whether it was a look of surprise or just her struggle to remain awake.

"Where you been?" she asked before inhaling the aroma of fresh espresso from across the room.

"Went for a walk." Meth's stilted brevity matched his mood. "Needed to think."

"Did you hear all those sirens?" she asked as she made her way to the coffee.

"Some tourist stepped in front of a bus," he explained. He followed her to the coffee, though he would never drink it in the middle of the night.

"Is he okay?"

"Dead."

"Dead?" she gasped. She turned from the pot and blew steam from her cup as she reestablished eye contact with Meth. "Are you always so blunt when people die?"

He scowled but said nothing. It was his easiest job in months: a well-placed foot, an inconspicuous shove, let the bus do the rest. It might not have worked had it been a taxi or a slower bus, but this job was done: quickly, easily, and effectively. *Now she wants to grill me?*

"People die every day," he said. "I have no interest in talking about it."

Meth's apathy—antipathy, really—left Hélène looking hurt and bewildered. If she chalked it up to a poor choice of words, it was because she didn't realize words were Meth's passion and he'd said exactly what he meant. His post-dispatch mood displaced all remnants of his humanity, at least for a while.

"The sirens woke me," she said, making another attempt at a reasonable conversation. "I just came down to get a cup."

They moved through the lounge and found two chairs. Meth sat quietly, pensively scanning the room.

"The leg again?" she asked, watching him drive his knuckles into the trembling muscles in his right thigh.

"That is why I went for the walk."

"Why?"

"I just told you why," he snapped.

"You told me why you walked," she clarified with a tolerant tone. She might have been less patient had she not already seen this behavior in Geneva. "But why does your leg tremble?"

"Just one of those things. I do not like to talk about."

"Why are you so sullen and abrupt when your leg trembles? It's like Geneva." She paused when Meth glared at her. She looked more concerned than intimidated, as if standing at the edge of a dark forest contemplating how far to proceed. "We can talk about something else, if you like, but someday we have to talk about this. You can't treat me this way, not if you want me to stick around. I care about you. I like you. But I *won't* be abused by you. I've got plenty of other things I can do with my time."

"I am *done* with your questions!"

He stood up. What he wanted to say was *Do not ask me about my business*, but that sounded too Godfatheresque and, as far as she knew, he had no business in London. "Mind your business," he substituted, feeling compelled to get the last word. "I do not want to talk when I get like this."

"So I've noticed," she said to his back as he started for the elevator. The scene was all too familiar. "But what *you* want isn't always the only consideration. I'm in this room too."

If she lacked any English skills or vocabulary, she wasn't letting it show. For the moment, she sounded more American than Spanish. Her speech and tone took him back to a conversation they'd never had—one he'd only imagined in his mind. He knew he had to tell her about his dark past, but he couldn't do it now. He kept walking toward the elevator.

"Meth!"

It was the first time he'd heard anger in her voice. He turned around, his fist clenched, rage in his eyes.

"I said I do not want to talk!"

She looked at his fist and his expression. She crossed the room, like a wolverine advancing on a bear—outmatched physically, perhaps, but unafraid—tilting her head back as she approached in order to maintain eye contact. She took an even and deliberate tone.

"Don't *ever* speak to me that way. I don't know how you're accustomed to addressing the women you date. I don't know what's going through your mind when your leg trembles. And maybe I ask too many questions. But a relationship with me demands mutual respect." She paused, her eyes leaving no question about her sincerity. "And, if that fist's for me, tell me now so I can pack my bags and catch the next train."

Meth stood speechless. He glanced down at his fist, wondering why he had never heard Adelaide speak to François like that. It was fear, he assumed, but why had she never demanded his respect? More pointedly, why was he imitating the behaviors of the man he loathed—the man he swore he would never emulate in any way? He felt confident that Hélène was running the same questions through her mind; he assumed she was too respectful to ask them aloud. He saw blood and bruises and fists, all in a flash. He heard cries and expletives and he smelled the vile combination of François' alcohol, sweat, and cigarette smoke. He wasn't sure how long he stood there, but the fleeting seconds seemed as endless as the panorama passing through his mind.

Hélène broke the silence, easing her voice as acutely as she had escalated it. She had said her piece. Apparently she was ready to move on.

"I think I'll just sit here and have a drink before bed," she said.

"Thank you," Meth whispered in a genuine, if not remorseful, tone.

He was stunned by the way she had fearlessly controlled the room. He turned again for the elevator, his head bowed and his shoulders slumped. Shame pressed upon him as the doors closed. A few moments later, in his room, he watched the alternating red and blue shadows of police lights through the sheer curtains. The sirens were silent; his mind was not. He wondered why he had clenched his fist—at the same time realizing his whole life was a clenched fist—and he wondered if he would do it again.

He sat on the edge of the bed. For the first time since Truman's death, he contemplated his life—his future and his past. He wondered why Hélène cared about him, why *anyone* would care about a person so cold and uncaring as he had become. All he could hear was François' reverberating: *You make me sick. You filthy dog. I hate you.* To be fair, he'd never heard François add that last phrase, but he assumed it was true. As the years rolled on, it just crept into the monologue with nothing to challenge or displace it. Meth struggled to clear his head, trying to remind himself of how little he cared about François' opinion, but the taunts charged forward, now with a different message: *She hates you. She will always hate you.*

Meth wanted to vanish—to check out of the hotel and disappear, to never see her again—but then he experienced something new. He realized he cared about what Hélène thought of him. (He couldn't recall ever caring what anyone thought of him.) Further, he wanted her to think well. The voices in his head fell silent when he entered her presence, like the noise of the gare disappearing behind soundproof doors when he entered the executive lounge. And, to his surprise, he found himself caring whether he lived to see another sunrise. Countering his inclination to leave, he longed to see Hélène tomorrow morning.

Forcing the emotions of his job and his growing feelings for Hélène into the same hour fractured Meth's defense. To a lesser extent, the same scenario had transpired in Geneva, but things were different then. Now his feelings for Hélène had changed, and his cold apathy about death and dying shuddered in the presence of her light and life. Tonight he couldn't miss the contrast or run from it.

He noticed the clock. He'd been fighting with himself for nearly an hour. He stood and walked across the room. He looked down at the still-flashing emergency vehicles. Guilt and remorse overwhelmed him. He hated himself for bringing Hélène into his darkness—for tainting what he was beginning to love the same way François had tainted everything he touched. On the sidewalk below, he saw a brown fedora floating along in the alternating red and blue lights. He recognized the bag moving along with it. He couldn't make out anything else, but he knew it was Hélène. A sickening emptiness overwhelmed him. The bag and hat moved off the curb toward the tube station. There was no time for thought or self-preservation. He raced from his room.

"Hercules!" he yelled as he exited the hotel. He scanned up Piccadilly, then down toward Regent Street. Nothing. He ran across the street and peered down the circular steel stairway into the tube station. He caught a glimpse of the fedora disappearing from the last step and rushed after it. He yelled again, but she didn't turn or slow down. He finally caught up with her halfway down to the next level. She stood calmly on the escalator; he huffed down the adjacent stairs to stay alongside her.

"Wait," he said.

"Wrong answer."

"Don't go."

"Wrong answer."

"Where are you going?"

"Wrong answer!"

"What's the question?!"

She finally looked at him, but only for a moment. They arrived at the next level. She stepped off the escalator and started for the platform. He hustled a few steps alongside to make his way into her peripheral vision. She refused to look. The tube train arrived. One person got off and walked away. Hélène kept moving toward the open doors. In a flash, he saw flowing blue ink on torn sheets of lined paper.

"I want you to stay," he exclaimed, his echo floating down the platform and back. "The fist was not for you. I want you to stay."

She stopped and looked at him. He'd never wanted a woman to stay. He thought about the word he'd never heard François say, the one he'd waited for so many times—not for himself, but for his mother. It was a word he'd never used, but he felt it forming in his mind and marching toward his lips.

"I'm sorry," he said between breaths. "I'll never speak to you that way again."

They stared at each other until the doors closed and the train pulled away. Her eyes searched his face, her expression still firm and serious.

"Right answer," she said quietly.

He extended his upturned palm.

She handed him her bag, and they started back to the escalator.

Like his namesake, Prometheus arrived a different man in the morning, his demeanor as calm as his leg. He entered the lobby and found Hélène in the same chair she'd occupied the previous night. She looked fresh in a dark pleated skirt, knee-high leather boots, a tailored red blouse (she had several red blouses, he'd noticed, and every one looked good on her) and a thick wrap-around sweater. She had her fedora in one hand and a newspaper in the other. She glanced up from her paper and smiled as though the previous night had never happened.

Meth released the breath he had held all morning, anxious to move on from their last encounter. He failed to understand how she could let things go so quickly—François would grind on a point of contention for weeks—but he was grateful. It was as if she had no reason to remain angry. She'd accepted his apology and his promise to do better. She had spoken her mind—a strong, determined mind with a valid point worth expressing—and then let it go. Meth agreed that the respect she demanded was deserved. And he was willing to acknowledge—if only to himself—that he could learn some things from her example.

"Déjà vu," she said as he approached.

Meth failed to register her meaning until she held up the headline.

"It's like Geneva all over again," she said, unaware of the depth of her observation. "This guy was some Italian senator."

Meth put his Alfred Sargent shoe on the arm of the chair and tied a loose lace. "Let's go find some breakfast," he said.

Hélène studied his expression and smiled. She stood and dropped the newspaper onto the chair. In her four-inch heels, she stretched only slightly to kiss him on the chin.

"Meth, did you just use a contraction?"

"I've been practicing all morning."

BY LATE evening, Hélène and Meth had seen much of London. They concluded their day with a concert at St. Martin-in-the-Fields and a walk, hand-in-hand, from Trafalgar Square back to their hotel. Meth didn't want the day to end. He didn't want to go back to Zurich or the darkness. When he listened to music at home, he increased the volume until it overwhelmed the dialogue in his head. He had never listened purely for enjoyment. But, when he spent time with Hélène, his thoughts calmed, like when he'd visited Murren. The concert, under the venerable hand of Sir Neville Marriner, had proven both soothing and invigorating. Without the crowd of messages in his head, he wondered if there might be room, not only for music, but also for another person. He couldn't bear the thought of losing her.

At the hotel, Meth walked Hélène to her room. The moment her door latched, his countenance darkened. He hurried down the back stairs to the lobby and re-entered through a rear door. Lars had apparently not realized it, but Meth had seen him in the National Gallery. While he and Hélène had admired Cima's *The Incredulity of Saint Thomas*, Meth had eyed Lars leaning against a pillar near the other end of the hall. When he'd entered the hotel with Hélène, he'd again spotted Lars, in a wingback chair in the dark end of the lounge—right where he had expected him to be, right where he would be himself if he were trailing a contract.

Meth slipped behind the bar and made his way to the other end of the room. Not expecting to see Meth again before morning, Lars had relaxed, intermittently closing his eyes. Meth inched his way along the wall until he neared the back of the chair. He swung his arm around the wing and clamped onto Lars' trachea so suddenly and relentlessly that the encounter was nearly over before Lars could stand up. Stand he did, however, when Meth hoisted him to his feet by his larynx, gripping it so tightly that Lars couldn't speak.

Lars grabbed the middle finger of his assailant and wrenched it until it cracked, dislocating at the first knuckle. Meth didn't flinch. He turned Lars toward him until Lars could see who was cinched around his voice box. When he saw Meth's face, he let go of the finger.

"This is the way I like you, Lars." Meth sneered and pushed him forcefully against the wall in the darkest corner of the room. "Quiet and cooperative."

They had hardly made a sound. No one had even noticed them in the corner. "I am going to let go of your neck now, and we are going to have a civil conversation. Otherwise I am going to point your nose toward the other ear. Agreed?"

Lars nodded—as much as he could, that is, with his neck in a vice. Meth released him.

"What are you doing here?"

"You know what I'm doing here," Lars replied, his Swedish accent now hoarse. He rubbed his throat. "It's business. It's what I do. You know. It's as standard and random as a tax audit."

Meth knew exactly what Lars was doing. He'd done it himself a decade earlier. Nobody liked it, but everybody had to take a turn. NEMESIS kept very close tabs on operatives, and everybody learned from observing one another. Meth knew the reasons, but he still didn't like it.

"Don't follow me, Lars, especially on my personal time. The job is done. Why are you still here?"

"You know the answers to these questions, Meth. You know I follow everybody occasionally, and you know I report to Karl. If you don't like it, talk to him."

"The job is done," Meth said again, walking away. "Go home."

The brouhaha was over in less than a minute. Meth relocated his finger without so much as a grimace. Lars straightened his lapels, cleared his throat, and started toward the bar.

"Farväl, Meth. Sorry about the finger. No hard feelings?"

Meth waved him off, like an exasperated customer swatting at a car salesman, and continued to the elevator. He wondered if Lars' presence in London was an entirely random assignment as he had said. He thought about François. He'd seen the address on that picture in the file. He knew François had returned Normandy—just as the proverbial Old Testament dog returneth to his vomit. *Maybe Karl was afraid I would end up Saint-Martin-des-Entrées.*

13

LE TRAIN BLEU

METH AND Hélène walked past a rack of touristy brochures and emerged from their hotel onto the busy London sidewalk. She held his arm with both hands as they admired an unusually azure English sky.

"I'm glad you invited me on this trip." She pulled his arm until she could whisper into his ear. "I'm looking forward to our night in Paris." She stretched and kissed his cheek.

Meth was glad, too, though not so open with his feelings. They stepped off the curb and disappeared into the tube across the street. Three hours and two transfers later, in Gare de Lyon, they found themselves within eyeshot of Hélène's new favorite restaurant; it had been Meth's favorite for decades.

"You're right about the planes," she admitted as they walked across the gare. "There's something nostalgic about train travel . . . Or maybe it's 'cause I'm traveling with you."

"'Cause?" Meth groused, at the same time smiling. "Is that one of your Americanisms?"

"I'm getting better, don't you think?" She didn't wait for his response. Instead, she diverged slightly from their apparent course and pulled his arm toward the stone stairs.

"Forget about America," she said. "We go Dutch. I buy you dinner."

Meth laughed. "That's not Dutch."

"What is this Dutch?"

"Each person pays for themselves."

"Oh. No. We don't go Dutch. I'm buying."

"I'm not sure we can," Meth said.

"Why?"

"I didn't make a reservation."

"You're not the only one who can use a phone," she giggled. "I have something special planned."

"I'm in your hands. Do with me what you will."

After Hélène tipped the maître d' and secured what she seemed to think was the perfect table, they began with Charolais beef tartar and duck foie gras. Time disappeared. Their conversation ranged widely, sometimes serious but usually light. They laughed. They visited across the table for nearly two hours, picking at their food, talking more than eating, barely breaking eye contact as each new course replaced another pair of empty plates. Sometime after sunset, a bus boy finally cleared the table from one end as their server presented dessert menus at the other.

"Crêpe Suzette, s'il vous plait," Hélène said, completely ignoring her menu. She glanced at Meth. He nodded agreement.

"Oui, madame," the server answered. He took the menus and left them alone.

"I'm enjoying this, Herc. It's been a long time since a woman bought me dinner."

"It's more than dinner, Primo."

Meth's brows elevated. His lids opened so wide Hélène could see white all the way around his deep green eyes. He waited, not sure what to say. She sat straight in her chair with a concerned look, apparently unsettled by Meth's expression.

"How did you know that?" he said. "Did I tell you that?"

"Tell me what?"

"Primo. My grandfather is the only person who ever called me Primo." She shrugged and smiled.

"In fact, I think the only time he ever called me Primo was in this restaurant."

"Meth, *you* told me . . . when we were here the other day. I like it. It fits you . . . I won't say it again if—"

"No, I like it . . . Especially from you."

Meth's expression softened. Hélène's concern disappeared behind her widening smile.

"Well then, Primo, I have something special for you. I bought you a present."

She pulled a small wrapped box from her bag and slid it across the table. It stopped short of the target. Before he could respond, she leaned forward and reached past her food to push it into his hand. The paper was torn on one corner from riding around Europe in her bag, but no secrets were revealed. She looked ready to burst with anticipation.

He wondered how she could have such a satisfied expression. *She just loves life.*

"Now?" he said.

"Certainly. Unwrap it. I want to see your face when you open it."

He pulled paper from the box, starting at the torn corner and working his way around. He dug through at least three layers before he saw the label. He froze and looked toward Hélène in astonishment, his eyes even wider than before.

"Perfect!" she said. *"That's* what I wanted to see."

"I . . ."

She relished in Meth's expression. She let the silence crescendo for a few moments before rescuing him from his speechlessness.

"It's just something I wanted to do. You told me you wanted one."

He stared at her until emotion forced him to look away. He dropped his eyes to the iconic Calatrava Cross on the box. Below the cross: Patek Philippe on one line, Geneva on the next.

"I . . ." Meth tried again. Still, nothing came.

"You deserve it," she said, her voice cracking. A tear coursed down her cheek, changing direction slightly as it touched the subtle division between her cheek and lip. It dropped onto her wrist.

"I think I love you, Primo."

They locked eyes again until Meth's lower lip quivered. He looked away. He hadn't expected the word. She, apparently, hadn't planned it. She seemed as surprised as Meth, but she didn't waver.

"I know it's sudden," she said. "I know it doesn't make sense, but I *feel* it. And life has taught me to trust my feelings."

Unable to verbalize a response, Meth resumed unwrapping, dropping the paper mindlessly onto the floor until he could open the distinctive box. He removed a beautiful gold watch with a brown alligator strap and a gold Calatrava Cross deployable clasp. He rolled it over and over in his hands, trying to tame the growing lump in his throat.

"A Perpetual!" he finally gasped. It was watch jargon, he knew, but it wouldn't be lost on Hélène. He was looking at a mechanical watch so finely crafted that it perpetually tracked the days of the week and month, right through leap years, and never required winding (as long as it was worn, that is). Most people wouldn't notice such a watch or admire the engineering and workmanship it represented, but Meth knew the quality and the value.

"Hercules," he whispered, "I can't let y—"

"Correction," she said with great satisfaction, still reveling in his awkwardness. "You can't stop me. Your reaction is exactly what I wanted, and you can't take it back. It's my gift to you; no strings attached."

Meth looked at her repeatedly, fleetingly, trying to bolster his almost-regained composure. He knew he couldn't sustain eye contact without becoming emotional. The feelings came fast and powerfully, pulling his heart and intellect in strange new directions. The women in his past had conditioned him like Pavlov's dog. *What does she want?* he wondered, disappointed with his cynicism. He desperately wanted to reciprocate, to say something in response to that L-word, but he just couldn't, not yet. He seemed unable.

Hélène must have sensed his apprehensions, because she addressed them head-on.

"Nobody's done anything like this for you since your grandfather died. You need to know that someone can . . . if you'll just open up and let them."

She paused, watching Meth tenderly slip his old watch into his pocket and place the new one on his wrist.

"This is more than a new watch," she said, waiting for him to look up. When he did, she continued. "It's a fresh start."

Meth struggled to speak, but he knew the time had come. He knew he had to say something. The gift was too large and the message too powerful to go unanswered. He squirmed and looked everywhere but to Hélène's eyes. When he finally made eye contact, he spoke slowly.

"My mother told me she loved me. No other woman has ever said it to me."

"*I* love you, Meth," Hélène whispered, as though she knew she had earned the right to say it.

"In my adult life, no woman has ever said that to me."

"I *love* you, Meth," she hastened, changing the emphasis perfectly.

"I'm trying," he choked.

"I know." She waited for him to breathe. "Read the inscription."

As carefully as he'd examined his new treasure, Meth hadn't noticed the inscription. He removed the watch to take a look. A stunned expression swept across his face; she'd shocked him three times in as many minutes.

"How did you know?" he asked, feeling unnerved. Before she could respond, he asked again, with a slight edge in his voice, "How did you know?"

"Know what?"

"The inscription, CHOOSE TO LOVE. That's the last thing my mother said to me. My grandfather said it when he gave me the watch, but I never told you. How did you know?"

He expected some elaborate explanation. Perhaps she had searched the cemeteries in Geneva until she found Adelaide's grave and read it on her headstone. There was no one for her to ask. How else could she know unless she'd been digging around where she had no business? What else did she know?

"It's on your old watch," she said. "I saw it. I thought you'd like it on this one too. Now you can retire your grandfather's watch, like you said, and still have the inscription on your wrist."

"I could never read it," he said, his nerves and suspicions dissipating. The words on the watch had been too worn for him to decipher. He had to admit, her answer was the epitome of Occam's razor—it was the simplest possible explanation. He wasn't sure whether the magnitude of her gift had given him cause to be more suspicious or to feel more guilt for harboring any suspicion at all. He hoped it was the latter.

"Now you can read it," she bubbled. "Nothing's as real as love, Meth. *Nothing*. When you choose to love, you choose to heal."

She waited. He was looking past her left shoulder toward the far corner of the restaurant. She jerked her chair a little to her left and leaned until she was directly in his sightline. He blinked and followed her eyes as she sat straight up again.

"Choose to love," she said.

He came around the table and embraced her. He couldn't say what he wanted to say, but he could do his best to show it. He kissed her long and gently on the lips. It was different from any kiss he'd ever experienced. It filled him with some inexpressible joy—a feeling entirely new to him—like a tiny fire had sparked in the center of his soul and spread outward until it had warmed every cell.

When their kiss finally ended, Hélène held him close and pressed her cheek against his chest, her eyes closed, her heart racing. She reached behind her back and found Meth's hand. She brought it to her chest so he could feel her heartbeat. She slid her other hand around the back of his neck and tugged until he lowered his head. She returned the gentlest, most sincere kiss Meth had ever experienced.

"Trust me," she said.

AFTER ANOTHER day in Paris, mostly at Musée de Montmartre and Clos Montmartre, Hélène and Meth shared a baguette au fromage and an evening walk on La Rive Gauche. The next morning they caught the Sunday train to Zurich. Meth grunted up the stairs to the second level of the train carrying the bags and a bottle of wine he'd purchased for Hélène at the vineyard. She offered to help, but he declined.

"Más cara que espalda," she said.

"More face than back? What does that mean?"

"Not so much in English," she said. "In Spain, we say it. It means, too big for one's trousers."

"Britches."

"What are britches?"

"They're trousers. In English, the saying is, 'Too big for your britches.'"

"As you say." She shrugged. "You carry too much for your britches."

He laughed. "It's my new watch. I feel stronger."

"I love your new watch."

Meth shoved the bags into the rack and sat down. He pushed the armrest out of the way and pulled her close.

"I still don't know what to say."

"Not too speechless, I hope."

"What do you mean?"

She gripped his arm. "We have to talk about things."

"Things?" His raspy voice, pitched higher than usual, telegraphed his concern.

"And I don't mean me talking while you restate my sentences as one-word questions."

"Restate?" he joked.

She drilled a playful elbow into his ribs.

"I'm not a good talker," Meth said, as is if revealing some great mystery. "Not much practice."

Even as the words tumbled out of his mouth, he knew the excuse was wearing thin. It might have worked at the beginning of the trip, but he'd spoken too much in the last few days to play that card now.

"I understand," Hélène said, "but I need a commitment."

"Commitment?"

She turned toward him with a stern look. This time he hadn't intended to do it.

"No, wait," he said. "I wasn't trying to be flippant. You just caught me off guard."

"Not that kind of commitment. I just need to know you'll open up—that you'll continue to share."

"I can try," he said, sounding relieved.

She didn't wait long to test him.

"When we met," she said, as if they had known each other for years, "I wondered who had hurt you." She moved to the opposite side of the table and looked him eye-to-eye. "I have to look at you, Meth. I have to see your face."

He looked away, trying to mask his anxiety. He rubbed his knuckles back and forth across his chin and gritted his teeth. By now, the train was gaining speed and approaching the outskirts of Paris. There was no conductor to ask for tickets, no tourist to divert the conversation. He was stuck. He finally looked back.

"At some point," she said, "I need to hear you say it. I need to hear you say, 'I love you.'"

They stared at each other, her request hanging in the air. Meth's face tightened as excuses queued in his head.

"Not now," she said, raising her hands, like a flagman stopping traffic. "Not before you're ready . . . but probably before you're comfortable saying it."

It seemed strange to Meth. He would readily admit his ignorance about women in general and romance in particular. Before Hélène, women had had one purpose only, but he'd read books and seen movies. *What woman wants a solicited declaration of affection?* Even if he felt it, he wasn't sure he could say it. And if he said it, and if he convinced himself he knew what it meant, he still wasn't confident he could live up to it.

"Do you love me?" she asked.

His eyes widened. His gaze darted from one inanimate object to another. He swallowed.

She took his face between her trembling hands and pointed it toward hers. She offered a cautious smile. Her voice softened.

"Do you love me?"

He nodded, moving her hands slowly up and down with his face.

"When you're ready, I need to hear you say it."

"It's not because I—"

"Not now," she interrupted. "Don't explain. You'll know. You'll just know. Do it then."

She let go of his face. He nodded again without changing his expression.

"Meth," she said, making sure she had his full attention, "before you can *really* love me, you have to love yourself."

"How?"

"We'll work on it."

Meth's affect flipped like he was Duc Tran. The mention of love triggered perverse feelings and messages from his past. He struggled to process them. His brow furrowed, his eyes narrowed. It happened so quickly it left Hélène looking bewildered and shaken. She noticed him gripping the armrest, his knuckles white, his fingernails buried in the upholstery.

"What makes a man hate his own son?" he said, unintentionally divulging his deepest insecurity—his deepest wound. "And how can that son feel deserving of love, even from himself? The very notion of love is a struggle."

Meth's words suggested vulnerability, but his tone was pure anger. The tangled confusion of love, anger, and hatred that he'd experienced as a child left him nearly unable to separate the feelings as an adult. Anger prevailed.

"He beat my mother. He killed my dog. He blackened my childhood and stole my self-respect. I could never contemplate marriage or children."

He jumped from one topic to the next, moving far too fast to notice the tears streaming down Hélène's face.

"What if I *love* my wife and children the way he *loved* us?" His emphasis highlighted his disdain for the perverted notion of love that swirled through his mind like a tornado through Kansas. He thought about his clenched fist in London. "What if I do the same things he did?"

"It's not in you, Meth. It's not who you are."

"It is! You saw it. What if—"

"You won't," she insisted. "I'll help you."

Meth was frustrated, not with Hélène for understanding, but with himself for failing to do so. He wanted to be in control. He prided himself on discipline. His anger left him feeling out of control, and that frightened him. And fear—that enemy he would never acknowledge—set off all his defense mechanisms and threated his destruction.

"How do you know what is in me?" he asked, reprising their conversation from The LaSalle. "How do you crawl inside my head and speak my thoughts? Or answer my unspoken questions? How do you do that?"

"Because I love you, Meth. I'm still getting to know you, but I love you. Already."

"I was not even seven years old when he did this." Meth pointed to the scar above his eye. "I have not cried since: not a single tear, not even at my mother's funeral. I do not have feelings—not like other people, anyway. I do not have tears. As a general rule, the only real emotion I have is hatred."

"Try not to hate," she pleaded. "It gets you nothing. It's poison. I know. I hated a man for years." She waited until Meth asked why. "He walked away from me . . . or ran." Her voice trembled. The tears she had wiped away returned. "After four years, he just walked away. He hurt me in the deepest, most personal way possible." She waited again. When he asked, she continued. "I couldn't conceive."

She swallowed hard. For a few moments, she bowed her head and wept, her shoulders shaking slightly. She looked back at Meth, courage in her eyes, and continued. "He just left. *He said I wasn't trying!* Can you imagine that? He abandoned me, and I hated him for it."

"Maybe it was *him*," Meth suggested, sensing the depth of her pain, unsettled by her vulnerability. He wanted to help. His feelings surprised him.

"Trust me. We tested everything. It was *me*. I hated him for years. I hated the situation, and I hated myself. I wanted more than anything to conceive a child. And when I couldn't, he made me feel like I'd betrayed him, and myself."

Hélène sat quietly for a few moments, catching her breath, softening her tone.

"When I met you, I wanted to ask why you hated yourself, but I knew I couldn't. It's not a question you ask on the first day, even if you want to, even if it's the right question. I recognized in you what I'd experienced, and I'd promised myself if I ever found a way out, I'd use all my experience to help someone else."

"Is that what this is?" Meth asked, his anger again escalating. "You do not *know* me! I share a few anecdotes about my past and you think you know me? Am I your project? Besides, what is in it for you?"

The words cut deep, particularly in contrast to the feelings they had shared so recently in Le Train Bleu. Meth saw the pain in her eyes before she looked away. He glanced at his new watch and felt the shame that had overwhelmed him in London. He checked himself. As hard as it was, he decided to listen instead of talk.

"No, Meth," she said, apparently recognizing his defenses and refusing to be distracted. "You know me better than that. Even after only a few days, you know me better than *that*. Initially I embraced the challenge of just getting you to talk. I admit that. But when you did, I couldn't help but listen and care. I couldn't help but love you. I'm just sharing my experience. You can do what you want with it. It's *your* life."

After an uncomfortable silence, Meth reluctantly asked, "What did you do?"

"I finally realized my hatred came from feeling hurt and unloved. When I realized he hadn't intended to hurt me, I stopped hating him. I found out later he didn't leave because he didn't care; he left because he knew his resentment of the situation hurt me and he couldn't bear to hurt me anymore. When I stopped hating him, I stopped hating myself."

Meth waxed introspective, staring beyond Hélène and into his past. Her explanation seemed a little too neat, a little too perfect. Was she suggesting François hadn't intended to hurt him? How absurd! He couldn't accept that. He wouldn't accept it even if he could.

"I'm not there yet," he muttered.

"That's okay. When you're ready, I'll help you find something better than hate."

Meth wasn't sure he wanted help. She was suggesting a paradigm shift. Hate was his fuel. It kept him moving—if not forward, at least still moving. As determined as he'd been in his London hotel room, decades of habit now grabbed him from behind and snatched him back. He just wasn't sure he wanted to give up the hate. And, even if he did, he was beginning to feel it might not be so easy.

"You just don't know me," he said.

"I'm trying."

"I'm not what you think. If you knew wh—"

"Tell me."

He shook his head. "I can't."

"You have to. Someday you'll have to. It might as well be today."

He shook his head again.

"I'll still love you," she promised, "no matter what you say."

"You just don't know."

"Try me."

He hated her pressure. He felt his anger escalating. He looked at the other passengers and kept his volume down, but his tone shifted.

"I can't." His eyes narrowed. He gritted his teeth. "It's not my choice."

"Whose choice is it? If you don't want to tell me, fine, but don't blame it on someone else. If you don't trust me, just say so."

"That's not it."

"Then what is it?"

They stared at each other until Hélène pulled Herman Melville from her bag and opened *Moby Dick* between them.

Meth studied the cover of her novel until his frustration boiled over.

"Some people are unlovable," he blurted out. "François was unlovable."

"Adelaide loved him."

"I'll never understand why."

"You don't have to. You're not Adelaide. And you're not François."

"I'm more like him than you think."

She finally lowered her book, revealing a concerned and inquisitive expression.

"You can't love me," he said without emotion.

"Why?"

He sat silent.

"I don't care about your past," she said. "I care about our future."

"You don't know my past."

"I don't care."

"*I* care."

"Then tell me."

They hardly spoke from Franse to Pontarlier. As they rolled past Lake Neuchâtel, Hélène stood up. She wore the same horrible sadness in her face that Meth had seen in Geneva. She stepped into the aisle, looking toward the empty seats at the other end of the car. Meth had no time to think. He feared she might walk away, driven by his hardheartedness—by the horrors of his past crawling relentlessly into his present. And, if she left, he feared she might never come back.

"Please don't go," he said, reaching for her hand. He caressed her fingers gently, making it clear he was inviting, not demanding. He had no obscure word or glib phrase. He had just tossed out the most visceral and genuine thing he'd said in years. He waited.

She pulled her hand away.

"Without love, there's nothing to work on. You have to trust me. I can't do it alone."

She gathered her belongings and moved down the aisle. She found a seat near a window facing away from Meth.

It was ninety minutes from Neuchâtel to Zurich. Then she'd be gone.

For an hour, Meth's mind raced. He contemplated a thousand scenarios. His answer came as a shattering slap in the face. He'd just done what he imagined François would have done. It was a revolting and sobering realization. Then he wondered: *What* should *François have done?* He gathered every shred of courage and humility he could discover and walked slowly to the far end of the car. He looked at her, waiting for an invitation to sit.

"You have to say it," she said, keeping her face in her book. "I'm not going to guess. And I'm not going to put any more words in your mouth. If you want to say something, you have to say it."

"Can we talk?" he said softly.

She slowly lowered her book and pointed to the empty seat with her eyes, her expression hard and skeptical.

"Sit where you want," she said. "It's not my train."

He settled into the seat across the table from her and studied her expression for a long moment. He could feel the consternation in his face. He assumed she could see it. "I'm afraid when you get off this train, I'll never see you again."

"I'm getting off at Aarau."

"You're not going to Zurich?"

"There'll be another train to Zurich. I'll take it."

"Just to get away from me?"

"You can't stand to be around yourself. How can you expect me to be around you?"

He had no answer. She was right. He couldn't stand himself or his life.

"What are you willing to give up, Meth?"

There was a long silence as the train began to slow at the outskirts of Aarau.

"I don't know who was on the other end of that phone call in Geneva," she said, "but I saw the change in you. And I saw it in London. You can't be that man and have me in your life. I've been in a soul-destroying relationship; I won't be in another. I can decide whether to be in a relationship, but I can't decide whether you're willing to change. That's your decision."

The Aarau signs moved slowly past the windows until the train stopped. They looked at each other. She raised her brows. Meth's mouth dropped open, but nothing came out. She tipped her head slightly and raised her brows even further. She leaned toward him as she stood.

"I'll tell you everything," he began, his speech pressured and nervous, "but it can't be today. I promise. I have to take care of some things first. And the time has to be right. This isn't the right time. It's not because I don't respect you. It's because I *do* respect you that I have to do this right. Can you trust me?"

"I can trust you. And I can wait; as long as I know we're in this together.

Are we?"

He nodded and reached for her hand. She met him in the middle and touched his fingers.

"Don't do this unless you're serious," she said. "I won't be hurt again—not like before. If you're not serious, I'm getting off now. You're afraid of being hurt, but so am I."

"Will you help me?" he asked.

She paused, obviously contemplating his question, and looked out the window at the Aarau sign.

"I like this town," she said. "I'm comfortable in this town."

"Help me."

Another long pause. She sat back down.

"Whatever it takes, Meth. I'm here. But it has to be a two-way effort. You have to work at it."

"Whatsoever thou spendest more," Meth whispered, almost mechanically, like it was programed into his DNA. He said it to himself, but Hélène overheard.

"What?"

The trained pulled away.

"'Whatsoever thou spendest more, when I come again, I will repay thee.' My grandfather used to say that when he'd go out of his way to help someone. I must have heard it a thousand times. He was always helping someone."

"What does it mean?"

"It comes from the parable of the Good Samaritan." The chill of their earlier conversation was gone. "Everybody knows about the Good Samaritan helping the wounded traveler. Most people know the Samaritan stepped across a broad cultural divide to help when neither priest nor Levite would stop. But that's not what most impressed my grandfather about the parable. He often became emotional when he related his favorite part."

Meth checked. Hélène eyes were fixed on his face, her expression sincere and inquisitive.

"After the Samaritan cared for the wounded victim, he took him to an inn and paid two pence for the room. Then he told the innkeeper—and this is the impressive part—'Take care of him; and whatsoever thou spendest more, when I come again, I will repay thee.'"

Hélène was speechless—a distinctly unusual circumstance for her—as though she couldn't comprehend Meth quoting scripture. Meth looked at her. He brought her hand to his face and kissed it.

"You remind me of the Good Samaritan," he said. "You promised to heal me in advance of even knowing the cost."

14

ST. MORITZ

METH AMBLED into the office sporting a smile Karl had never seen. He was, to use his paraphrase of Dickens, as giddy as a schoolboy. In keeping with his English background, Truman had insisted they read *A Christmas Carol* together each December 24th. Meth could recite lengthy chunks of the tale. What Ebenezer Scrooge actually said was, "I am as merry as a schoolboy. I am as giddy as a drunken man." Meth liked *giddy*; he was not so keen on the drunken man. Every time he eyed his new watch, or felt it on his wrist, he thought of Hélène. And every time he thought of Hélène, he was Scrooge on Christmas day.

Karl didn't notice Meth's watch or the folder in Meth's hand, perhaps because it looked like every other folder piled on his desk.

"Here's a bonus," Karl said, passing two envelopes. He complimented Meth on London. "No back-up. No cleanup. No trails. You're worth it."

"There's always a trail," Meth said.

It was the beginning of a conversation they'd had before. Meth wasn't interested in having it again. Karl paid no more attention to Meth's use of contractions than he did to the watch or the folder. In his younger years, when he did Meth's job, Karl never missed details. "Wear your holster higher," he'd once said when he noticed the uneven lie of Meth's blazer. Karl had barely transitioned into his desk when Meth arrived at NEMESIS. He'd taught Meth the importance of details. Now Karl seldom needed such details. Meth wondered about a life with less stress and fewer details. He still wondered about the trail to his family and to Cambridge. It gnawed at him, but not enough to ask. *Some questions*, he thought, *are best unanswered . . . or unasked.*

Preoccupied with more important things—anything more important than money or contracts was a new concept for Meth—he pocketed the envelopes without checking their contents. He showed no interest in business or in his frequent pastime of antagonizing Karl. He dropped François' file on the desk without explanation. His weekend with Hélène had left him determined to forget about François and to find a way out of NEMESIS—an antagonistic process that included appearing before a committee to justify the breech of his employment contract. It meant a loss of pension and eviction from the NEMESIS-owned home. He wasn't ready to talk about it, at least not with Karl.

"Shit, Meth, that's quite a smile."

"Noun or verb?"

"Huh?"

"Feces or defecate? I always wonder when people say that whether they mean the noun or the verb."

"You're shitting me, right?"

"No. That would be the gerund." Meth offered a tortured smile.

"Yeah, whatever."

Karl picked up François' file and thumbed through it, offering his own version of the shit-smile. He thanked Meth before dropping it back into the chaos on his desk. He didn't resuscitate the François row by asking questions.

"I'll be gone for a few days," Meth said. "I'm skiing at St. Moritz with a friend."

Karl looked more than surprised. Amazed might be a better description. The return of the file was cause enough for shock, but he'd never heard Meth speak of recreation, let alone friends. Amazed or not, Karl was about business. He was always looking to the next job.

"I need you to check on someone while you're there."

"No," Meth said. "No business on this trip." His tone was new and energetic.

Karl straightened. His eyebrows elevated. Meth had always been engaged in his work to the exclusion of virtually everything else in his life, and he'd always been poised for his next assignment. If anything, he had seemed to resent downtime. Though obviously surprised by Meth's reluctance, Karl persisted.

"You don't have to complete a contract. Just check the guy out."

Karl extended the folder. It looked like every other folder—like the folder Meth had just returned—except for the ID code in the corner.

"Just take the file," Karl prodded. "Nail down the usual stuff. We'll take care of the rest later."

Meth wanted nothing to do with the assignment. He resented the intrusion into his weekend plans. In fact, he resented his job altogether. On the other hand, he wasn't being asked to dispatch a target. Resisting Karl was difficult. It might have been easy to say no if Meth hadn't spent so many years consistently saying yes. He was habituated to his catch phrase.

"I'll take care of it," he finally said, eyeballing Karl, silently debating for a few more moments before reluctantly snatching the folder. Like some fiendish gremlin, the file made its way into Meth's bag and onto the train to St. Moritz.

EVEN SEASONED travelers noticed the scenery along the narrow gauge rails from Chur to St. Moritz. Chur claimed to be the oldest town in Switzerland. And the railroad to St. Moritz boasted UNESCO World Heritage status. The vistas, the snow, the tunnels, and bridges were all beautiful. Meth and Hélène, in casual cool-weather attire, enjoyed the scenery from the dining car—an eighty-year-old, wood-paneled, brass-trimmed restaurant-on-wheels, complete with linen and candles.

As they ate and visited, the train climbed more than one thousand meters and the snow steadily deepened. They crossed high, stone-arched bridges and passed through tunnels along the way. They stopped briefly at Tiefencastel, where one young woman waited on the outdoor platform.

"I love the ride to St. Moritz," Meth said with a mischievous grin. "The men get richer; the women get younger and more beautiful."

"Hey," Hélène said, feigning offense.

"Hey, yourself," he joked. "Being with a beautiful woman doesn't make me blind."

It was Meth's version of a compliment. He never expected compliments and seldom offered them. He cared so little about other peoples' opinions, he assumed they were likewise indifferent to his. If he had looked, he would have seen the warmth in Hélène's eyes and her smile.

"Look as you wish," she said.

"I only see you."

"Hasta el rabo, todo es toro."

"'Until the tail, everything is bull?' Are you saying I'm full of bull?"

"It means, uh, 'I know you are telling me this, but I believe it when I see it.'"

"Actions speak louder than words? Is that what you're saying?"

"Sí. Sí." She nodded as she spoke.

"I'll act better."

"I'm glad you came," she said. "Sometimes this is hard for me."

"Hard? Why?"

"I should've told you earlier." She hesitated, uncertainty in her eyes.

He looked at her and waited. Leaning a little closer, he absent-mindedly folded and unfolded his napkin.

"I'm not going to St. Moritz just to ski." She paused and swirled her wine before taking a sip. She reached for a macaroon but stopped as if she could procrastinate the inevitable no longer. "I go for another reason. Skiing is just a bonus."

She looked wistful and cautious, almost tearful. Her lower lip quivered.

"Olin is buried in Maloja near St. Moritz. It was his favorite place. I come every March twenty-first, the day he died. I go to the cemetery and then take a walk around Lake St. Moritz." She took a few audible breaths. "You remind me of Olin. He was quiet, like you. It was hard for him to talk to people. Some thought he was arrogant, but he wasn't, just quiet and . . . and afraid."

As their train continued through the tunnels and past the high banks of snow, she opened her heart.

"Olin's why I didn't leave you in London; he's why I didn't get off the train in Aarau."

Meth finally dropped his napkin on the table and extended his open palm. She rested her hand in his and launched off on one of those monologues that left him impressed with her English skills.

"He was so different from me. It was hard for him to communicate. I resented how people faded out of his life because of his unintended stern expressions and his short, to-the-point comments. He came across as curt. At one point, even I began fading away, but I reconnected and came to appreciate how good he was. Sometimes I'd stand close to him at parties just to support the conversation and help him feel comfortable. I wanted people to know the real Olin. I'm sorry I didn't tell you. I just didn't want to be alone this year. I didn't know how to bring it up. You don't have to go to the cemetery."

"I'm glad you invited me, Herc. I'm happy to go."

"Primo?"

He saw tenderness and concern in her face. He nodded, leaned forward, and listened more intently.

"Are you okay if we share a room this trip?" she said.

In the flash of modern mores, it might have seemed an odd question, but Meth understood. He'd been wounded and he knew she had been as well. They'd put their physical relationship on hold. She knew from their conversations that Meth was apathetic about women that wanted only a one-night tryst. "They are good for something," he had said in an awkward moment, but it was not anything he wanted to continue or anything he and Hélène wanted together. They'd concluded that trust was as important as love in a relationship, perhaps more so, and that trust hinged inevitably on respect. It was clear to Meth that she knew what *she* wanted. Her question reflected an unselfish concern for him.

"Of course," he whispered. He nodded, raising one corner of his mouth. "Of course."

He took her hand and stepped away from the table. He dropped some money next to their glasses as she grabbed the last green macaroon. They moved through three coaches to the observation car. Meth gestured her toward the window seat.

"I'll go to freshen up," she said. "I'll be right back."

He slid to the window and watched Hélène disappear down the aisle. Then he turned his attention to the scenery. Snow fell fast, huge flakes with occasional swirls from the wind of the passing train. People played in the snow not far from the rails, including one well-bundled woman watching a boy build a snowman. Meth's mind drifted. He saw his mother, gaunt and pale, wrapping one more scarf around her cachectic neck as she exited their home to sit on the covered porch. Meth saw nine-year-old Prometheus positioning the head on his growing snowman. Giant flakes accumulated quickly on the yard, leaving the landscape quiet and white.

"Momma, you will get cold. You can watch through the window."

"I can *watch* through the window, Prometheus, but I can't hear from inside. I can't share your experience through the window. I want to be with you, Son."

He couldn't appreciate her sacrifice at the time; he later realized how much pain she had endured to treasure every second with him. Her remaining moments, by then, were few and precious.

Meth found two sticks and promptly transformed them into snowman arms.

"That's quite a snowman," she said. "What's his name?"

Without answering, young Meth continued his work, kicking ice from the edge of the frozen flowerbed to uncover two perfect stones. Twisting the stones into their would-be eye sockets, he pressed a little too hard and sent the snowman's head plummeting. It broke into several pieces. Too angry to speak, Meth knocked the snowman over and kicked it incessantly until nothing remained but a small pile of snow and two sticks. Then he stomped the sticks into splinters.

Adelaide winced with every kick. Out-of-breath and too exhausted to continue, Meth came to his mother's side. She pulled him close and felt the trembling in his right leg. She massaged his quivering muscles until his leg became still. As soon as the trembling stopped, Prometheus smiled and snuggled closer.

"Are you all right now?" she asked.

"Yes, Mamma."

On the rare occasions when young Prometheus lost his temper, the rage flowed like lava, explosive and destructive. It worsened with each beating and persisted after François left. Adelaide held him close, with a troubled expression, obviously worried about what the rage might lead to after she was gone. She turned his head and looked directly into his eyes as if to make him *feel* what she was about to explain.

"Prometheus, I want you to remember something. I won't be here to remind you, so it's important that you listen carefully. Can you do that?"

"Yes, Mamma," he promised.

"Look at the snow. It's pure and clean. It's quiet and beautiful. It's god's gift to his children. Do you hear me, Son?"

"I hear you."

"God gives us snow to remind us that there are new beginnings. It comes to remind us of his love. When you see the snow, think of him. And think of me . . ." She cleared her throat and blinked away the tears, trying not to alarm her son. "Because I will always love you. Do you hear me?"

"Yes, Mamma. Yes, I hear you."

"Choose to love."

Those became her last words to Prometheus. She quietly passed in her sleep later that evening. He gave the phrase little thought as a child, but he seemed unable to escape it as an adult.

"Isn't it beautiful?" Hélène said, snapping him back to the present. "I love the snow."

Meth nodded, still hearing his mother's words. He thought of her whenever big, heavy flakes made things quiet.

METH STEPPED from the taxi in front of Hotel Schweizerhof and extended his hand to Hélène. Snow continued to fall, adding four centimeters an hour to the meter already on the ground. She removed her glove, as if to maximize the intimacy of a simple gesture, and slipped her bare hand into his. She stepped into the crisp St. Moritz air and started with him toward the hotel, their breath misting behind them as they walked.

"I like your taste in hotels," Meth said.

"It's my favorite in St. Moritz. We have a beautiful suite."

"We?"

"I know we didn't discuss it until today, but I gambled on your answer." She gauged his expression for a long moment. "I won."

"*I* won," he responded.

Staff nearly surrounded the car, taking luggage and skis to the hotel.

"I can't wait to hear some great music," she said as they continued toward the entrance.

"Music?"

"The St. Moritz Music Summit is this weekend. Every year. Live music all over town."

Their walk through the hotel seemed more like a promenade than a ski weekend. The hotel manager stood in the middle of the luxurious lobby, keycard in hand and a bright smile on her face. "Your suite, Ms. Ingebretzen," she said in German, handing the keycard as they passed. Even Meth was impressed.

"They know me here, Meth," she said as they walked toward the elevator. "After twelve years, they should. They even know about Olin. My annual trips have slowly transitioned from mourning his death to celebrating his life."

They stepped onto the elevator and Hélène swiped her card.

"The staff see me differently this year," she said as the doors closed. "You're the first person to ever come with me."

When the elevator opened on the eighth floor, they strolled out into their private hallway. Beyond the windows, the ski slopes loomed in the near distance, almost obscured by the cloud of falling snow. Meth and Hélène were too preoccupied to notice. On each side of the hallway, a bellman held open one of the heavy doors to their suite.

"I hope we find time to ski," she whispered, smiling, as they approached their room.

She pushed a handful of francs into the nearest bellman's hand without breaking stride. The bellmen released their respective doors simultaneously, like they had rehearsed it for a role in some romantic movie, allowing Meth and Hélène to disappear into their suite as the doors closed behind them.

HÉLÈNE FELT a tremor in Meth's hand. She looked at his leg. It was still.

"Are you okay?" she asked, seeming to sense his nervousness.

"I'm fine." He smiled.

She gripped his hand when she heard him use the contraction but didn't comment. She turned toward him, resting her head against his chest and shoulder. She pulled him into a tight embrace as if hoping the moment would never end.

"Thank you for coming."

Meth's mind raced, like his heart. He'd determined before leaving Zurich to divulge his secrets today. He'd planned to tell her what even Karl didn't know: that he intended to quit. He didn't know yet how that would happen—he could still hear Karl, from years ago, saying, *never speak of NEMESIS* and *no one leaves*—but he'd made a decision. He would work out the details later. Now, he couldn't imagine bringing it up. Not telling her seemed almost a lie, but divulging his dark talent on their first night together would be like dumping tar on a Rembrandt. He couldn't do it.

"Where are you?" she asked, breaking the long silence. She'd drawn her head back from his lapel to look up into his eyes. "Tell me."

"There are things I need to tell you," he admitted. "All those things I promised to share . . . but not tonight. Tonight is just for us."

He coaxed the parka from her shoulders, pushed it down her slender arms, and tossed it into an overstuffed chair in the corner. His coat promptly followed. Still standing just inside the doors, as if moving from that spot might somehow disrupt the magic, he slowly ran his hand up her arm, over her shoulder, and behind her neck. As he slid his fingers from her sweater onto her soft skin he heard her breathing quicken. His other hand found the small of her back and pulled her close until he could feel her heart race against his lower chest. She tipped her head back, using his hand as a headrest, and closed her eyes.

Meth tenderly kissed her, first on her forehead, then on her cheek, and then her chin. He rested his cheek next to hers and inhaled the perfume he had come to adore. Every time he smelled it his heart fluttered, like a teenager at Bal de Printemps. He held her in a long, silent, motionless waltz, as if waiting for the music to begin. He moved one hand from the small of her back to her wrist and then to her fingers, continuing to caress her neck with his other hand. He lifted her tiny, adorable hand and studied every delicate curve and texture. He kissed each knuckle. Then he turned it over and kissed the tip of each finger before pressing it against his face and kissing it again.

He traced each feature of her face, first with his eyes, then with his finger. When her eyes opened, he did his best to silently communicate his profound feelings. It wasn't like the passing glances on the TGV or the awkward and interrupted eye contact at Le Train Bleu. He offered a deep steady gaze that seemed to last forever, passing through her eyes and into her soul. Then he carefully kissed her neck, jaw, and ear, working his way back to her forehead.

"You're beautiful," he said, his voice quiet and tender; he was strangely unafraid of loss or abandonment or of revealing too much. "You're the most beautiful woman I've ever seen."

"I love you, Meth."

"When you touch me I can't breath. When I look in your eyes, I see hope."

By now, Hélène had untucked the tail of Meth's shirt and was slowly exploring the small of his back, occasionally digging her perfect nails gently into his skin. Her other hand crept from his face to the back of his head and closed snugly around a handful of hair, tightening his scalp and sending a pleasant shudder down his back and to the furthest reaches of each extremity. It was all so much more intense than anything he had previously experienced, so much more tender and genuine.

He wanted to reciprocate her words and sentiment. He tried to say it. He hoped she knew. He convinced himself he could will the message through his eyes and touch—he had never touched a woman so slowly, so tenderly and unselfishly—but he still couldn't *say* it. He had never told a woman that he loved her. He didn't think he'd ever loved a woman, but he was convinced he loved Hélène. Still, he could not say it.

She caressed his back and neck as she tipped her right ankle so far to the side that the outer edge of her four-inch heel rested flat on the floor. Then she stood on it with her left foot and pulled her right leg out of the tall leather boot without reaching or looking away from his eyes. She repeated the process with her left boot and suddenly dropped to where she could tease her chin over Meth's top button and kiss him in that sensitive hollow just above his sternum. Meth shoes came off more easily. He kicked them across the carpet. Then, in unison, as if they both heard Carla Bruni singing the first few bars of "L'Amour," they drifted into the bedroom and swung the doors closed behind them.

15

THE MONSTER

"**YOU MUST** ski a lot," Meth observed as Hélène plopped down next to him on the lift, still catching her breath.

"Since I was four. Learned at Grandvalira, in the Pyrenees. How can a person live so close to St. Moritz and not ski?"

"I love snow," Meth said.

Hélène looked as surprised as Meth felt. He'd said it, even if only to reference the snow. The last time she'd heard him use the word it was with distain and resentment. Today it came out naturally, leaving no foul taste in his mouth. Maybe, thought Meth, if he said it more often and in less threatening circumstances, he could eventually say it to her.

"I love big flakes, falling fast, piling high on the ground." He looked at Hélène and took her hand. "Mother said god sends snow to remind us there are new beginnings."

"She was right. Look at us!"

THE ST. MORITZ Music Summit filled the Hotel Schweizerhof nightclub with live music. The club bustled. Couples danced. Hélène and Meth, after a day on the slopes, nursed their usual drinks—his Pellegrino, hers red wine—and chatted over the second verse and chorus of "Please Return to Jesus."

"I love this music," Hélène said. "Who is he?"

"Bap Kennedy. He's one of my favorites."

Meth liked most of Bap's songs, but not this one. The reference to Jesus reminded him of things he'd tried to forget. He sometimes resented the biblical passages and references to god that ricocheted around in his head, but he couldn't get rid of them. They came from his mother and grandfather and from his theological studies at Cambridge. They were part of who he was and where he'd been.

"Bat?" she asked, shouting over the music.

"Bap. B-A-P. From Belfast."

Meth had listened to Kennedy for years. He'd even attended one of his concerts in Belfast.

"Come on," Meth beckoned. "Let's dance."

"Let's?" she echoed. "Did you just say let's?"

"Yeah. Let's."

Meth had danced a lot at Cambridge, not so much the first year, but with Adi's help, more often as time went on. He was good at it. Hélène pressed her cheek against his shoulder, tightened her left arm around his low back, and gave herself to his effortless lead. He floated her across the floor so smoothly that one couple, then another, stopped to watch. As the music slowed, Hélène became silent. Meth looked down just in time to see her wipe away a tear.

She gripped his hand a little tighter, pulled his head close, and whispered in his ear. "This has been a perfect day, Primo."

They danced until they were both warm and out of breath. They whispered in one another's ears and laughed like a normal couple. Meth hoped they could be. He kissed her forehead so tenderly they forgot they were dancing. They stood motionless until brushed back into reality by the swirling skirt of a tall blonde spinning at the end of her partner's arm. They decided it was time for a break.

"I wish you had let me go to the cemetery," Meth said, following Hélène from the dance floor to their table. She'd wanted his presence in St. Moritz for the weekend, but she'd been assertive about going to the cemetery alone. He liked her confidence and independence. He felt secure when she showed initiative, whether skiing, reserving their hotel suite, or just leading a conversation.

"Next time," she said. "This morning was personal. I just wanted to talk to him alone."

Meth understood. His topic had been very different, but it had only been a few weeks since he'd visited a cemetery for the same reason, to speak to the dead. She'd taken a taxi the sixteen kilometers to Maloja and paid the driver to wait for her. It wasn't a long visit—they'd become shorter over the years—but it was important to her to be there. Meth and Hélène snacked and sipped as they spoke. He surprised her when he explained that he knew of the Maloja Mountain Cemetery. He'd been there.

"Giovanni Segantini is one of my favorites," Meth said, "He's buried there." Meth explained that forty-one-year-old Segantini had been painting in the area when he contracted peritonitis and died in 1899. "One of his paintings depicts that very cemetery."

"Espectacular," she said. "I know Segantini. I visited the Segantini Museum in St. Moritz. I saw . . ."

She trailed off as Meth's expression turned abruptly to frustration. He pulled his vibrating phone from his pocket and eyed the caller ID.

"Don't answer it," she said. Though polite, her voice was firm.

"I have to."

She inhaled deeply through her nose. Her smile disappeared as she turned away. She stroked her hair from her face before looking back.

"You *choose* to," she said, pointing at the phone. "Let's be clear."

"I have to."

She shook her head, unwilling to argue or make a scene. "I'm going to the room." She pushed back from the table and walked away.

Her sharp response surprised Meth, but he felt compelled by habit or some relentless sense of responsibility. He slipped into the lobby to answer. Hélène had headed for another exit but found her path blocked by the crowd. As she struggled back toward the lobby doors, she heard Meth's end of the conversation from around the corner.

"*No!*" he insisted. "I can't . . . Okay, then, I won't . . . No. Not here. Not now."

Hélène looked increasingly concerned as she heard Meth's escalating frustration.

"Not in the snow," he said, followed by another long pause. "It matters to me . . . It's not silly to me." More silence. "This isn't Geneva. No. It's not London either, or Paris . . . François? No."

Hélène's eyes widened as the tumblers clicked into place. She'd seen the headlines. A look of terror swept across her face. She couldn't bear another word. She turned back into the club and ran across the dance floor to a distant exit.

"I'm fed up, Karl. I'm not doing it. Not here. Not now."

It had been a short call, but Meth felt exhausted. He stumbled back into the club to compose himself before going upstairs. As he saw it, his first step away from Karl and NEMESIS would be his final step toward Hélène. He'd already determined to tell her everything, but he hadn't decided what to say or how to say it. He sat down to breathe and prioritize his thoughts. He found himself, instead, haunted by unfamiliar music and Bap's rendition of an old Hank Williams song that asked him if he was ready to meet the Angel of Death.

A dark emptiness stormed through Meth's world. He felt sick. He couldn't explain it or turn it away. It felt like his last day at Cambridge, when he learned of Truman's death. He imagined he felt the same way when his mother died, but those memories were locked away too tightly to be sure. He finally returned to his suite an hour after the call.

As he entered, Meth saw his packed bag near the door, his coat and scarf draped over it. The ominous manila folder sat on top. His eyes locked on the file. He felt life and hope drain away, like Achilles' blood disappearing between the slats of the porch.

Hélène sat in a chair across the room, the lower half of her frame visible in the light of the shaded lamp; her face and upper torso were almost indiscernible in the shadows. Her open laptop sat facing away from her on a table. Squinting, Meth could read the Paris newspaper headline he'd shown Karl. Even with the shadows, Meth could see her eyes were swollen and red. He crept forward and knelt near her chair.

"Do I need a gun?" she said in a cold, merciless tone—no fear.

In that moment, Meth knew everything he had hoped for was gone. He thought about leaving but felt compelled to make an attempt, no matter how futile.

He extended his arm. "Hercules, what—"

"Don't touch me!" She shuddered and pulled away. "Don't *ever* call me that. Who the hell are you? What kind of a despicable person are you?"

Meth inched closer, knowing but desperate. "What did I—"

"Don't." She shook her head. Her eyes told him too much. She'd been prying words from him for weeks. Now she refused to let him speak. "Paris. Geneva. *London!* You took me to London to kill a man? How stupid could I be? I sat there and read the headlines and flirted with a monster." She pointed at the computer. "I saw the Paris headline, too. Are you proud of yourself?"

"Let me—"

"Explain? You think there's an explanation? Are you going to kill someone here too? Is that what that file's for? You'd defile my sacred place with death? You're despicable! I can't believe I'm sitting here. I should be running for my life. I should be calling the police. What . . . what am I doing? Get out of my room! Everybody knows you're here. They all saw us check in together. You can kill me but you won't get away with it."

His mind raced, but he had no response. Still kneeling and frozen, he saw some version of himself pacing the room, struggling for an answer. *You make me sick; you filthy dog.* That's what he heard, only this time it was his own voice.

"Hélène," he again attempted, "I need to—"

"Need?" She stood and stormed across the room in silence, her back to Meth. When she turned, she began speaking again but refused to look in his direction. "I loved you. You let me love you. How dare you? You let me give myself to you. I slept with death. *Get out, Meth! I hate you!*"

He couldn't speak; even if he could, what would he say? He no longer believed his own rationalizations. It *wasn't* just a job. Karl might tout the virtues of NEMESIS; he still believed. But Meth could no longer justify his actions. He forced himself from his knees and slowly backed away.

"Where now?" she asked. "François? You think your leg will stop trembling then?"

Her words startled him. Every syllable inflicted another wound. She'd verbally vivisected him. And it was all too true. His confused emotions churned, infuriated one instant and heartbroken the next.

"Plea—"

"Don't. Don't come around me. Don't . . . don't . . ." She shook her head and brought her clenched hands toward her face. "You asked how I knew your feelings. I know about senseless violence." She paused, as if deliberating on how to deliver her next blow. "Do you know how my brother died? *He was murdered!* Olin was murdered. How dare you inflict that horror on others?"

She turned away, struggling to regain her breath. When she spoke again, she seemed objective, almost detached, as if she'd decided to not waste another shred of emotion. Her voice was cold.

"You avoid alcohol and tobacco because your father drank and smoked and because he burned you with a cigarette. You don't like French because *he* spoke French. You would do anything to not be like him, but you *are* like him, only worse."

Meth still couldn't speak. He just stood there, like a statue about to crumble. She had remembered everything. She had internalized it and now hurled it back at him. His realization of how attentive she had been only propped him up for her next brutal injury.

"You think you're going to kill *him*, but you'll only be killing yourself."

She walked past, just inches away but still refusing to look. When Meth reached his hand toward her, she recoiled and swung her arm away from his touch.

"I'll never be able to forget you. Every time I read a headline about someone's death, I'll think about you. I'll think about the time and energy and emotion I wasted on you. I hate you, Meth."

She disappeared into the unlit bedroom and hurled her last dagger from the darkness.

"You deserve your pain and your life. No wonder François hated you. Maybe he saw what you would become."

Meth felt like London after the Great Fire. François' beatings had never cut so deep. He wanted to lie down and cry, but he'd given up on crying decades earlier. Though he wanted to explain, it was too late. Slowly, reluctantly, now alone, he lifted his coat and scarf with his right hand and draped them over his left forearm, drawing his eyes to his treasured new watch. He opened the clasp and watched it slide from his wrist. He placed it carefully on the table next to her gloves. He struggled to let go of it, remembering the words and feelings they had shared in Le Train Bleu. He opened the door and looked back. He hated himself, but what could he do?

What could he say? He did the only thing he could. He left.

16

ONE FOR YOU: ONE FOR ME

METH RUMINATED in the gray shadows of his study, the lights off and the early morning sky overcast. He'd been up all night. Only the rain against the glass, punctuated by an occasional clap of thunder, invaded his silence. Drops coalesced and streamed down the windows as their shadows slid across the walls, desk, and floor, giving a sense of movement to the entire room. The half-empty bottle of Kilbeggan cast a sallow shadow across an ashtray filled with butts and a glowing half-smoked Davidoff. The acrid aroma of smoke and alcohol would have reminded Meth of his childhood horrors had he been sober enough to recognize it. A strike of lightning shot a blue-gray jag across the walls and illuminated the ascending smoke that slowly embraced the bottle.

Meth saw his own hand come into view, the black-and-white image bespeckled with shadows of raindrops, as if he were watching a noir movie. The seemingly detached hand dropped his BDM onto the desk next to the Irish whiskey and tipped another dose from the bottle into the adjacent tumbler. He watched the fingers first caress the cigarette and then the glass before hoisting both toward his face. He gulped the alcohol and continued watching as the hand lowered the empty glass back to the desk and then brought the cigarette to his mouth. He took a long drag.

Continuing his out-of-body experience, Meth watched his estranged hand snub out the butt, drop it into the ashtray, and pick up the gun. The closer the weapon came to his face, the more meticulously he inspected it, seemingly from every angle. The autonomous hand slowly turned the gun until Meth could count the riflings through the muzzle. As the barrel came closer, he drew a deep breath. With his mouth wide open, he closed his eyes.

The gun tasted like death, like the blood that had dripped into his mouth the day Achilles died.

IF ANYONE had asked Meth later that morning what had happened, he'd have had a hard time answering. He remembered pouring a glass of Kilbeggen and lighting a cigarette. He had done that every day since leaving St. Moritz, trying to keep the voices at bay. He'd become all too good at it. It was the only way he could stomach himself. He'd tried to ignore Karl's calls, but the vibrations had seemed endless—before he silenced them, that is. A large piece of the phone still dangled from the torn Nesvadba; the rest huddled in a pile on the floor.

Meth felt like a character in one of Bap Kennedy's songs about insanity, demons, and a sea of alcohol. He'd never understood the lyrics; now he did. He couldn't remember much of the night or early morning, but he remembered the gun in his mouth. He'd decided then that he had one more task to complete before pulling the trigger. He'd do what he did best.

His open bag waited on the bed for its last few items. Wielding the short-handled axe he'd packed once before, he crossed the room and dropped it carelessly into his bag. He hoisted a rocks glass of whiskey—no rocks—from the marble-topped nightstand and emptied it down his throat, swallowing just once. He studied the empty glass, as if it had something more to offer. He wasn't sufficiently steeped in the culture to know it as a rocks glass—it was just part of a set—but he liked the heavy feel in his hand. He looked at the mirror across the room. Disgusted and resigned, he hurled the glass, shattering his revolting reflection. He pulled open the drawer of the nightstand, lifted his Browning, and checked to confirm it was loaded.

"To hell with making it look like an accident," he said. "What do I care?" Any inhibitions about talking to himself were gone. "One for you," he said, looking at the axe in the open bag, "and one for me," dropping his gun next to it. He glared at the shards of his reflection, some still in the frame, the rest now on the floor. He pulled the strap of his bag over his shoulder and headed for the door.

Walking to the gare, Meth saw a handful of characters who looked nearly as bad as he felt. Seeing them reminded him of the fireworks and noise he'd forgotten from the previous night. While he'd tried to burn his personal demons with alcohol, the town celebrated Sachsiluute, a holiday unique to Zurich, when they burn winter in effigy, usually on the third Monday in April. He'd been too drunk to remember until he saw his fellow hangovers. He hadn't been sober in a month.

He left Zurich on the train, no computer on the table. He had nothing left to write and no reason to write it. He looked as he felt: tired and unkempt, his face nearly expressionless, his usual three-day beard now a week old. He'd gained five kilograms, all in his belly—no exercise and a two-carbon diet. He stared at his bag with its unseen weapons and then at his watch—the one his grandfather had given him—and then out the window. His only twinge of connection to life or love was the left-handed Patek and the story behind it. As the train rolled on, he drifted into a half-drunken dream of better times.

FOURTEEN-YEAR-OLD PROMETHEUS carefully wiped his mouth and placed his napkin back in his lap as he'd been taught to do by his English grandfather. He watched a nearby server carve a lamb shank tableside. Another, at the next table, flamed a young couple's crêpe Suzette. Truman Hamstead, a slender, soft-spoken, gentleman's gentleman, looked around the restaurant, inhaling the nostalgia and tapping his chest as if he were gently touching his heart.

"Soak it in, Primo. I've been coming here since I was your age, when my grandfather brought me."

Buffet de la Gare de Lyon, as it was called when Truman first visited, was renamed Le Train Bleu in 1963, after the famous train. Little else had changed over the decades. Truman swallowed hard to control his emotions as he reminisced about his grandfather.

"He believed in tradition and family," Truman said, again tapping his chest. "He believed in love. He brought me here and gave me something very special. 'One day,' he told me, 'you will bring your grandson and you will do the same.'"

Their meticulous server, in a black tie and jacket, finished preparing their plates and positioned them carefully on the table. He filled their water glasses and added wine to Truman's goblet before leaving them alone. He returned periodically, quietly, inconspicuously anticipating their every need. Their conversation drifted widely but Truman adroitly shepherded it back to the things that mattered most.

"You're my only son," he said.

He chose the word carefully. He'd used it since rescuing Prometheus from Saint-Martin-des-Entrées.

"I had one daughter. When your mother died, I didn't know how I could live. I was broken. But these past five years with you have healed my soul. You have the power to heal, Son, and to love. Choose to love."

Prometheus stopped eating and fixed his eyes on his grandfather. He had never heard him say those words.

"Mother said that when François burned my hand. I never repeated it. I never believed it." Sounding more like an adult than a teenager, he continued: "She said it again the day she died. Those were her last words to me. I have always wondered how you came to put them on her headstone."

"I didn't get that from her," Truman said. "She got it from me. And I got it from *my* grandfather the day he brought me here." Truman spoke with a crack in his voice. "Someday you'll believe it. When you feel it, you'll be able to live it." He took a sip of wine and continued. "It's about choices, Son."

"Choices?" Prometheus snarled, clenching his jaw. He could see where this was going. At least, he thought he could. "What choice did I have?"

"Wait. Wait," Truman begged. "Wait. Don't go there. Don't let that feeling come into this place. Let me finish."

Their server approached at the least opportune time. "Les desserts, messieurs?"

"En quelques minutes," Truman said, politely waving him away. Then he turned back to his grandson. "The heartache and darkness in your life came from François' choices and from the cancer that none of us chose. The future—where you go from here—that depends on *your* choices. No one can make them for you. Choose to live, Primo. Choose to love."

Prometheus shook his head, suppressing his anger and doubting himself. "I will try, Grandfather."

"There's a soft voice that speaks to our souls, Primo, a gentle hand that writes upon our hearts and makes us who we are. You struggle to hear or feel it because of your past, but you can choose your future."

Truman had said enough. He decided to lighten the mood. "Crêpe Suzette, s'il vous plaît," he said, offering a festive wave to the server who was waiting dutifully nearby. Then he turned again to Prometheus.

"I have something special for you, Son, to remember this day. I received it from my grandfather. To me, it's priceless."

Truman reached under the cuff of his sweater and unbuckled his watch. He stretched across the table and gently wrapped his hand around his grandson's wrist. "You've seen this before," he said, "but now it's yours." He pulled Meth's arm out straight and slipped the Patek Philippe 1925 Grogan into his hand. "Take care of it, S—"

METH'S PLEASANT memories stopped as abruptly as his train. He awoke not quite sober and surprisingly angry, as if his rage from the present had hovered on the edge of his dream, waiting to invade and invalidate everything he had learned from his grandfather. He pushed the warm feelings from his past safely behind the blackness of the present. He had business to take care of. *This is no time for sentiment,* he thought. *No place for love.*

17

THE EXPRESS TRAIN

METH HIT the button to open the train door and stepped into the early morning air of Saint-Martin-des-Entrées. He'd seen the address. He knew François had returned to the scene of his crimes. Emotion nearly overcame him on the open-air platform. It all looked the same. It smelled the same. The last time he was there, he'd stood next to a carved mahogany casket. The memory caught him completely unprepared, but he pushed forward.

He crossed the platform and pulled a glass door to enter the ticketing area. He passed through the small gare quickly and exited onto a narrow lane on the other side. He looked right, then left, then he crossed the lane and walked a short distance to a small patisserie. It wasn't the café where his mother had worked as she wasted away—he couldn't make himself go there—but it was on the same street. He found a seat where he could suck down refills of espresso until his mind cleared. He knew the coffee wouldn't hasten sobriety (as depicted in movies), but time would clear his mind and caffeine would keep him awake.

It was a cold, gray day. Patches of dirty snow dotted the streets and buildings. Puffs of steam floated from villagers' mouths as they greeted one another outside the patisserie. Frost filled the corners of windows. Smoke escaped innumerable chimneys. Icicles refused to release even a single drop. It was a day as cold and gray as Meth's existence without Hélène.

He sipped espresso for three hours before venturing out again near noon. Patrons remaining in the patisserie saw him cross the lane and converse with a local who pointed down the lane toward the gare. The stranger had confirmed Meth's suspicions; François still went to the gare at noon, and most of the villagers apparently still knew it. Meth would never have asked such a question had he been on assignment, or if he cared about being caught. Since he had already planned his own fate, he didn't care who knew. He shook the man's gloved hand and moved on.

Back in the gare, Meth found a locker for his bag. He had no intention of coming back for it; he just needed to have his hands free. He removed the weapons from his death kit, slid them discreetly into his coat, and locked the bag behind a dented metal door. He glanced around the room. No one seemed to pay him any notice. He took a few slow steps toward the glass door. Reversing his path of earlier in the day, he pushed on a brass plate and emerged into the icy air on the other side. He saw a bundled mass on a bench at the other end of the platform, just as the villager had promised. He felt the chill of hatred convulse in his chest and surge to the tip of every digit. His leg began to tremble.

Hélène's comment about his trembling leg staked a claim in Meth's mind. He pushed it away. He'd drunk the voices into silence after St. Moritz, but now he was sober. *You'll only be killing yourself,* he heard her say. He longed for unconsciousness. Soon the voices would finally be still.

He marched slowly and deliberately the full length of the empty platform until he stood directly in front of the pathetic figure hunched on a bench against the wall. The unshaven inebriate was wrapped in a worn-out overcoat, a corked flask extended from one pocket. He sat with his hands in his pockets, perfectly still, except to puff occasionally on the cigarette that dangled from his nicotine-stained face. Meth had long since dispensed with wondering why there was a file. He didn't care. This was personal.

He squared his shoulders, his back toward the rails, his right hand gripping his visibly trembling thigh. He'd imagined this encounter innumerable times—the words he would say, the anger he would unleash, the accountability he would exact—but he had always heard the dialogue in English. Now he realized that nothing would transpire as he had imagined. Moreau didn't speak English; even if he did, he was in no condition to understand or respond.

"François Moreau?" Meth shouted.

François looked up, making only a meager attempt to raise his head. It seemed he was trying to squint his world back into focus. Meth was struck by how strange the name—first and last—sounded coming from his mouth. He had refused to say it for so long, it almost felt forbidden.

"Are you François Moreau?" he demanded in French.

When François spoke, every hair on Meth's body stood erect. He recognized the same slurred French he had heard on his seventh birthday. "Oui," François mumbled. "Qui diable êtes-vous?"

"I am Prometheus," Meth said with a pride in his name he'd never felt, his right eye twitching. It angered him that his father, after so many years, could still trigger the tic. Their exchange continued in French.

"Can you spare some change?" François asked. "Or a cigarette perhaps?"

Meth's eyes fixed on the animal. He drew his right hand from his trembling leg and pushed it past his lapel and into his coat. He closed his fingers and pulled back until the sharp edge of the axe peeked from his jacket. He could feel the throbbing in his carotid arteries. He could see the oscillations in his vision with each heartbeat. He had taken a half-step toward his target when a rail worker stepped through the door and onto the platform. Meth caught the motion in his peripheral vision and pushed the axe back out of sight.

"Prometheus?" François muttered. "I had a son named Prometheus."

The employee disappeared down the platform, leaving Meth and François alone again. The infrequent trains at the small gare afforded Meth the relative privacy he desired.

"You *never* had a son," Meth snapped, remembering François' repeated references to him as The Dog. He'd never felt like a son, and he'd never thought of François as a father.

"Yes, I did," François insisted. "I had two. One died. The other couldn't speak right."

Meth fought his rage, at the same time finding himself intrigued by François' words.

"What are you talking about?"

Drunk and only marginally interested in the conversation, François labored to finish his sentences. He shifted slightly on the bench and sucked a long breath through his cigarette.

"He couldn't speak right. I slapped him every time he fumbled his words, but it only made things worse."

"You slapped *me*, you miserable drunken wretch! And I hated you more every time you did it."

François squinted again and struggled to get a clearer look.

"Prometheus? Is that you?" He belched. His expression became more curious, almost frightened. "Perhaps it did work. You speak fine now." He belched again. "How did you find me?"

"How did I *find* you?" Meth was almost yelling into the wind. "Everyone in town knows where you are at noon."

"Yeah," François acknowledged, again rearranging himself. "I'm here . . . every day."

"You make me sick," Meth said, disappointed in his inability to say something more descriptive, more hurtful. His passion for obscure words had completely failed him. When he'd rehearsed his attack, the adjectives had rolled off his tongue with great abundance and precision. He'd thought himself the grand orator until humbled by Hélène's punishing demonstration. Now he struggled just to be coherent.

"Get in line," François said. "I sicken most people, including myself."

Meth couldn't stand it any longer. He walked away. He could hear François mumbling something, but he kept moving. A quarter-century of hatred and distain had come to a boil. He was so enraged he had to calm down to complete his plan. He saw his mother's swollen eye. He saw Achilles bleeding near the porch. He heard Hélène: *I hate you, Meth*. He walked the full length of the short platform, turned around, and walked back. François had stopped mumbling.

"You are the cancer that killed my mother. You are the real disease: the implacable, soul-destroying poison." He'd finally struck his practiced rhythm and vocabulary, his contractions fully overcome by rage. "Your abuse is more malignant than any tumor. You consumed her love and gave nothing in return. You befouled everything in your path and left a trail of sorrow and despair."

François offered no defense or rebuttal. He just nodded in agreement. "When Achilles died, I escaped my sorrow with booze. I haven't been sober a day since."

Infuriated, Meth again reached into his jacket. "You were bathing yourself in liquor long before you butchered my dog with an axe, you contemptible, malevolent coward."

François perked up a bit, pulling the cigarette from his mouth and flipping it toward the tracks. He straightened slightly and looked intently at Meth. He'd registered more of the conversation than Meth had realized. He finally fired back.

"Not your dog, you idiot. Your brother! You only gave your dog that name because you'd heard it so often in our home . . . our once happy home."

François looked down. His shoulders slumped, as if his last shred of self-respect had just drained away and left him empty.

"Every time I saw you, or heard you call that dog's name, another piece of me died."

"What brother? What are you talking about?"

"We were here, on this very platform, at noon." François now spoke clearly. "The express train barreled toward us. It didn't slow down because it was the express train. Achilles was four. You were a year old, in your mother's arms. Achilles jerked away from my hand."

François seemed almost sober now. He paused and pointed, checking his emotions and building momentum as he spoke.

"He fell off the platform right behind you, right in front of the train, right in front of your mother and me."

As he spoke, François drew the flask from his pocket and flung it carelessly in the general direction he had pointed, as if to punctuate his statement. It skipped off the edge of the platform, cleared two pairs of rails and broke against the concrete base of a rusted switch stand. Meth's eyes reflexively followed the bottle. He saw the last drops of cheap vodka roll off the edge of the stand. Shards of flying glass spooked a nearby booted eagle. It launched from its half-eaten rodent and flew directly at Meth and François, as if it knew they had caused the disturbance. Then it turned and quickly disappeared into the gray horizon.

Turning back to François, Meth's expression softened slightly, his mind racing, re-contextualizing his entire childhood. How could he not know this? Why hadn't he been told?

Large snowflakes began to fall, fast and hard. He turned to his left and noticed the falling snow at the near-end of the platform. He heard a flash of his mother's voice saying something about new beginnings. *You'll only be killing yourself,* he heard Hélène say. His expression continued to change, first to contemplation, then compassion. He looked down at his leg, now still. He removed his hand from the still-concealed axe. Could he have been that wrong about François? About everything?

"Adelaide and I could never look at each other again," François said. "I insisted you were better off not knowing. I killed one son, destroyed the other, and disappeared into a drunken oblivion. I hear his voice. The only time I don't hear his voice—the only time I can tolerate myself—is when I'm falling-down drunk."

"I . . . I never knew," Meth stuttered, catching a hint of ozone in the rapidly shifting wind.

Despite the ravages of alcohol and decades of self-abuse, François now spoke as the educated man who had once cared, whose only escape from caring too much had become his soul-destroying addiction. Meth heard the pain in his father's words.

"That's why I'm here . . . at noon . . . every day. Sometimes he feels closer when I'm here. I want to be with Achilles. It's finally time, Prometheus. Now you're here, now you know; it's finally time."

"Time?" Meth mumbled aloud. He looked at François more intently, without comprehending. He had so many new twists to unwind. And now he had another reason to hate François.

"I had a brother? All these years? How could you not tell me?"

If François heard Meth's questions, he chose to not respond. "Srecko?" François yelled, looking down the platform. He looked back at Meth. "Is that your back-up?"

"What back-up?"

Meth turned to see Srecko Knezevic, the marksman who had tutored him at the range. He stood at the far end of the platform, reaching toward the lump inside his coat. Meth stepped between Srecko and his father, suddenly wondering how François could have known his name. At the same time, Meth noticed the speeding express train approaching from the far end of the platform. Because of the wind, he had not heard it coming.

Srecko moved to the right and leaned to see François. Meth mirrored Srecko's movements, blocking his sightline. Meth hadn't seen the CZ 99, but he anticipated its arrival. He repositioned the steel axe in front of his heart. When he turned back, he saw François launch from the bench with an agility that betrayed his decades of drunkenness. The man Meth had hated for so many years dashed past him in a blur and leapt from the platform. The train struck him in midair.

Meth's eyes widened. A gust from the passing train pushed him back a step. He looked away from the horrific scene to the opposite end of the platform. Srecko had already disappeared.

18

WHO BURIED ACHILLES?

SUNLIGHT CREPT into Meth's dark entryway through the transom and sidelights that surrounded his custom front door. The antique brass hardware used to control the transom had been salvaged from a building in Zurich. Meth hadn't touched it since before St. Moritz. For weeks his hideout had been sealed and silent. Now the bell rang impatiently as Meth's leather heels thumped across the hardwood. Pulling the door, he drew his first breath of fresh air in a fortnight; he hadn't even ventured out for food. Karl stood on the other side of the threshold, looking more professional than usual, his shirt pressed and tucked in, his face clean-shaven.

"Why was Srecko there?" Meth immediately asked, his tone anything but inviting. He squinted in the sunlight, his eyes more accustomed to dimly lit rooms. Karl had called Meth at St. Moritz two months earlier; they hadn't spoken since.

"NEMESIS doesn't send back-up. There wasn't a contract. So why was Srecko there? And how'd François know his name?"

"I can explain."

"You can try," Meth said, his still-acerbic tongue drawing a pleasant grimace from Karl. Meth's difficulty with contractions had died with François. If Karl noticed, he didn't comment. Meth's five-kilogram weight-loss also went unmentioned; he was off the two-carbon diet and not eating much. Meth and Karl eyed one another as if they both realized how much they had missed their toxic tête-à-têtes.

"It's time to talk," Karl said.

Meth felt ambivalent about talking. He wanted answers, but getting them meant talking to Karl. He stepped back and silently gestured toward the study. Meth hadn't been in the study for weeks—too much light, too many memories. They took a few steps together before resuming their conversation. The house was warm and quiet. The smell of cigarettes had long since dissipated.

"I'm done, Karl," Meth declared as they settled into burgundy leather chairs. "I told you before I left St. Moritz."

"I assumed as much, but we have to talk. It's not that simple."

"Simple? It's plenty simple."

"They'll pay you double and give you more control."

"They? Who are *they*?"

"C'mon, Meth. Don't do that. I'm just the messenger. And, by the way, you're still under contract."

"Eat the contract, or put it somewhere else. I'm not coming back." Meth's words lacked the tone he'd used in the past to egg Karl on. He was cold and serious. "What are you going to do, kill me? I'm ready."

Karl extended two envelopes. "Take some time off," he said. "Then come talk."

"I don't want it. I'm done. Done with the contracts. I'm done with you and that filthy lucre you're always pushing at me."

"Easy on the sanctimony, Moses. I've been in this game longer than you, and I wasn't always behind that desk. I was good when I was young. Not as good as you, but I was good. I know what it feels like."

"Really? *Really*? You know what it feels like to see the degenerate figure that had once been your father decide that death was better than life? To see his frame dismembered and strewn along the track, his blood splattered on the platform? He'd still be alive if I hadn't gone."

Meth paused for a breath.

"No," Karl said, "I can't imagine . . . I don't know what *that* feels like. But you're not the only person beaten down by life. Most of us struggle the same way at times. I've got a life experience too. I have plenty of resentment, but I believe in what I'm doing. I was on your side of things for years before moving to that office. And, by the way, pushing those folders across the desk isn't exactly a warm-puppy experience."

"I thought I'd feel better after his death, but he robbed me even of that. Maybe he *did* love me in his own sick, distorted, drunken way. Maybe he was just too consumed and cankered by grief. Maybe he left because it was the only way he could stop destroying us."

Meth hadn't thought of it previously, but as he heard the words come out of his mouth, he recalled Hélène's comments about her ex—about how he had left to avoid causing her further pain.

"You referred to him as your father."

"It's a step," Meth said, almost resentfully. He stood and paced through the shadows of the sunlit room.

"I've loathed life since my grandfather died, passively suicidal for twenty years, actively so when I went to Saint-Martin-des-Entrées. I fully intended to finish him and then myself. I longed for death, even as I inflicted it on others. And yet, I think *he* hated life even more. Is that possible?"

"He had to leave, Meth. After he killed your dog he was terrified of what he'd become and what else he might do . . . to you, to your mother."

Meth's stunned expression silenced Karl. They stared at each other like prizefighters waiting for the bell.

"I know what happened," Karl said. "I know a lot."

Meth wanted to know, but he refused to ask.

"I made a promise not to tell," Karl continued, "but you need to know. I should've told you years ago." He spoke with compassion. He reflexively reached for a cigar—something to keep his hands busy and to placate a craving—but he caught himself and left it in his pocket.

Meth squirmed, anxious about what Karl might say. He wanted to hate his former boss, but he'd always felt Karl cared, even when he yelled and swore.

"I knew your father."

Meth's expression stiffened. Color drained from his face like sidewalk chalk in a rainstorm.

"You called him Le Soûlard, but—"

"Don't call him that!"

"I'm not," Karl said, sounding apologetic. "Like I said, *you* called him Le Soûlard, but he was *my* friend, and I had to keep my mouth shut when you'd say it. We worked together. He did what you do."

"Did."

"Yeah, what you *did*. Didn't you read the file?"

Meth stared at his shoes and shook his head.

"François was a good man. He was a damned good operative . . . better than either of us. He and Srecko were friends. They took the toughest contracts together."

"Then why'd you send him to back me up?"

"I didn't send him. And he wasn't there to back you up. I didn't even know he'd gone until it was over. He loved Franco. He went to protect *him*, not you."

"Who's Franco?"

"François. Your father. I called him Franco. He came to me after your dog died."

"You mean, after he *killed* him." Meth felt a hint of compassion toward François, but that didn't excuse his killing the dog.

"Yeah, after he killed your dog."

On another day Karl might have traded barbs, but not today. He let the interruptions roll off unchallenged and kept moving.

151

"I was in Lyon, on vacation—holiday, as you call it. I hadn't seen him for a couple of years. He'd faded away and caused no problems, so NEMESIS didn't bother him. He was already a devotee of the bottle but sober enough to make sense. If he'd come to the office, I wouldn't have seen him, but he flopped into a chair at my table in front of Le Sud. We'd been friends for years, and I had nowhere to go. So I listened."

"You know about my brother?"

"Achilles? Hell yeah. For crying out loud, I was his godfather. François loved that kid more than life."

"How could you not tell me?"

"Like I sa—"

"You could have told me!"

"Like I said, I made a promise. We were good friends. I loved your father." Karl unconsciously grabbed the cigar again and started fiddling with it. This time he got it briefly into his mouth before returning it to his pocket.

"He looked like death waiting to fall. He'd lost thirty or forty pounds—hadn't shaved in weeks. His breath could've peeled paint. I was glad he was sitting downwind."

Karl looked through the window, gazing out as if he were reliving their exchange. His voice softened.

"'Aidez moi,' he said, so I listened."

"He wanted your help?" Meth asked. Karl spoke French so seldom Meth almost forgot he could.

"Yeah. He asked for help. I bought him lunch. Don't know how long it'd been since he'd had any calories from someplace other than a bottle."

Karl's tone drifted, sometimes talking to himself, sometimes to Meth. He unfolded François' whole story, starting with details about NEMESIS. He described the endless agreements, treaties, extradition arrangements, and multi-national authorizations, as if Meth didn't already know. He explained how shortly after his arrival at NEMESIS he had met François and started calling him Franco. Within weeks, everybody in the office was doing the same.

"He trained me," Karl said with a wistful expression. "He was the best."

Flipping back and forth between French and English, Karl continued, sometimes narrating recollections, sometimes paraphrasing François. "Aidez moi," he said again, unconsciously translating as he spoke. "Help me . . ."

"**HELP ME,** Karl. I can't go back. I can't hurt them anymore."

"What are you doing in Lyon, Franco? What are you talkin' about? You look like you've been run over by the shit wagon."

"I killed the dog. I killed Achilles. Now I've killed the dog."

"You didn't kill Achilles. It wasn't your fault. It's been years; you've gotta let this go."

Karl had attended the funeral. He'd witnessed his friend's suffering. François had remained stoic throughout the service, even as a tear trailed off his cheek and dropped onto his slate gray suit. Karl had spent a week with him before heading back to Zurich. François hated himself for letting Achilles pull free and he feared Prometheus would grow up hating him as well. Before Karl left, the grief-stricken father swore Adelaide and Karl to never speak of Achilles, to never let Prometheus know. "And that includes your father," François had said to Adelaide, insisting that his youngest son never be told of the unforgivable sin. No one could persuade him otherwise.

After the funeral and several days with François, Karl had headed back to Zurich. There had been no dog *then*. He knew Prometheus and Adelaide, but he'd never heard of any dog. Now François was intruding on Karl's lunch in Lyon, frantic about some dog.

"What dog?" Karl asked. "Whose dog?"

"Prometheus. He named his dog Achilles. He kept saying Achilles, over and over. I just couldn't stand it anymore. I killed him. I was drunk. I'm always drunk. I—"

"Wait, Franco. Is Prometheus okay? Is Adelaide?"

"Yes, but it's just a matter of time. I can't control it. I snuck back to the house. I buried the dog, but I couldn't face him. I'm never going back. I love him too much, Karl. Will you take care of Prometheus?"

They looked at each other for a while, François trembling in shame and remorse; he wasn't dry enough to tremble from withdrawals. He demanded again and again that Prometheus never know.

"I loved that name," François said quietly. "Prometheus never gave up."

"We can get you help," Karl promised.

"There's no help," he said. "I've tried. I loved her. I loved the boys. I'll never go back. Promise me you'll take care of Prometheus. *Il a la douleur d'un chien sale.*"

METH'S HEAD snapped around. They locked eyes. Karl had retold the encounter with François in such detail Meth felt he'd viewed it from the next table, but that phrase crashed him back into the moment.

"*Il a la douleur d'un chien sale?*—He has the pain of a filthy dog?—That's what he said?"

Meth leaned forward, impatient for an answer.

"Yeah. He said it all the time after your brother died, or some version of it. He said it to sympathize with people when they were going through a tough patch. It means—"

"I know what it means!" Meth said. "Everybody knows what it means."

153

"Well, I didn't. I always treated my dogs well. I thought a dog's life was something to aspire to. Trust the French to turn it into something painful."

Karl kept talking—at least, Meth thought he did—but Meth had gone to another world. Maybe, all those years ago, François hadn't said, "*Vous êtes la douleur d'un chien sale*"—You *are* the pain of a filthy dog. It was hard to know. François had been drunk and bordering on incoherent; Meth was young and terrified at the time. Perhaps he had said, "*Vous avez la douleur d'un chien sale*"—You *have* the pain of a filthy dog. The phrases sounded almost identical. But, even if that's what he'd said, was he talking about his son or himself? And, even if that's what he'd said, he'd still been the source of Meth's pain. A whole new set of questions marched through Meth's mind. When he finally reconnected with the present, Karl was still talking.

"He sat there at my table and sobbed, and not like a blubbering drunk at a party; he wept like a devastated child. He begged me to take care of you, and to never tell." Karl described every word and feeling, his voice sometimes cracking, as if he bore the burden of François' demise, as if Meth was his own son. He gave Meth a stern, fatherly look.

"You still drinking?"

Meth recoiled. He shot a defiant stare at Karl, then looked away in shame.

"Word gets around," Karl continued. "I know these things. NEMESIS knows. I'm not asking about your job, Meth. I'm here as your friend."

"A friend would have told me."

"A friend made me promise not to. I was an egg in vice. Listen, let's talk about your job."

Meth walked across the room and shoved a dozen books along the shelf to expose a small keypad. One book fell on the floor. He left it there. He punched five numbers into the keypad and a small door popped open. He grabbed his BDM and took two steps toward Karl, who was watching carefully. He pointed the butt of the gun toward Karl and pushed a button on the right side of the grip—the magazine release, just behind the trigger—allowing a spring in the handle to shoot the loaded magazine into Karl's lap. Then he opened the slide, locked it in place, and caught the additional cartridge from the chamber. He dropped the gun and cartridge into Karl's open hands.

"It's *not* my job! I'm done."

"Let me help you do this right. You're entitled to a pension and this house."

"I don't want a pension. I'll live in a shack."

Meth spoke louder and faster with each sentence. He walked back to the open lockbox. He buried his hand in the back corner and pulled out his closed fist. He threw his Ferrari keys and a small leather wallet at Karl.

"Take it all. I don't want it."

"What's this?"

"Poison. Remnants of NEMESIS. That's what's left of my signing bonus and my number to one of those infamous Zurich bank accounts. Twenty years of death. I'll find another way to live. I don't want it. I don't need it."

"No. You need a friend."

Those were the first of Karl's words that Meth actually registered. Silence reverberated throughout the house, louder than had Mahler's Resurrection Symphony several weeks earlier. Meth's expression changed.

"Yeah," Karl said. "Nobody's ever said that to you before, have they? You don't know what it feels like to have a friend, or what to say. I could've been a friend, Meth, if I hadn't been trying so hard to be your boss. When your grandfather died, I thought I could look out for you better if I had you close by. It all got out of control. You were too good."

"I've never had a friend. I got close once in college, before your Suits snared me. I've never had a meaningful relationship that . . ." Meth stopped mid-sentence and swallowed hard.

"I know about her too," Karl said, only to draw another resentful scowl. "Don't pretend you're surprised. NEMESIS knows these things. They have to. You know how it works. Governments don't just lay out cash without accountability; well, maybe in the States, but not here. After you abused him in London, Lars followed you to St. Moritz. We kno—"

"I stopped drinking a few months ago," Meth said, as if Karl's earlier question had just clicked. "Cigarettes too. I'd avoided them because I hated *him*. I gave it all up because I hated *me*. I hated what I'd become." He looked at Karl and raised an eyebrow—the good one. "I'm still not too fond of me."

Karl tried to respond, but Meth kept talking. He hadn't spoken in six weeks, and now, as he spoke to Karl, his feelings flowed out like water from a hydrant.

"Do you know where the term melancholy comes from?" he asked, his question largely rhetorical. "In Greek, it means black bile, from an ancient belief that the body's humors need balance. A person becomes depressed when they have too much black bile or melankholia. The blackness is real— maybe not in the bile, but it's real."

Karl tried again to speak, but Meth wasn't done. He sounded like a despondent dictionary. "The blackness is pervasive, Karl. It's ubiquitous and nefarious. It's palpable and unbounded, consuming everything in its path. The blackness is alive and insatiable: a soul-destroying emptiness, feeding on all that's good. It destroys the present with discouragement and despair. It consumes the future when it lays waste to hope." He paused and looked at Karl. "As an adult, I've only felt hope once."

"Go feel it again. You know where it is."

"How?"

"Just go."

"She hates me, Karl. She called me a monster—the same word I used to describe François—and she was right."

"You're here, referring to him as your father, admitting he may have loved you. Knowing the truth changes things. She needs to know."

"She hates me."

"She loved you."

"She loved what she thought I was."

"No. She loved *you*. She hates what she *thinks* you are."

Meth shook his head in disbelief.

"She knows," Karl said. "But she needs to hear it from you."

"What do you mean, she knows?"

"Lars had to tell her. It was the only way to keep her from going public. She'd already called the police. Lars managed the whole mess, but he couldn't tell her much; you know that. She knows you're not a murderer, but she needs to hear the rest from you."

Meth paced around the room, running scenarios in his mind. He didn't hear the dialogues in his head anymore, but he still had a tendency toward obsessive thoughts.

"Love doesn't die," Karl whispered. "She may hate you. She may never speak to you again. But you still have to try. You have to know."

Meth stared at him, wondering what he knew and how. He'd never conversed with Karl long enough to know his past or perspective. Now he felt a tiny spark of trust.

"Do you believe that?"

"A lot of people don't," Karl said, "but I do. Love may rot and stink and hurt—hurt like hell—but it doesn't die."

In a flash, Meth remembered Karl laughing about his fencing days in college. He'd spoken of his three daughters; all had attended college in the States; all had married and settled there. Before her death, Karl's wife had traveled often to see their grandchildren; she was gone more than she was home. Meth had never given Karl's situation much thought because—well, frankly—he didn't care. Now he saw decades of sacrifice and regret in Karl's face and a love for those whom he'd lost.

At that moment, their conversation—and their relationship—turned a corner. They spoke for hours. Meth divulged his anxieties and aspirations. Karl taught him about François: about the love he'd had for his young family, his dedicated service to NEMESIS, and his inexorable descent into addiction. Karl promised he'd work through the details of Meth's release from NEMESIS. Then he all but pushed Meth out the door to go find Hélène. What Karl couldn't do for François, or for himself, he would do for Meth.

19

THE RETURN OF HOPE

KARL DISAPPEARED after his only visit to Meth's home—at least that's the way it seemed to Meth. They had embraced on the front step. Meth had reiterated his determination to walk away from everything NEMESIS, including Karl. Karl had thanked him for his service and friendship and went back to doing what he believed in. Meth moved on to more important things. He concluded that finding Hélène meant first finding himself. He'd never wanted to find himself; he'd never wanted to look.

Meth's emotional journey began with one physical step. After learning about his brother and witnessing the demise of his father, his first difficult step was to get back on a train. For all the horrible things he'd recently learned and seen, trains were still his salvation, and the smell of ozone was still strangely pleasant. Healing meant writing, and writing meant trains.

Meth traveled with a different heart and eye. He saw people and places he'd previously ignored. He wrote with emotions and insights not previously accessible. He wrote what he *felt*, not just what he saw. He walked through stations—whether they be gares, bahnhofs, stazioni, or in some other language—at a relaxed pace, determined to enjoy the experience. He contemplated relationships differently, carefully listening when he overheard conversations, startled by how little he knew about people's motives and struggles and, as Karl had promised, how similar their feelings were to his.

On the west bank of Lake Maggiore, in Meina, Italy, Meth stopped, literally, to smell a rose. He'd never done that. He marveled at the tender interactions of a mother and daughter on a train. He watched a father teach his son how to dribble a ball on a football pitch in Lugano. And, much closer to home, on a bright and beautiful day in Lindenhof Square, he introduced himself to a man who was at least twice his age and spent the rest of the day playing chess.

With every meaningful experience, the harsh voices grew more distant. He hadn't heard them since François' death. Now he hardly remembered them. He studied a young couple—from New Zealand, he thought, from their accent—affectionate, smiling, seeing the sights, but looking more at each other than the scenery. He contrasted them with an elderly couple sitting on a park bench quietly holding hands, less frequently looking at each other because they had memorized every curve and shade in their partner's face over a lifetime together—at least, that's what Meth wrote as he continued coaxing words from his keyboard.

He made a special trip to the Galleria d'Arte Moderna in Milan to see *Love at the Fountain of Life*, a Giovanni Segantini painting Hélène had described and admired: two young lovers approaching the fountain, a feminine winged angel protecting and dispensing the source of life. After he saw it, Meth liked Segantini all the more. And he missed Hélène.

Meth's good days got better and more frequent, but his bad days refused to surrender. Sometimes paralyzed, he'd sit in his den with the lights off, listening to Mahler or in silence, thinking about his past and his future. Continuing forward meant facing his past. Karl had said something that still hung in Meth's mind like dark matter, unseen but warping his perception of the universe. He had to return to Saint-Martin-des-Entrées.

Meth had walked the platform in Saint-Martin-des-Entrées next to his mother's dead body. The last time he was there he'd watched his father leap to his death. The thought of returning made him physically ill. He loved the rails in Europe, but he couldn't take the train to Bayeux. He decided to drive. After an unusually friendly chat with Zeta Fritz—the attractive broker who'd taken his 456 in-trade and sold him his Berlinetta—and after Meth exaggerated his interest in purchasing a new car, she let him take a Porsche 918 Spyder for a weekend "test-drive."

The 900-kilometer route forced Meth into six hours of solitary confinement (nine hours for a normal driver in a normal car). Driving meant he couldn't bury himself in his writing. He had nowhere to hide. He churned out some tough realizations along the way. By the time he reached Normandy, his growing catalogue of faults and weaknesses left him feeling like he needed a larger car. He was ashamed of the way he'd treated other human beings. He didn't know his brother because he was dead, but he didn't know the rest of the world because of his own choices.

Meth rolled into his childhood village on Rue William Kennedy Ferguson. The main street through town had had a different name when Meth lived there. It was renamed on June 6, 1994, the fiftieth anniversary of D-day, to honor Sergeant William Kennedy Ferguson (posthumously commissioned and promoted to Pilot Officer) of the Royal Canadian Air Force. Ferguson's Spitfire EN-183 was shot down on Friday, January 15, 1943. On the day of his burial, as a show of support, villagers had gathered for his funeral. Germans had arrested several and sent some to concentration camps; a few never returned. Ferguson's headstone still stood in the local cemetery.

Meth parked nearly a kilometer down the rue so he could stretch his legs after the long drive. Inside the gate, he paused at Ferguson's marker and contemplated the stories Truman had shared about the sacrifices made by World War II soldiers and civilians throughout the world. He wanted to salute, but having not served in the military, he feared a salute might seem disrespectful. He nodded his appreciation and moved on.

In the northeast corner of the small cemetery, near an aged yew tree, he found two graves, just as Karl had described. Karl had seen both graves filled. In fact, he may have been the only person present on both occasions. Karl, François, and Srecko were of the same vintage. Meth now knew they had been friends. If Srecko had accompanied Karl to Saint-Martin-des-Entrées, Karl hadn't spoken of it. There had been no funeral for François, but Karl had arranged for a headstone. Both markers were simple; on the left, ACHILLES MOREAU FILS BIEN-AIMÉ (BELOVED SON); on the right, at the head of the still-struggling turf, FRANÇOIS MOREAU. Dates appeared below the names.

The afternoon sun warmed Meth's shoulders and cast a conspicuous shadow that fell between the stones. He stood, it seemed, for an hour, wondering what he should feel. He wanted to be happy about knowing the truth, but he resented having never felt like a beloved son and having never known his older brother. He was still angry with François but his leg no longer trembled. Without his rage, he ran segments of his childhood through his head and made an attempt at empathy. His recent bout with loss and alcohol afforded him a tiny glimpse of the humanity in François. It was something he could work with; it was enough for the moment.

Meth felt embarrassed and petty for thinking it, especially while standing at the graves of his father and brother, but he wondered where François had buried the other Achilles. And what had he done with that would-be marker? Meth paced around the small cemetery for two more hours, stopping occasionally to read an epitaph. He didn't speak to the graves as he had at Cimetière des Rois, but he found better answers. He couldn't undo what he'd done or what had been done to him, but he could get right with himself and his future. On the way out, he stopped again at Ferguson's grave. He touched his heart while nodding his respect—a salute of his own making—and headed home via Mont Saint Michel.

THE PRIME Tower, at 126 meters, claimed title to the tallest building in

Switzerland from 2011 until 2015, when the Roche Tower in Basel was finished. Meth liked Clouds, a restaurant on the top floor where he could see much of Zurich and write. It was one of the few places he could write without the sounds and sensations of a moving train. Hélène would like Clouds; Meth knew that. It had large windows, beautiful views, and great food. He would scan the tables when he entered, but she was never there.

He arranged a corner table with a 270-degree view on alternate Wednesdays. The manager liked him because he arrived in the slowest part of the afternoon and complimented the quality of the establishment. The chef liked him, and treated him well, because he ordered the chef's pleasure and complimented his creations. And Meth's tips always pleased Svenja. She kept his glass of Pellegrino full and the tables around him empty. After his late lunch, he would pump out several pages. He looked forward to his afternoons in the Clouds.

As his manuscript accumulated pages, Meth rewrote himself and his future. Every admirable trait he imagined for his character became his own quest. He slept better. He looked forward to getting up in the morning. He ran and cycled and generally enjoyed life. He smiled and interacted with those around him. Every time he recognized a negative thought, he replaced it with something positive. After a few drafts on his own, he sent his work off to Twitch. Then, after a two-week break in Orléans, France, he followed his pages to Twitch's office.

When Meth arrived, Twitch waved the dog-eared manuscript around like he was a manure salesman swatting flies. He sat on the corner of his oak desk, his shoulder occasionally jerking, one foot swinging like a pendulum as he spoke. He rambled on in endless sentences, just as he had at Cambridge. He thumbed portions of the manuscript, stopping occasionally to show Meth red notes and to expound. His explanations were fast-paced and unreserved, as if any decent writer should already know everything he was saying.

"Listen," he said, "I care about the feelings of my authors, but I care more about the quality of the books I publish. Set all this dialogue crap aside and concentrate on the story and the structure, but stop wordsmithing and finish the B story and you can go back later and punch up the dialogue to make it more edgy. Stop worrying about the words. Worry about the feelings—tell the story—and the words will take care of themselves."

Sometimes lost in Twitch's barrage of ands and buts, Meth was grateful for the occasional period. He plied Twitch for every morsel and embraced his critiques gratefully. He watched and listened intently, nodding acknowledgment along the way. The defensiveness that had marked his conversations with Karl was gone. He no longer felt like he had something to prove. Despite his harsh review, Twitch finished with an encouraging grin and a promise to publish. Meth shook Twitch's boney hand, pushed open the glass office door, and disappeared into the busy streets of Zurich with a bounce in his step.

IT WAS nearly sunset when Meth ambled down Station Road, surprised by a comfortable sense of returning home. He walked through a cascade of pleasant memories and wondered what had become of Duc and Adi. He turned right, onto Hills Road, and continued through the crisp autumn air to Regent Street near the outskirts of the University of Cambridge. He felt invigorated by the familiar environs. Just beyond Parker's Piece, where 15,000 guests had gathered in 1838 to celebrate the coronation of Queen Victoria, Meth turned into the University Arms Hotel. The original inn had opened a few years before the coronation. It was currently undergoing renovations, yet again, but that didn't matter. As a student, Meth had vowed he would someday stay at the most prestigious hotel in the area. *Today is the day*, he thought.

After a good night's sleep and a shower, Meth ventured into the hotel restaurant for a traditional English breakfast: pork sausages, fried eggs, baked beans on toast, and broiled tomato halves. He pushed the black pudding aside; Truman had liked it, but Meth wasn't *that* English.

He strolled across campus to Trinity Street and into the outer office of the Vice-Chancellor, Professor Sir Alfred Townsend, ten minutes before his 9:00 a.m. appointment. Truman's friend, Sir David Kipling, had served as Vice-Chancellor until 1996. Townsend began his seven-year term in 2011, the 345th Vice-Chancellor since the institution's founding in 1209.

Precisely on the hour, Townsend's door opened, revealing a warm, sixty-two-year-old smile. He gestured an invitation to Meth.

"Prometheus?" he invited, confirming the name on his schedule.

Meth made his way across the outer office, the young secretary's eyes following his every step. He approached the Vice-Chancellor, whose hand was extended.

"I have hoped for your return," Townsend said, offering a firm handshake.

"And I, sir, for the return of hope."

"IT'S A lot better," Twitch said in his office several weeks later. "At least you've got a story here now though it still needs work but it's less mechanical and more engaging."

Meth found himself more amused than usual by Twitch's run-on sentences.

"Where have you been, by the way? I haven't heard word one from you in months and I thought maybe you'd given up."

"Not giving up," Meth answered. "Just going through the process. I took some time to study. I went back to Cambridge. I finally finished the paperwork for my degree. And I learned a little more about writing."

"You learned a lot," Twitch quipped, surprising Meth with the compliment. "Your style's more relaxed and I don't have to read with a dictionary in my hand though you still use too many polysyllabic words"— he winked—"and you're starting to get some feeling into the B story but you have to amp it up. What's she going to do? What's *he* going to do? Where do they end up and how do they get there? Your main character's still too flat emotionally."

Twitch paused for a breath. Sometimes that seemed to be the only reason he'd pause. If it weren't for that troublesome necessity, he would talk perpetually. He thumbed through pages as he spoke. "Make your character *do* something to find his heart and give it a voice. If you want this out by spring," he cautioned, "I need the finished manuscript by the end of the year. No exceptions." Referring to their shared years at Cambridge, Twitch agreed to do the final edit himself and to a prelaunch in Zurich. "We'll make sure people know," he promised.

THROUGH THE night, Meth quietly repeated Twitch's last suggestion, like some mantra from his writing guru: *do something*. Twitch had spoken of a fictional character in a novel, but Karl, when he'd pushed Meth to find Hélène, had pressed him into life: *do something*. At sunrise Meth set out on a long run. His breath steamed along in puffs behind him as he ran past the Zurich landmarks and out into the countryside, still perseverating: *do something*. He greeted people and waved to pedestrians and cyclists as they passed. About eight kilometers out, he noticed a hand-painted sign on a rough piece of wood, WELPEN ZU VERKAUFEN (PUPPIES FOR SALE), with an arrow. He studied it for a long moment, like a cryptographer trying to decipher some hidden message, still breathing hard. The letters suggested a child's touch.

"Do something," he puffed, now jogging in place. Meth stared down the long, narrow lane. Beyond a clump of trees in the distance, he eyed a benevolent column of smoke escaping a single chimney. He glanced again at the sign and headed off in the direction of the arrow.

ON THE floor of Meth's new apartment, a large envelope, torn open at one end, leaned against his wastebasket. It had three addresses and a twenty-year-old postmark. The return address had no name, just Lowestoft, England. Truman's address had been crossed out. The third address was to Global Resources, Inc. in Zurich. The handwriting of the first two addresses was Adi's—Meth had long ago recognized it—the third, Meth assumed, was the hand of some barrister called upon to settle Truman's estate. The envelope had arrived several weeks after Truman's death, but Meth had never opened it. He knew what it was; it had the familiar muffled jingle he'd unwrapped once before. Until today, he'd never wanted to hear it again.

Meth had spent much of the morning talking on the phone with Karl. They hadn't spoken in weeks.

"All of it?" Karl said.

"All of it."

Meth switched his phone to speaker and placed it on his small table so he could entertain his new pup with both hands. Apollo was a smiling chocolate lab. He wore the collar, now with two new holes to make it smaller, and the blue nametag Adi had purchased so many years ago.

"There's almost three million euros in that account, Meth."

"All of it: the money, the Ferrari, the house, the savings, the pension. All of it."

"I worked hard to get that stuff for you." There was a long pause. "Well, Srecko did most of the work."

"What did Srecko do?"

"You know he has more seniority than anyone? You know that, right?"

"Yeah. What'd he do?"

"Hell, he doesn't talk much. Right?"

"Right, right, what did he do?"

"We were in this committee meeting—high stress, drama, all that shit— and all of a sudden Srecko says his seven words for the week: 'He's sacrificed enough; let him have it.' That was the end of the discussion. And now you want me to give it all away?"

"I don't want any of it. None."

"You told the guy I was your financial advisor?"

"What'd you want me to tell him? I was going to call and give you a heads-up, but I got busy. I knew you'd figure it out when he told you he was from Cambridge and started talking about an endowment."

"Achilles Moreau?"

"Right. The Achilles Moreau Memorial Scholarship. Orphans only."

"That's a shitload of money."

There was a long pause. Meth smiled at Karl's discomfort and laughed as Apollo nipped at the chew toy Meth swung back and forth in front of him.

"Alright," Karl said. "It's your money."

"It never should've been."

METH CONTINUED to travel. He had to travel to write. On one trip to Geneva, he finally visited the Patek Philippe Museum on Rue des Vieux-Grenadiers. He lost himself among the timepieces and paid no attention to Elise, a svelte, well-dressed, twenty-something museum staffer. She followed from a distance, leaning discreetly to better see his watch. Then she disappeared and returned with a smartly dressed elderly man. They passed unnoticed, whispering to one another, until Meth finally turned and saw them.

After an awkward silence, Elise spoke: "Bonjour, monsieur."

"Bonjour, madame, monsieur," Meth said, no longer resentful of the language.

"Please pardon our intrusion," she continued in French. "We were just admiring your watch."

"Oh, thank you."

"Hello, sir," the gentleman interjected. "I am Weldon Andrew, the museum curator. Do you still prefer English?"

"English is fine," Meth answered. "Have we met?"

"Yes, sir, I believe we have. As Elise said, we were just admiring your watch. It is very rare." Weldon's precise diction reminded Meth of Truman.

"It was a gift from my grandfather."

"Truman?" Weldon asked, his expression suddenly forty years younger. "Is your grandfather Truman Hamstead?"

"You knew him?"

"I loved him," Weldon responded, "and *his* grandfather, Ivory, as well. I arranged for Ivory Hamstead to receive that watch as a retirement gift. I engraved it for him."

"How's that?" Meth said, sounding incredulous.

The curator nodded and smiled, resting his gnarled hand on Meth's shoulder as if he'd known him for years. Meth recognized something comfortable about his touch.

"Young man," he began (Meth had not been called a young man by anyone in a long time), "I'm ninety-seven years old. I first met you when you were a young boy in your grandfather's home. We met again on the day of Truman's burial."

Meth looked carefully and smiled. He began to nod. "I remember."

"Long before volunteering here, I worked for Patek. I began in 1939, when I was just nineteen. Ivory had nearly forty years with the company by then. He finally retired in 1945. He worked on the Graves Supercomplication in the early thirties. For more than fifty years that was the most complicated watch in the world. Ivory was a master. The only things he treated better than the watches he worked *on* were the people he worked *with*. Everyone loved him."

Seeing Weldon's passion, and hearing it, Meth slipped the watch from his wrist and passed it over for a closer look. Weldon immediately turned it over to read the inscription.

"This is a 1925 Grogan. You know that? The only left-handed watch Patek ever made." Meth nodded. "Ivory was a great comfort to many through the war. When coworkers lost loved ones, he'd remind them of the unconquerable power of love. 'Choose to love,' he would say. That's why I engraved it on his watch. Everyone wanted to give back what he'd so freely given. Your grandfather, Truman, was the same way. We worked together for many years. I loved him."

"I've never seen another one like it," Meth said.

"Oh no," Weldon agreed. "There are very few. A 1925 Grogan sold at Christie's in 2006 for two million U.S." He carefully handed the watch back to Meth. "Would you like to see the rest?"

"The rest?"

"The rest of the collection."

"I think I've seen most of the museum," Meth answered.

"No, sir. You don't understand. Truman loved watches, particularly Pateks. He collected them. He searched high and low, scraping together every resource he could find to acquire them, and using his considerable skills to repair and maintain them."

Meth shook his head. "He never told me."

"He placed the collection on loan here, but it belongs to you. I tried to explain when we last met."

"I'm sorry," Meth said. "I wasn't ready to talk that day."

"Do you still go by Prometheus?"

"Prometheus Hamstead," Meth answered, impressed by the recall of Weldon's ninety-seven-year-old mind. "When Grandfather died, I took his last name."

"Mr. Hamstead, please come with me."

Weldon's formality amused Meth. The elderly curator led him into a private room and turned on the lights, revealing glass cases containing dozens of beautiful watches. Meth scanned the cases from the doorway then moved closer to examine the individual watches.

"These are all yours, to do with as you choose. It's an honor to finally have you here."

"I never knew," Meth said, shaking his head in amazement. "He never told me."

"Your grandfather was very concerned about you. He worried about your future, but he took great joy in your studies at Cambridge. He spoke often of his love for you."

Meth came to the last case. It contained a single watch, a 1953 model 2526, Patek's first self-winder. The watch captured his attention momentarily until he noticed something else. The timepiece rested unceremoniously on a small slab of barn-wood. It was rounded and smooth on the edges from being touched innumerable times. Near the watch, two almost imperceptible letters—A. M.—were scratched into the wood. The initials, carved years earlier, were now nearly as oxidized and gray as the rest of the surface.

Suddenly Meth was seven years old again, wielding a small spade, struggling to care for his fallen friend. He felt the rock in his hand, scratching away at the wood. The board was smaller than he remembered, the carvings not as deep. He swallowed the lump in his throat, glad for the moment that he didn't have to speak.

"He intended this collection to be your graduation gift," Weldon said. "He stipulated that you must come here of your own accord to receive it. We have all longed for this day."

"What about this piece of wood?" Meth pointed, leaving a fingerprint on the glass.

"He said you would know. He kept it on his workbench after your mother died. He said she wanted you to have it. After he passed, I put it in that case with the last watch. Does it mean something to you?"

Meth looked at the wood. To him it was more precious than the watch. He swallowed again, thinking of Truman, laboring away at his workbench to keep him in school, to heal him. He felt a deep urgency to follow the example Truman had set. He regretted how harsh he had acted toward his mother that day when he had tried so hard to bury Achilles, when all she had wanted to do was help. He suddenly realized that all she had ever wanted to do for him was help—that she'd done her best.

"It means they cared," Meth said to Weldon, scanning the collection of watches. He tried to comprehend Truman's sacrifices on his behalf and how he must have felt when his only daughter died. He looked at the last case, at the watch and the wood. He nodded and whispered to himself: "It means they cared."

20

FINDING METH

METH NEARED completion of his six-kilometer run along
Lake St. Moritz. Apollo, now four months old, wandered
through nearly a meter of new snow. When he returned to the
trail, he shook the snow from his head and back and wagged his tail so
briskly his hind paws slid back and forth on the slick path. Giant flakes fell
just the way Meth most enjoyed them, leaving his morning quiet and white.

Out ahead of Meth, Apollo made friends with a woman on the trail, his
tail wagging with even more vigor. Meth quickened his pace and called for
his dog. When Apollo ignored him, Meth ran faster and called a little
louder. He approached, apologizing, while the woman still faced away and
played with Apollo.

"I'm sorry," he said. "He's still young."

"He's beautiful," she answered, still looking away. She accepted a nuzzle
and a lick on her cheek while ruffling Apollo's ears between her fingers.

"I'm sorry," Meth said again. "I should have him on a leash."

The woman turned around with a life-affirming smile that warmed
Meth's soul. It was a smile he knew well. He saw it flash in his mind: on the
train from Paris to Basel, in London, in Le Train Bleu, at St. Moritz a year
ago. He suddenly realized how the memory of that smile had sustained him
through the last year—how it had pushed him forward—though he was
never sure he'd see it again.

When Hélène saw Meth's face, her smile vanished. The anger Meth had
seen a year ago returned. She opened her mouth, but nothing came out.
Meth's heart sank. She looked out across the frozen lake and shook her
head as if she just wanted the whole encounter to disappear.

"How's your leg?" she finally said, her tone full of distain.

"I don't do that anymore."

"I can't believe you're here."

She turned and walked away. Meth froze for a moment, still caught off guard, and then he hustled to catch up.

"Leave me alone," she said.

"Wait . . . please. I had to come. I have to tell you some things. I have to explain."

"What? The same things Lars told me a year ago? How you're some heroic protector of humanity? You kill people . . . for money!"

"Not anymore. I don't do that anymore."

"You did it. It's done." She kept walking.

"Every soldier on the battlefield gets paid."

She stopped and glared back at Meth. She didn't need to say a word. Her expression was as cold as the frozen lake. She started walking again. He ran around her and then walked backwards in front of her.

"Wait," he said. "Please." He brought his hands forward, palms down, as if to still the already frozen waters. "That's not why I'm here. I shouldn't have said that. I don't want to justify it. I don't want to argue. I've done what I've done. I'm not proud of it. But I can't change it. That's not why I'm here."

"You lied to me."

When he slowed down, she walked around him and kept going. Meth followed, talking to her back.

"I couldn't tell you. I wanted to . . . but I . . . I was going to tell you."

She stopped and turned back.

"Oh really?" She took a step toward him, as she had in London—full of confidence, no fear. "When?"

Meth looked at his feet and then out across the lake. He spoke quietly. "The night you found out. I quit that night. I was coming to the room to tell you everything."

Apollo hopped around, frantically trying to get some attention.

"There's nothing left to say, Meth. You can't change what you did."

"Please," he begged. "Just five minutes. I'm right down here"—he pointed—"at Badrutt's Palace, at the end of the lake. Just a cup of espresso. That's it. Then I'll go. Please."

She offered a resentful nod.

WHEN THEY arrived at the Polo Bar, Meth dashed Apollo to the room upstairs and returned with two objects in his hand—a paperback book and a tiny leather box. Hélène sat near the open fireplace, her coat on a chair, her hat and gloves drying on the hearthstone. Tendrils of steam rose from their mugs—his on the table, hers between her pink hands, doubling as a hand-warmer.

"Five minutes," she said as Meth sat down. "Don't get too comfortable."

"I don't want to talk about the past. I don't want to try to convince you of what's right or wrong. Your views are as valid as mine. I just want to thank you. That's all. Just thank you."

"Well, you just did. Are we done?"

Meth held up one finger. "Five minutes. Please. You promised."

The last time he'd come to St. Moritz, Meth had locked all his dark apparitions in a trunk—or a manila folder—hoping to let them out one at a time so he could control them and manage his image with Hélène. This time he had nothing to hide. His humility softened the creases in Hélène's expression. She set her coffee on the table and leaned toward him.

"I'm sorry about your father."

Her comment sucked the air from the room and left Meth stunned.

"Karl came to see me," she added. "I know how you felt about François, and I know how I feel about you, but I'm still sorry for your loss."

"Thank you. I . . . I had a brother."

"He told me."

"I never knew him, but I had a brother."

"Brothers are hard to come by," she said. "And they're hard to lose."

Meth sipped his espresso, mostly to prevent his lower lip from trembling.

"I'm sorry about Olin," he said.

"It's been a long time. It still hurts."

He nodded.

"Karl told me about the organization. About why they do what they do. I understand it, but I just can't condone it."

"You don't have to."

"He told me things you don't know."

Meth raised his brows and waited.

"The folder on François; he said you didn't want to know."

"I do now," Meth said.

"His addiction destroyed him. When the organization tried to help, it only made things worse. He started talking to people about everything. He jeopardized lives and the whole operation. They were going to bring him in one last time and try again to help, but then . . . well, you know."

She looked at Meth, watching the wheels turn in his head. She blew on her espresso and took another sip.

"He didn't have a choice after the first few drinks," Meth said. "He surrendered his god-given agency to alcohol. His addiction made his choices after that. I felt it, just in the few weeks I was drinking. I knew if I didn't stop, I'd never be able to."

Meth didn't want to talk about his father anymore, or his past. He pushed the paperback book across the table. It had a crimson cover, the title in raised white letters: *Finding Meth.*

"I've been writing."

"About us," she said, "I know." She picked up the book and thumbed the pages. Her face brightened slightly. "You should have changed your name. It sounds like you're a drug dealer." She almost smiled. "Thanks for not using my name."

"You've read it?"

"Of course . . . published in Zurich . . . it was in the store right around the corner from my house. Achilles Moreau is hardly a mysterious nom de plume. Why'd you write about us?"

"I could never tell you how I felt. The book helped me find the words."

"Is it real?"

He nodded.

"That's how you feel—that stuff you wrote in the book?"

He nodded again.

"You should have told me. You should have said it out loud."

"I know. I couldn't."

"It's too late now. I've moved on."

"That's okay. I understand."

"You can't just walk back into my life. Things are different. I'm different."

"So am I," he whispered.

She looked like she might cry but quickly stiffened.

"Your time's disappearing," she said, gathering her gloves. "I have to go." She was every bit as abrupt as Meth had been in London.

"Alright. Alright," Meth nodded. "Just one more thing, then I won't bother you again."

He lifted the leather box from the table and put it directly into Hélène's open hand. She gave a skeptical, almost angry look. Then slowly opened the box.

"Don't be ridiculous, Meth!" She was almost shouting. She put the box on the table and stood up. "You can't buy me with a diamond!" She shook her head and took a deep breath. "A giant pile of bollocks, no?" Her twist of the English idiom might have been funny in other circumstances, but she was dead serious. She turned and walked away. Meth jumped up and followed.

"Wait. That's not what it is."

"It's not a diamond? Are you crazy? I know what it is."

"Well . . . yes, it's a diamond, but that's not what it's for. Please. I have two more minutes. Just let me explain."

Hélène's eyes broadcast regret for promising five minutes. She gritted her teeth and shook her head, but then relented. They made their way back to the table. She slowly sat down. She looked at the translucent stone shaped like two small pyramids joined base-to-base.

"It's not a gemstone," he said. "It's an octahedral. It's—"

"*I know what it is!* Don't you remember what I do for a living?"

"Don't think of it as a diamond," he said. "Just think of it as perfection—a mole of pure carbon." He picked it up and placed it in her reluctant hand.

"A mole? You gave me a mole of carbon?"

"Six point zero two two times ten to th—"

"Avogadro's number," she interrupted. "I know what a mole is. I have a Master's in geology. I don't need a chemistry lesson. And you can't influence me with a fifty-carrot diamond."

"I'm not trying to influence you."

"Then what are you trying to do?"

"It's sixty carrots, one mole, exactly twelve grams. That's what makes it perfect. It was hard to find. I had to go to Yakutia. But it's *not* to influence you. It's a gift, pure and simple."

"I don't want your blood money!"

"It's not blood money. I gave all that money away."

She glanced at his wrist.

"Where's Truman's watch?"

"In your hand."

"How could you give up your grandfather's watch? Four generations. Why would you do that? You make me so angry. This won't work, Meth. I can't be with you."

"I'm not asking you to be with me. That's not why I'm here. Truman gave me that watch to teach me about love and sacrifice. He'd be proud to know that you finally succeeded. That's why I want you to have this."

"Even *that* watch wouldn't buy *this* diamond."

"I had others. Truman left me a whole collection. But the diamond's nothing compared to what you gave me."

Hélène finally stopped protesting long enough to admire the treasure in her hand. Almost twenty millimeters at its base, it was nearly as large as the twenty-Rappen coin in her pocket. Her resolve softened just enough to give him a coy look. "I could have saved you some money."

"You saved *me*," he said. "It's a thank you. That's *all* it is." He abruptly stood up. "My time's up." He nodded a slight smile, as though he'd won, and started for the elevator.

"I can't take it," she said.

"It's my gift to you," he said over his shoulder, "no strings attached." He kept walking.

"You saved yourself, Meth"—he kept walking—"Wait!"

He stopped and turned around. Hélène met him in the middle of the room.

"Are you really leaving?"

He nodded. "I'm done. That's why I came, to thank you."

"And, you don't want *anything?*"

He shook his head.

She turned back toward the table. "Whatsoever thou spendest more," she whispered.

He heard it—at least he thought he did—but he couldn't believe it. He waited.

"You helped me today, Meth. Things have been hard the last few months. Your kindness just helped me. I really needed it—not the money—the kindness."

"I'm not here to manipulate you. I'm not trying to make you feel guilty. You don't owe me anything. I learned something . . . I don't . . . I didn't realize it until later, but the voices stopped when I was with you. Do you remember when I lifted your bag on the train, when I first called you Hercules?"

"Sí. Of course."

"It wasn't because of your strength; it was because Hercules rescued Prometheus from endless death. Even then, when I'd never admit it, I secretly hoped you'd save me. My eagle was my hatred, eating me every day."

"And now?"

"I'm alive—no more hate—and it's because of you."

"Listen, Meth, there's someone waiting for me at my hotel. I have to go. I can't be late." She stopped, as if reconsidering what she was about to say. She shook her head. "There's someone I want you to meet." She sounded almost restful. "¡Ay!"—she growled—"I can't believe I'm doing this!" She waited and slowed her breathing. She looked at the fire, then out the window at the snow. She glanced back at the book and diamond on the table. Then she offered a kind but reluctant look to Meth. "Will you join me for dinner?"

Meth hesitated and turned his head away. He look back through the corner of his eye.

"You understand I'm not here to work things out, right?"

She nodded.

"That's not what this dinner's about?"

"No," she said.

He looked away again, and then back, debating.

"Okay." He paused. Then nodded. "I'll come."

They walked back to the table. He lifted her scarf from the back of the chair and placed it gently around her neck, the inescapable smell of

Shalimar exploding a flash of memories and emotions through his mind and heart. He struggled to maintain his composure. She grabbed his book from the table and handed it back to him.

"Bring it with you," she said. "Write something special."

METH ARRIVED in his room just in time to see Hélène through the window. She turned the corner and disappeared as she walked back to her hotel. He sat at a table near the window for two hours and hardly moved. Apollo remained surprisingly quiet, wagging his tail intermittently, eying Meth from the braided rug in front of the fireplace.

Meth looked back and forth between the frozen lake and the novel on his table. He thumbed a few pages, wondering what to write. He wished he had a fountain pen with blue ink and the calligraphy skills to use it. Hélène's note in Basel had been so brief and so powerful.

For no apparent reason, Apollo stood up and walked across the room. He licked Meth's hand and then rested his head on Meth's leg. Meth stroked the fur on Apollo's neck. Then he picked up his pen and began to write.

21

THE B STORY

METH WALKED the short distance from Badrutt's Palace to Hotel Schweizerhof. He tried to put aside his nerves but he couldn't forget the concerned look in Hélène's eyes as they parted. *Who does she want me to meet?*

He entered the lobby after dark, brushing snow from his jacket before stuffing his gloves into the pockets. He saw Hélène across the room. She appeared comfortable in a soft chair, sipping sparkling water. When their eyes connected, his heart relocated to his throat—right where Hélène had kissed him a year ago—and thumped so hard he could feel it in his jaw. He hadn't wanted to feel this way. It surprised him. He thought he was past it. Determined to keep his emotions in check, he started toward her, dropping his hat and coat into the extended arms of the bellman. He pulled his novel from his back pocket as he walked.

Hélène stood and smiled. She hugged him, grabbing his childhood innocence and optimism and caressing them into the present.

"You have a new line," she said, gently tracing her finger across his brow. "I memorized every line, and this one's new."

"Oh, well . . . ah . . . thanks?" he said.

"Sí, mi querido amigo. Right there." She bounced her finger on his forehead and started to laugh. "It's from smiling. It looks good on you."

Meth breathed a deep sigh of relief. He was so grateful to see her smile. He slipped the novel into her hand as they sat down.

"Did you write in it?"

He nodded and smiled.

She opened the book and looked for the inscription, but a server interrupted with a clean glass for Meth and a new bottle of Pellegrino.

"I ordered your favorite drink," she said, closing the book. "I hope you don't mind."

The server filled the glass. Meth took a drink.

"So why's your dog named Apollo?"

"It goes all the way back to a friend in college." He didn't elaborate. "It's a good name for a dog. He helps me talk about my feelings. He's a good listener. And Apollo's a god of healing, so it works."

"But Apollo was the son of Zeus. I didn't think Prometheus would hang out with the son of his tormenter."

Meth shrugged, surprised by her familiarity with Greek mythology.

"I finally realized no one should be held accountable for the deeds of their father. Besides, Hercules was also a son of Zeus. You know, Hél—"

"Hercules," she said.

"Pardon?" Meth looked confused.

"Call me Hercules."

"You told me to nev—"

"I'm telling you now . . . it would mean a lot if you would call me Hercules . . . I mean, if you're still comfortable with it."

"Yes, of course. I'd like that."

Meth studied her face as she looked at the book.

"What about the B story?" she said.

"It's just a book. Books have happy endings. You know I always mess up the B story."

"You didn't come here to work on your B story?"

"No," he said. His tone was firm. "I'm working on my *A* story. No hidden agendas."

"Let's talk about it over dinner?" she said, pointing to the restaurant, her expression turning serious. "We need to talk."

"Grab a table," he said. "I'll wash up and be right back."

WHEN METH exited the bathroom several minutes later, he looked across the lobby and saw Hélène, not in the restaurant, but near the elevator. She stood on her toes and waited for an athletic, fair-skinned man to lean down so she could kiss him on the cheek. She tenderly cradled a baby, a tiny head visible beyond the pink blanket. As the man straightened, she gently passed the bundle into his arms and affectionately lingered, as if still bonding. She caressed the child's hands and face, reluctant to let her go. She kissed her forehead and stretched to again kiss the man at her side. She held his forearm as he backed away, as if she longed for the encounter to continue.

Meth stepped behind a pillar, out of sight, and watched as the man with the pink bundle backed into the elevator and disappeared. Hélène watched intently until the doors closed. Then she walked back into the restaurant and requested a table.

Meth had long ago dismissed any romantic notion of sweeping Hélène off her feet to some fairytale ending, but the sight of her with another man injured him deeply. He'd assumed she was seeing other men but witnessing it shattered his composure. His appetite disappeared, replaced by an emptiness he'd hoped to never feel again. He wobbled back into the bathroom and approached a stall, unsure if he could keep down the sparkling water. He felt the blood drain from his face and he sunk to one knee. He leaned to the side, grabbing the stall for support, but his sweaty palm and fingers found no traction and slid along the smooth metal, further worsening his balance. He thought he might fall. He contemplated lying on the floor, unseen germs notwithstanding, to avoid passing out. He dragged his tongue across is his pallid lips in a futile attempt to restore some moisture. There was no saliva, not on his tongue or his lips. All the moisture was on his palms and in beads across his forehead. He teetered before pulling on a sink to return to his feet. He tried to slake his thirst with a few cupped-handfuls of water, but he found it impossible to swallow. He waited, wondering when his strength would return.

A specter from the past, Yesterday's Meth, peeked through the darkness to see what would happen. He would have run, first from the hotel, then from St. Moritz. Forgetting the weakness in his legs, he would have run all the way to Zurich or, better yet, died trying. The blackness Today's Meth had worked so hard to dispel sat poised to close in on him, to steal his hope and leave him in despair. But Today's Meth had worked too hard to give up. He saw an alternative. He'd be a proper English gentleman. He'd do what Truman would have done. He borrowed a smile from earlier in the day, washed his hands, and left Yesterday's Meth dying in the bathroom. He started for the restaurant, his strength and composure increasing as he walked.

"I think I should go," he said, approaching Hélène at her table.

"What? Why? I thought we were going to have dinner and catch up."

"I don't want to intrude." He turned and started for the exit, his head bowed despite his best efforts to look composed.

"Wait!" she said, jumping from her seat and grabbing his arm. "Intrude on what? What's going on? Where are you—"

"I wrote what I hoped," he interrupted. "It's just a book with a happy ending. It's not real. I thought I could just walk away. I'm trying to be polite, but it hurts. I'm sorry."

He took another step toward the lobby, playing tug-of-war with his own arm, Hélène pulling at the other end.

"I gambled," he said, studying the floor. "I lost."

"No, Meth," she said, looking confused. "You won! *I* won! At least, I thought I did."

With Meth at a temporary halt, Hélène still gripping his wrist, she reached into her pocket and pulled out a closed fist.

"Here," she said. "I want you to have this. I don't know what's going on or why you're leaving, but you have to take this."

With one hand, she turned his wrist until she could see his open palm; with the other, she released the Patek he'd left behind a year ago into his cupped hand.

"I want you to wear this," she said, a tear streaming down her cheek. "And, someday, I want you to give it to your grandson."

Meth stood paralyzed. How could she say those things? *There will never be a grandson,* he thought. *Just let me go.* He wanted the torment to end. He wanted to be gracious, but he was leery of his ability to maintain.

"I love you, Primo. I never stopped loving you. I'm still . . . so . . . so *mad* at you." She shook her head. "I don't know if I'll ever get over it. We may never be together, but I'll always love you."

As hard as he tried to remain silent, he could no longer contain himself.

"I saw you kiss him when I came out of the bathroom." There was a long silence. "I saw you kiss him and hand him the baby."

"Kiss him?" she wondered aloud. First confusion swept across her face, then relief. "Oh, Ivan. You saw Ivan."

Meth nodded without knowing whom he had seen. He was hurt and humiliated and embarrassed. He just wanted to leave. He wanted to be gentlemanly and kind, but he wanted to leave. He leaned away from her and toward the exit.

She smiled and wiped away another tear with one hand while refusing to release his wrist from the other.

"Meth, it's not what you think. I invited him to join us for dinner, but that's not who I wanted you to meet."

As if on cue, Ivan came around the corner, babe in arms.

"Did you get the bottle?" Hélène asked Ivan.

He nodded and carefully balanced it in the baby's mouth. He looked more at the baby than at Meth.

"Ivan's my brother," she said. "He came with me to Olin's grave this year."

Meth struggled to regain his composure. He could hardly keep up with his rapidly changing perception of events. He swallowed hard, leaned toward Ivan, and shook his hand. He drew the blanket just enough to see the baby's face and the tiny dimple on her chin. He turned to Hélène.

"Then this must be your beautiful niece?"

"No, Primo." She wept and smiled, shaking her head. "She's *your* beautiful daughter."

Meth looked back at Hélène, then at the baby, then at Hélène, unable to speak. Emotions he had never experienced swelled in his chest as tears filled his eyes. A euphoric thrill permeated his entire being like a warm spiritual embrace that defied all understanding or description. His euphoria gave way to an equally exquisite sense of peace and reassurance.

"It's her birthday," Hélène said. "She's three months old today."

Meth paused, counting the months in his head. He didn't need his Cambridge degree for that.

"One time? One night?"

"One miracle," she nodded.

"I didn't write *that*."

"What you wrote was good. What you *did* was perfect. Do you want to hold her?"

Meth's head was bobbing again, back and forth between Hélène and the baby, like a spectator at a tennis match. Ivan leaned forward and passed the baby to Meth. He received her with a first-time fatherly awkwardness.

"I'm giving you *one* chance," Hélène said. "I swore I'd never have anything to with you but, when she was born, she changed me. I waited so long for a baby. I prayed endlessly for a baby. When I learned I was pregnant, I promised myself you would never be in her life. But, when she was born, I saw you. And when you gave me that gift today, without asking anything in return, I knew I needed to give this gift to you. You never had a father. I'm giving you one chance to be this girl's father—one chance to be the father you never had. This isn't about us; this is about our daughter."

Meth admired his daughter. He looked at her eyes and counted her fingers. He looked at Hélène, then back at the perfect little life he held in his arms.

"She looks like you," he said as a tear trailed from his cheek. "Name?" he whispered.

"Hercules," Hélène replied.

"No. The baby. What's *her* name?"

"Hercules," she reiterated.

"Hercules?"

"You're not the only one who reads Greek mythology, Meth. I know something about saving Prometheus too."

"I love her," he said, almost too quietly to be heard, his eyes fixed on life's greatest miracle. "I *feel* it." He looked back at Hélène, his lip quivering. "And I love *you*."

Hélène took the watch from Meth's closed hand as he continued to hold their daughter. She slipped it onto his left wrist and snapped the clasp into place. She studied his eyes as they scanned the face of little Hercules. She pushed closer and embraced him. She lifted his novel from the table. In her kindest voice, she read Meth's inscription: "CHOOSE TO LOVE."

ABOUT THE AUTHOR

Jeff O'Driscoll has been an emergency medicine physician for more than twenty-five years. He has been writing for more than thirty. He has published works of history, biography, theology, medical science and healthcare administration. He has also recently published a series of children's books available at MucktheDuck.org. *Who Buried Achilles?* is Jeff's first novel. Jeff and his wife, Sheila, have been married for thirty years. They have five children and two granddaughters. They are anxiously awaiting the arrival of their third grandchild.

A word from the author: Thank you for reading my debut novel. If you enjoyed this story, please share a positive review and tell a friend. If you have constructive criticisms or corrections, feel free to send me a message through JeffsPublishingCompany.com.

Made in the USA
San Bernardino, CA
27 June 2017